PRAISE FOR
DANIEL KALLA

FIT TO DIE

"Timely and relevant. Exposing the dark side of the wellness industry, this electrifying, ripped-from-the-headlines thriller will keep your heart racing from the first page to the very last."

JENNIFER HILLIER,
USA Today bestselling author of
Things We Do in the Dark

"A compulsive, fast-paced thriller that'll keep you flipping those pages well into the night. Filled with twists, turns, and shocking revelations about the diet industry, this is one heck of an intriguing must-read. I devoured it (guilt free)."

HANNAH MARY McKINNON,
internationally bestselling author of
Never Coming Home

"Combines a timely plot with a well-paced thriller I became addicted to, fast. This is a gripping page-turner crafted by a skilled, intelligent writer."

MARISSA STAPLEY,
New York Times bestselling author of *Lucky*

"Tight and tense with great dialogue and snapshot descriptions that crank up the believable. Daniel Kalla is one hell of a writer and *Fit to Die* is one hell of a thriller."

DIETRICH KALTEIS,
award-winning and bestselling author of
Under an Outlaw Moon

"This is one of Kalla's best."

The Globe and Mail

"Kalla's characters are well-developed across the board, be they victims, heroes, or the long list of suspects. The original and twisty plot helps this taut thriller stand apart."

Publishers Weekly

"Once again, Kalla demonstrates . . . his ability to focus [his] lens square on hot topics."

Vancouver Sun

"A timely and relevant story."

The Miramichi Reader

"[A] timely thriller. . . . [Kalla] balances interesting medical details with empathy and a pacey plot, without getting preachy."

Zoomer

THE DARKNESS IN THE LIGHT

"*The Darkness in the Light* is a gripping, heartbreaking, and enthralling suspense so vividly immersive that I was hooked from the first page. With crisp, powerful writing and two extremely compelling voices, Kalla draws you in to the remote, intriguing world of the Arctic and the tragic, inexplicable suicide clusters that have ravaged a small, tight-knit town. Kalla is a clever master of surprise, dropping subtle clues and expertly changing course, so you can't possibly look away until the mystery is solved. It's an absolute must-read from a remarkable talent."

SAMANTHA M. BAILEY,
USA Today and #1 nationally bestselling author of
Watch Out for Her

"Kalla is unparalleled in his ability to create compelling characters that embody societal trauma and medical complexities. *The Darkness in the Light* explores rural northern health care, the unrelenting pressure of depression, and pharmaceutical treatments with great care. Both heart-breaking and brave, this is a boldly written story that fans will love and new readers will devour."

AMBER COWIE,
author of *Last One Alive*

"This book, with its well-written descriptions of the far north, is one of [Kalla's] best."

The Globe and Mail

"Emergency room physician Danial Kalla is one of Canada's best-selling and most impressive writers, and his latest novel, *The Darkness in the Light*, demonstrates why."

Zoomer

"Kalla's Alaskan whodunit delights. . . . Just remember that Vancouver E.R. doctor Daniel Kalla not only writes superb medical thrillers with a pronounced social edge—his books are also terrific murder mysteries."

Winnipeg Free Press

"A very good read, and very timely."

CBC's *The Next Chapter*

LOST IMMUNITY

"Kalla ratchets up the suspense as a cover-up is exposed . . . a truly scary scenario from a writer who knows his medical thriller lingo down to the final line."

The Globe and Mail

"Kalla . . . has a knack for writing eerily prescient thrillers."

CBC Books

"Always there to hold up a mirror to society—his last book, *The Last High*, took on the opioid crisis—Kalla's new *Lost Immunity* book sits smack dab in the middle of what the world has been going through for the last year."

Vancouver Sun

THE LAST HIGH

"A thrilling, front-line drama about the opioid crisis."

KATHY REICHS,
#1 *New York Times* bestselling author of
The Bone Hacker

"Kalla has long had his stethoscope on the heartbeat of his times. . . . In his latest, the focus is on Vancouver's opioid crisis. . . . A lively story."

Toronto Star

"A riveting thriller. . . . This important, must-read book is not only well-researched and entirely realistic, it gives a human face to a devastating epidemic."

ROBYN HARDING,
internationally bestselling author of
The Arrangement and *The Party*

"Kalla is terrific at building suspense as the case progresses, uncovering a web of dealers, sellers, and users."

The Globe and Mail

"If you want an engrossing, edge-of-your-seat thriller that combines good detective work, corruption, savage criminal practices, a dark, seamy portrait of a large Canadian city, and a hard-hitting lesson on the medical and emotional effects of opioid drugs, then *The Last High* certainly fills that prescription."

Montreal Times

ALSO BY DANIEL KALLA

HIGH SOCIETY

DANIEL KALLA

PUBLISHED BY SIMON & SCHUSTER

New York   London   Toronto   Sydney   New Delhi

SIMON &
SCHUSTER
CANADA

A Division of Simon & Schuster, LLC
166 King Street East, Suite 300
Toronto, Ontario M5A 1J3

This Simon & Schuster Canada edition May 2024

SIMON & SCHUSTER CANADA and colophon are trademarks of Simon & Schuster, LLC

Simon & Schuster: Celebrating 100 Years of Publishing in 2024

For information about special discounts for bulk purchases, please contact Simon & Schuster Special Sales at 1-800-268-3216 or CustomerService@simonandschuster.ca.

Manufactured in the United States of America

10 9 8 7 6 5 4 3 2 1

Library and Archives Canada Cataloguing in Publication
Title: High society / Daniel Kalla.
Names: Kalla, Daniel, author.
Description: Simon & Schuster Canada edition.
Identifiers: Canadiana (print) 20230533825 | Canadiana (ebook) 20230533833 |
ISBN 9781668032510 (softcover) | ISBN 9781668032527 (ebook)
Classification: LCC PS8621.A47 H54 2024 | DDC C813/.6—dc23

ISBN 978-1-6680-3251-0
ISBN 978-1-6680-3252-7 (ebook)

For my wife, Leeandra

HIGH
SOCIETY

PROLOGUE

Two years hadn't dulled the pain. If anything, the hole in her soul had grown bigger. Holly didn't think she could miss her father any more than she already did, but being this far away from home made the memories of him feel fuzzier, his absence more acute.

What am I doing here with all these old burnt-out hippies and weirdos?

Holly resented her grandfather for dragging her to this primeval Peruvian jungle, five thousand miles from home. But even the struggling eighteen-year-old realized he had only acted out of love and concern.

Holly had been in a downward spiral ever since the accident. Her grades had plummeted. She was disconnected from the few friends who had stuck with her through her grief. And life alone in the house with her melancholic and withdrawn mom felt more like living in a tomb. More than once, Holly had eyed the bottles lining her mother's medicine cabinet, imagining what a relief it would be to just swallow all the pills.

"Trust me, Koala," her grandfather had promised her with a sad smile as they boarded the plane for Lima. "This will help you."

But this was his world, not hers. Everything about it felt foreign to Holly. At times, nightmarish. The twisted tangle of branches forming such a thick canopy that Holly couldn't see the sky. The constant hums, thrums, buzzes, and chirps. Even the smells—a combination of vegetation, moisture, soil, and decay—made her want to puke. It all gave her the unsettling sense of being just another rung on the food chain of the living ecosystem that engulfed her.

Holly was the youngest one on the retreat by at least fifteen years. She had been mortified that first morning when she had to shed her clothes and immerse herself in the communal plant bath—basically just a deeper pool in the muddy stream that ran beside their encampment—in front of all the other women in the group. And she found the ceremony that followed it on the dirt floor of that weird circular hut, with its smelly inhalants, purgatives, and poultices, to be just as unnerving.

None of this mystic bullshit will bring Dad back. Or make me any less responsible for what happened to him.

That evening, the group gathered after dusk in the clearing for what would become a nightly ritual. By the time Holly sat down with the others around the roaring fire, she could feel the panic welling inside her chest. Sensing her growing distress, her grandfather reached over and gently took her hand in his, giving it a reassuring squeeze. That helped for a while. Then the kettle dangling above the dancing flames began to hiss, and the bitter, acrid stench of the special tea brewing inside turned her stomach and reignited her apprehension.

As she reluctantly brought the clay cup to her lips for the first time, feeling nothing but dread and regret, Holly would have never guessed that her life was about to be transformed.

CHAPTER 1

Monday, April 1

Any perceptive observer would recognize that the windowless room has been engineered for maximum calm. The light-taupe walls are sprinkled with pastel acrylic abstracts. The LED lighting is comfortably dim but not dark. A neutral ecru rug covers much of the hardwood flooring. The exit is clearly demarcated by the string of soft red lights lining the top of the door. And the relaxing scent of sandalwood floats through the air, the diffuser nowhere in sight.

Mocha-colored leather recliners form a crescent around Dr. Holly Danvers. Each of the seven seats is occupied. And what a hodgepodge of occupants they are: a rock star, a CEO, an activist, a fashion designer, a lawyer, a socialite, and even one of Holly's own colleagues. To one another, they're members of the same eclectic self-labeled "tribe." But to Holly, they're clients, a term she much prefers over *patients*.

All of them are equipped with identical black blindfolds and headphones. Each has a blood pressure cuff already wrapped around their arm and an IV bag suspended above their chair with tubes dangling below, waiting to be hooked to their forearms. But that's where the physical similarities end. Race, size, gender, age, sexuality, and dress vary from one client to the next. Holly feels particularly protective over each of them today, but the therapist in her reminds her it's merely a reflection of her own sense of exposure and vulnerability.

After all, today is the day the experiment leaves the laboratory.

Holly has been working with them for almost three months. They have made genuine progress, as a group and as individuals, through their weekly ritual: first, a potent intravenous dose of the psychedelic agent ketamine, followed later the same day or next by individual therapy and then a group session.

But they're still addicts. Each with their own habit, ranging from sex and gambling to opioids and alcohol. Their hold on sobriety is new and fragile. One of them hasn't even reached that point, but that is a secret only she and Holly share.

Eleven weeks into group therapy, Holly recognizes that all of them still have obstacles in their paths: truths they aren't willing to admit and past traumas they are unable to confront. But her gut tells her that they're as ready as they ever will be for a session under dual doses of two powerful psychedelics. A new step for them. And for her, at least in the clinical setting.

But Holly isn't nearly as confident as she projects to the group. While ketamine-enhanced therapy is legal and largely accepted, none of the same holds true for the off-ramp she is about to lead her clients down. She's going to supervise them as they self-administer a second psyche-delic that has no legitimate pharmaceutical supplier and no sanctioned medical use, and in so doing, she will expose herself to potential legal and professional risk. She has reservations about a few of them, especially Elaine and Salvador, the two most anxious members. Salvador had a dys-phoric reaction—what laypeople would label a "bad trip"—during one of his previous sessions. And Elaine's needle phobia only worsens with each subsequent IV insertion.

Then why do it?

Holly sees it as a calculated risk, one worth taking if it will help to free them from the shackles of addiction. At least, that's what she tells herself. But she realizes she's motivated by more than simply altruism. There's potential glory in it for her, too. Not to mention material gain—in terms of research data as well as free publicity for the book she has been contracted to write. That is, *if* she can demonstrate that adding a second psychedelic provides a stronger and more permanent form of abstinence.

As Holly was taught during the month she spent shadowing an anesthetist friend from med school, she has already preloaded the ketamine into the IV bags that now hang above the chairs. After the clients arrived, she tested each of their MDMA tablets using her laboratory-grade analyzer and found the pills to be pure. The group had to procure the MDMA on their own, albeit through a site Holly recommended, since she can't prescribe it. No physician can. Besides, even in the exploding world of ketamine clinics and other plant-based wellness centers, none offer therapy combining two such potent psychedelics. Or if they do, none dare to publicize it.

Elaine Golding squeezes her eyelids shut and whimpers as Holly inserts the IV needle into her forearm. Fortunately, it slides into the vein with ease. Elaine gasps with relief, as if she has just jumped back onto a curb and narrowly avoided an onrushing truck.

Once all the IVs are secure and the last of the seven clients have swallowed their MDMA tablets, Salvador Jimenez raises his arm as if about to ask a question in class. Despite his meteoric rise in the LA fashion world, the designer looks and sometimes acts like a child. It doesn't help that his round face is accentuated by an ever-present, undersized ball cap.

"They call this kitty flipping, don't they?" Salvador asks with a giggle.

Holly frowns. "They?"

"Y'know. Like on the street."

"The mean streets," Baljit Singh grunts. "That makes us sound so bad-ass. So *Narcos*. Not the whiny bunch of entitled elites we actually are."

The real estate CEO gives off almost the opposite vibe as Salvador. Baljit isn't much older than him, but with her impenetrable self-assuredness and edgy cynicism, she could pass for his mother. And her outfits—like the tailored blue blazer, matching skirt, and gold hoop earrings she wears today—epitomize the power executive look. Still, Baljit's gambling addiction is just as self-destructive as Salvador's dependence on Adderall and cocaine, though she tries to hide it with a "baller" attitude.

Holly offers them a patient smile. "Remember, our sessions have nothing to do with recreational use."

Clients often ask, particularly members of this group, how it's possible to treat addiction using psychedelics. *Aren't you just substituting one habit for another?* is the common refrain. But Holly always takes the time to explain how psychedelic agents like ketamine, MDMA, or even LSD represent an alternate class of medication, which works differently on the human brain. How, despite the recreational use and abuse of LSD, it was still the most widely studied psychiatric drug in the 1960s. How it showed more promise for treating alcoholism than any drug has before or since. And how, unlike other psychiatric medical treatments, such as antidepressants, psychedelic therapy is limited to a finite number of sessions over weeks to months.

"Why do recreational users call it 'kitty flipping'?" demands Dr. Liisa Koskinen.

Fair-skinned, with a stern blond bob and always garbed in formless dresses, the middle-aged client is also a colleague—a clinical psychologist, not a psychiatrist like Holly—who happens to suffer from a crippling Xanax addiction. Liisa rarely misses an opportunity to question Holly's therapeutic approach.

Holly nods. "Among recreational users, a psychedelic experience with just ketamine is considered a trip. And one with MDMA—"

"Ecstasy, right? The love drug?" interjects Justine Jang, or "JJ" as everyone refers to her, including herself. The third-generation Southern Californian of Korean heritage is a household name in Laguna Beach. And not only because she's the heiress to one of the region's largest family fortunes. Because she stands barely five feet tall, JJ's bubbly, larger-than-life personality is even more striking relative to her tiny frame. Holly knows JJ to be in her late forties, but she can't tell if it's genetics or Botox that keeps her face wrinkle-free and ageless.

"Some call it Molly, too," Elaine points out. The activist is pale, and Holly suspects anticipatory anxiety.

"Not here," Holly says. "Here we only use proper pharmaceutical names."

"They say that if you trip on ketamine and you roll on MDMA—" Salvador begins.

"Then you flip when you combine the two!" roars Simon Lowry, the aging rock star, whose lionlike mane of gray hair and beard shakes as he laughs.

"I won't let you flip." But even as Holly says it, her gut rumbles again. "No question, combining psychedelics is a more intense sensorineural experience. One that is usually accompanied by markedly altered perceptions."

Elaine shifts nervously in her recliner. With her haunting good looks, gaunt but with exquisite bone structure, like Kate Moss, she could have become a runway model instead of one of the most vocal advocates for opioid recovery. Even while she was continuing to secretly use them. "You mean hallucinations, don't you, Dr. Danvers?"

"Those, too. Almost always, in my experience," Holly says, but what she really means is in her self-experimentation. "And, it's during that fully dissociative state when the deepest breakthroughs occur."

"All of which you explained in detail last week," sighs Reese Foster. Tall and willowy, Reese has cropped brown hair, a heart-shaped face, and deep-set hazel eyes that come together in a distinctive but attractive visage. The Newport Beach–based lawyer sometimes approaches these sessions as if she might be losing billable hours. And Reese is clearly impatient to proceed as she fiddles with her blood pressure cuff.

"You totally did, Dr. Danvers!" JJ interjects, practically beaming as she nods to Reese.

All seven clients came into group therapy as strangers, but Holly has noticed how often JJ tends to side with and defer to the younger lawyer. Holly often catches them sharing glances, laughs, or even eyerolls. She wonders if the bond between the two of them is related to the fact that they're the only members of the group who share an addiction: alcoholism.

But Reese is right. At the end of the previous session, Holly had explicitly warned the group of the potentially terrifying fracture of reality that can result from combining psychedelics and the inevitable serotonin storm they provoke inside the brain. It didn't deter them. All seven members willingly—maybe too eagerly—agreed to proceed. And they all signed waivers.

"I still need to confirm it with you here and now that you're aware of the risks," Holly says as she scans the sets of eyes focused on her. "If any of you have doubts or second thoughts, the MDMA tablets you already ingested will be more than enough for our later counseling debrief." She glances over to the far recliner on her left. "Salvador, would you still like to proceed with the ketamine?"

He utters another nervous chortle and twists his ball cap around backwards. "Sure. Let's flip this kitty."

With a smile almost as wide as her face, JJ is vehemently nodding even before Holly asks her. The other clients each reiterate their consent with a nod, a thumbs-up, or, in Simon's case, a fist pump along with a holler of "Fuck, yeah!"

"All right," Holly says. "Remember it's all about the—"

"Set and setting!" Baljit moans. "We know. This isn't exactly our first rodeo."

"Maybe so, but I'm going to remind you every time. A positive mind-set coupled with the calmest surroundings guarantee the best possible experience under psychedelics. So, please lower your blindfolds and go to your warmest and happiest memory or place in your mind."

Fifteen minutes later, with the MDMA absorbed from their guts and the ketamine pumping through their bloodstreams, the clients are all under the influence. Technically speaking, they're anesthetized.

Reclined in their chairs with the blindfolds down and headphones on, each manifests a different response to the potent combination of drugs. JJ's huge smile is glued to her glossed lips, and Holly knows where she must be in her head: on that lanai in Kauai, proudly holding up her positive pregnancy test to show her first husband. Reese is dead still in the recliner beside her. Baljit rolls her shoulders as if they're being massaged. Salvador wiggles in his seat. Elaine grips both armrests, her knuckles white. Liisa picks at the air above her. And, not surprisingly, Simon is singing.

Aside from Simon's soft falsetto and the near constant buzz of one or the other of the blood pressure cuffs automatically inflating and deflating, the room is otherwise quiet. No sound leaks out from under the headsets, which play individualized soundtracks, ranging from nature sounds to jazz, as chosen by the clients themselves.

Soon, Baljit, Elaine, and Salvador go still, too. Even Simon stops singing. And while Liisa continues to strum the air above her, the motion is as peaceful as if she's playing an imaginary harp.

But for some paradoxical reason, the tranquility surrounding Holly only heightens her vigilance. She holds a syringe full of midazolam—the powerful, short-acting version of Valium—ready to dose anyone who experiences a dysphoric rection.

Why do I keep expecting the worst?

A little voice inside responds: Because the worst already happened, and it's been haunting you ever since.

CHAPTER 2

Where the hell am I? Elaine wonders from where she sits, in the heart of a meadow encircled by endless rings of wildflowers.

The explosion of color is overwhelming, almost painful on her retinas, but also impossible to turn away from. The beauty is beyond breathtaking. Beyond words. Hers, anyway. All those brilliant hues: aubergine larkspurs, frothy pink-and-white milkweed, daisies as bright as the sun, and forget-me-nots bluer than the sky. An unseen creek burbles in the background while birds chirp overhead. The sounds are as soothing as a warm hug.

There is peace here. Maybe a deeper peace than she has ever experienced. No selfish politicians blocking the provision of lifesaving harm-reduction measures to desperate users. No speeches to write or rallies to organize. No infighting among her own community. No opportunistic upstarts angling to steal her thunder. No paralyzing anxiety. No predatory uncle. No sweet temptation from the pills. No one dying alone in the street.

And no little brother incapable of forgiveness. If Tyler could be here with her now, surely, he would he finally find it in his heart to forgive her.

There is, Elaine suddenly conjures the word, *acceptance* among the wildflowers.

She sweeps her hand through an inflorescence of violets without feeling anything on her fingertips. This only makes her laugh. As she reaches out again, the nearby stems rustle almost imperceptibly. But it's warning enough. She withdraws her hand as if burned.

He's back!

Jagged teeth, whiter than ivory, appear one-by-one between the blooms. The rest of his bloody snout, shaped to rip flesh from bone, materializes, then his huge gray head. Once more, she's being devoured by those ravenous black eyes.

Even Elaine is startled by the bloodcurdling scream that arises in her belly and blasts out of her mouth.

CHAPTER 3

Holly relaxes her grip on the syringe full of midazolam and turns to her laptop. She normally records her detailed notes after a session, but since all the clients are drowsy, she types a few quick lines now. "11:24. Clients sedated. Psychomotor activity is minimal, except Liisa continues to strum."

Holly is about to add more when she catches movement out of the corner of her eye.

Suddenly, Elaine balls up into a fetal position on her recliner and screams, "Leave me alone!" Her arm jerks up so violently that the IV rips out of the vein. Fresh blood leaks down her forearm. She whips the blindfold off her face with her angled wrist, smearing blood across her cheek and forehead. "*No!* Go away! Go away!"

As soon as Holly reaches her, she pinches the skin over Elaine's other shoulder and jabs in the needle. She injects the full dose of sedative into the muscle but realizes, with concern, that it will take longer to calm Elaine than an intravenous dose would have.

Elaine's bloody hand shoots out, barely missing the tip of the needle, and grips Holly's wrist. Her pupils are fully dilated, and her expression is frantic. "I can't, I can't . . ." she whimpers.

Holly feels for Elaine. Not only sympathy, but guilt, as well. Their therapy together had forced Elaine's deeply buried memories of child-hood sexual abuse at the hands of her uncle to the surface. While Holly saw confronting that trauma as necessary for Elaine's healing, and ulti-mately her sobriety, she can't imagine how overwhelming it must be for the frail young woman trembling in front of her now. It's no wonder that Elaine always shows up early for sessions and is so desperate for more time with Holly.

"*He*'s here!" Elaine sobs. "I saw him!"

Holly squeezes her arm reassuringly. "Only those you can trust are here."

Elaine lunges forward and wraps herself around Holly. The hug is almost crushing. Elaine's narrow rib cage trembles against Holly's breast, and she can feel the other woman's heart pounding.

"Hold me," Elaine murmurs. "Please."

Despite her discomfort, Holly doesn't break off the intimate embrace. But her gaze sweeps the room to ensure the other clients still have on their headphones and blindfolds. They do. "It's OK, Elaine." She strokes the back of her head. "It will be over soon. You'll see."

Elaine clings to her for long seconds. As much as Holly would love to slip out of the uncomfortably tight hug, she senses it would only agitate Elaine, so she surrenders to it.

Suddenly, Elaine gasps and jerks herself free, pushing Holly away with both hands.

Lips trembling and eyes dark with suspicion, Elaine gapes at her. "What do you think you're doing, Dr. Danvers?"

CHAPTER 4

Holly can feel her shoulders relaxing. The tension from the morning's group session loosens the moment she steps through the doorway and into the open-concept living room which, thanks to its vaulted ceiling, has always seemed bigger than it is. Though Holly has never lived here, nowhere feels more like home. Sleepovers spent in the mid-century California rancher, perched in the hills above Dana Point, are among her happiest memories from childhood.

Ten years after her grandmother's death, her grandfather still refuses to downsize. Even at the age of ninety, Dr. Walter Danvers insists on doing much of his own yard work, gardening, and pool maintenance.

"Papa?" Holly calls out, though she already knows where she is likely to find him.

"In the cave!" Walter replies in the baritone that has lost some of its rich timbre but is still reassuring to her ears. She thinks of rainy Saturday afternoons long ago, watching old movies with her grandfather in the den while Grandma made grilled cheese sandwiches for lunch.

Holly heads over to the third bedroom, which serves as her grandfather's undersized office. She sticks her head inside to find her grandfather seated in his chair staring at the computer screen on the desk, which is crammed between filing cabinets and piles of other boxes. The walls are covered with framed black-and-white and Kodachrome portraits. Most of the faces belong to pioneers of the psychedelic movement. In one shot, a young Walter has his arm slung over the shoulder of a much older Albert Hofmann, the brilliant Swiss chemist and creator of LSD. In another, Walter is sandwiched between a laughing Timothy Leary and Robert Anton Wilson, two of the sixties' most famous proponents of acid.

Holly wouldn't have invested as much of her career in psychedelics were it not for her grandfather's influence. But when she was a child, those faces lining the walls meant nothing to her. They were only relics from the sixties. Like psychedelics themselves. It wasn't until she had her own catharsis under the influence of ayahuasca that she came to share her grandfather's passion.

That experience made her a true believer. It also saved her life.

Walter spins his chair to face her. "Koala!" he says, using the same pet name as he has for the past thirty years, ever since the then-eight-year-old Holly scaled halfway up a eucalyptus tree in the backyard. He points a knobby finger to his screen. The magnified font only partially compensates for his macular degeneration. "Did you read this latest article out of New Zealand? On the need for more precise phenomenology in objectively assessing psychedelic-assisted psychotherapy?"

"It's great to see you, too, Papa." Holly laughs. At ninety, her grandfather is as single-minded as ever about his lifelong mission, despite how much the quest has cost him, professionally and personally. She steps over to him, wraps him in a hug, and kisses the top of his balding head.

"I read it, yes," she says. "And I totally agree. Mainstream psychiatry will never accept the wildly impressive clinical results that we're seeing with psychedelics until we start measuring outcomes using the same accepted scoring metrics. In other words, speaking their language."

"Precisely!" He pats her arm affectionately. "I've been beating that drum for decades. Rigorous science! None of this airy-fairy bullshit."

Holly thumbs to a photo on the wall. "Says Timothy Leary's pal."

"Tim was a self-aggrandizing prick," Walter grunts. "He helped turn LSD into a party drug. Did more to set back the cause of serious psychedelic research than almost anyone. He knew better, too. Tim was *once* a legitimate academic."

Holly chuckles. "Then how come his picture's still up on your wall?"

"Bob's in the photo, too. I always liked him. But enough about us dinosaurs." Walter rolls his hand with a flourish. "I'm in the company of the future of psychedelic therapy."

"As if!"

"How's the book coming along?"

"Really, Papa? I just signed the book deal."

"You've got to strike while the iron's hot. You have the platform. And the credibility. That's a rare combination, my darling."

Holly clears a box off the only other chair in the room and drops down onto it. "It's also a ton of pressure."

"You've always thrived on that. Gold medal winner in your med school class. Chief psychiatric resident. Associate professor by the age of thirty-five." Walter winks a watery eye. "Pressure is like eucalyptus leaves for you, Koala."

"It might be too much this time," Holly says. "Ever since Simon Lowry told his millions of Instagram followers that he was in therapy with me . . . I can't keep up with the demand."

"That busy, huh?" Walter asks with a pleased grin.

"I had to close my waiting list a couple of months ago. I've been bombarded with media requests. I even had to hire a publicist!"

Walter nods to the photo of himself with Leary. "Old Timothy must be spinning in his grave to see someone else get that kind of attention."

"It's too much, Papa. It feels like I'm under the microscope. But on the other hand, psychedelics are finally getting the serious attention they deserve. For the first time since Nixon derailed your career." In 1970, with a sweep of his pen, the former president had banned LSD as a controlled substance, putting it in the same criminal class as heroin. Nixon did so largely out of his intense hatred for Leary, but the result was disastrous for psychedelic research and for the careers of serious academics who studied the drugs, especially Walter. "But if I screw this up now?"

"You won't." Walter's hand trembles slightly as it wraps around her wrist. "Besides, who the hell is Simon Lowry, anyway? You want to talk real stars?"

She rolls her eyes. "Here we go . . ."

Holly has heard the story countless times. How in 1960, as a young post-doctorate researcher, Walter got a chance to intern under the legendary Dr. Mortimer Hartman. Despite being trained as a radiologist, Hartman performed group therapy in Beverly Hills with clients who were under the influence of LSD. He became the talk of Hollywood, especially after Cary Grant publicly acknowledged that he himself was a patient and a true believer.

"Such a kind man, Mr. Grant!" Walter says. "Not only a movie star, but a real gentleman. He always shook my hand and remembered me by name."

"The Cary Grant story again? Really?"

"There are parallels to your current predicament," Walter tsks. "Like you, Dr. Hartman was also overwhelmed with interest in his practice. Especially after Mr. Grant asked *Good Housekeeping* to share his story. You want to talk about an explosion in demand?"

"Fair enough." Holly sighs. "Maybe I don't have anything to complain about."

Walter eyes her with that penetrating stare. "What's really troubling you, Koala?"

Holly hesitates. "I took another step today."

He tilts his head. "Which step?"

"Dual therapy."

"Dual therapy?" His voice catches. "Two psychedelics *simultaneously*?"

"Yes. MDMA and ketamine."

Walter's eyes widen. "And?"

"Six of the seven clients tolerated it well."

"And the seventh?"

"Not so well." Holly describes Elaine's intense dysphoric reaction and their awkward embrace. "The irony is she's my only pro bono client in the group. Elaine came to me desperate for help after hiding an opioid addiction for years. She melted my resistance with her neediness."

"You always did have a penchant for bringing home strays. Remember that kitten you found and foisted on your grandmother and me?"

"It's different with Elaine. Turns out she suffered terrible sexual abuse as a young girl. And those memories only surfaced during our therapy."

"The poor woman." Walter sighs. "Still Holly, you can't afford even one tiny misstep."

"She'll be OK," Holly says, sounding more certain than she is.

"Why try dual therapy now? When your work has the attention of those who really matter?"

"We discussed this, Papa. You agreed. It's the next frontier for psychedelics."

"But the timing is poor. As you said, you're under a microscope. If it doesn't go perfectly, this could be the final frontier."

"That's a bit melodramatic, isn't it?"

"Maybe. Don't forget I've lived through this before."

"Lived through what?"

"The repercussions of serious people, including doctors and scientists, being too ambitious, too aggressive, with psychedelics. People not unlike you."

Holly dismisses the suggestion with a flick of her wrist, though she understands her grandfather's concern. Why introduce dual therapy now when her newfound fame only adds to the risk?

But Holly knows exactly why. She intuited that the group needed more than a single psychedelic agent to hang on to their sobriety—or in Liisa's case, to find it. And if she could show that dual therapy is effective for the most recalcitrant of addicts, imagine how many others could be helped? Maybe even cured? And how good would that be for her own reputation and career, not to mention sales of her upcoming book?

"What does the esteemed Herr Professor Laing think of your new clinical adventure?" Walter asks.

"Let's not go there."

"He doesn't approve?"

"You'll have to ask Aaron. We're still separated."

"But will you remain so?"

"Only time will tell, Papa," she grumbles, but her grandfather has reason for his skepticism.

Holly and Aaron have been separated for six months. The second separation in their volatile ten-year marriage. Both times, Aaron's professional insecurity and jealousy over her professional success—which often manifested as derision or spite—coupled with his possessiveness, had pushed Holly to the breaking point. And their issues are only compounded by Graham, the troubled one of Aaron's two grown sons from his previous marriage. But Holly acknowledges that her laser focus on her own career has also affected her ability to prioritize Aaron's needs.

After their first separation, Aaron convinced Holly he had changed. And he did, for a while. But he eventually reverted back to old habits. He once even spoke up in the middle of her presentation at a psychiatric conference, to disparage her conclusions on psychedelics. She thought that was the final straw. It wasn't. There has always been an inexplicable, and not necessarily healthy, magnetism between the two of them. And despite her current resolve, she isn't convinced this separation will end differently than the first one.

"Are you two on speaking terms?" Walter asks.

"Of course. Aaron and I are still linked professionally. Financially, too."

He raises an eyebrow. "But not emotionally?"

"It's complicated."

"Hmmm." Walter eyes her quietly for a moment. "You remember Peru?"

As if Holly could ever forget.

She and Walter left for Lima exactly two years from the day of the car crash that killed her father, and Walter's only son, Martin. Holly, who was sixteen at the time, had been in the station wagon, too, when it flipped and rolled. Aside from extensive bruising and a lingering concussion, she emerged physically intact, but she couldn't shake the darkness and loneliness that followed. And while she had no memory of the accident, she felt somehow responsible. In the two years that followed, her pervasive guilt and hopelessness inched ever closer to suicidality. Her mom, who had never been emotionally well equipped, basically shut down after the accident. Only Walter recognized how dire his granddaughter's situation had become. He forcefully persuaded her to accompany him on the ayahuasca retreat.

Though she left for Peru feeling nothing but doubt and dread, she returned with a new lease on life. The experience converted her into a devotee of psychedelic therapy. And she's still in awe of its restorative power.

"What does my separation from Aaron have to do with Peru?" Holly asks.

Walter views her with an amused grin. "At the risk of sounding like a fortune cookie, Koala, sometimes you need to travel far away to make lasting changes at home."

Holly can't tell if he is encouraging her to reconcile with Aaron or to make the break permanent. And, at this point, she would rather not know.

CHAPTER 5

Tuesday, April 2

Simon Lowry tries to swing his leg over the armrest of the padded chair but is stopped by a twinge of pain. The discomfort in his left groin reminds him that sooner or later he's going to have to have that hip replaced, too, just as he did with his right one.

What kind of self-respecting rocker has two prosthetic hips? he wonders again. *If Jeremy could see me now, he'd be kitty flipping in his grave.*

Like Jeremy, his best friend and cofounder of their band, Simon was convinced they would both die young. Only one of them realized the self-prophecy. Then again, it wasn't a fair comparison since Jeremy had taken his own life after he found his naked wife in Simon's bed with her arms and legs bound to the bedposts and her face still flushed with arousal.

Pushing aside the uncomfortable memory, Simon sits up straighter and focuses on Dr. Danvers. She's seated in the matching chair across from his, one leg crossed over the other and hands folded in her lap, as still as the aloe vera plant on her desk.

"Trust me, Dr. D, I've dropped a ton of acid in my day." Simon chuckles. "Shit, being in the music industry all these years . . . there isn't a drug I haven't dabbled in. But I got to tell you that trip with MDMA and ketamine, now that was something!"

Dr. Danvers leans forward in her seat. "Something good or . . . ?"

"Something amazing."

"Elaborate, please." Dr. Danvers shows him one of those cute closed-mouth half smiles, as she pushes her glasses back up her nose.

Simon loves that look. It reminds him of his sixth-grade teacher, Miss Mullen. How he used to crave that shy grin of hers, too. And the resemblance between the two women is uncanny—both lean and flat-chested, with narrow hips, mid-length dark hair, long angular faces, and soulful eyes that ooze sensuality behind their glasses. Before he even realized the world of BDSM existed, Simon used to fantasize about binding his teacher's limbs with rope and taking her like that. On her desk. On his desk.

Simon has had similar thoughts about his therapist, too, but there's nothing sexual in what he's experiencing now. All he wants at the moment is Dr. Danvers's approval. Maybe his second wife was right? Maybe his whole life has been spent trying to compensate for his perpetually detached and disapproving mother?

"I went places . . ." Simon struggles to put yesterday's wild double psychedelic trip into words. "Like I saw and heard things. Plants that walked. Animals that talked. It's so weird. Like it was so intense, but it was also so . . . peaceful."

"A paradox?"

"Yes!" Simon snaps his fingers. "Exactly!"

"And how do you feel today?"

"In a word or three? Fan-fucking-tastic!"

"And the urges?"

"Nothing. Not a sniff."

"Even right now? You're not sexualizing me at all?"

"No." He scoffs, but his cheeks heat.

At times, Simon wishes he hadn't been so candid with Dr. Danvers. When he first came to her clinic, Simon claimed it was for treatment of his habitual cocaine use. But after a few sessions, he also confessed to his sexual addiction and compulsive fantasies. Without, of course, sharing everything.

"I'm telling you, Dr. D, ever since we—our tribe—started the ketamine, my urges have faded. All of them. And honestly, since yesterday, not one single filthy thought has crossed my mind."

"You do understand, Simon, that some of what you're feeling is probably due to a placebo effect?"

Simon bellowed with laughter. "I don't care if you flushed me with salt water and gave me a sugar pill."

"I didn't give you any pills—"

"I know. I know. Those MDMA pills just fell off the back of some truck." He chuckles. "Point is, Dr. D, I saw what I saw. And I felt what I felt."

He's rewarded with another one of the doctor's small smiles.

CHAPTER 6

Wednesday, April 3

Elaine is the last of the seven in the group to arrive for her one-on-one debrief with Holly, a day after their dual MDMA and ketamine session.

Before Elaine even reaches the chair, Holly can tell that her client has had a vastly different response to dual therapy than the rest of the group. To start with, there is no light in her eyes. The others have all described the experience in glowing terms such as "life-altering," "transformative," and even "a brush with God." Holly might have predicted such enthusiastic responses from perpetual optimists like Simon or JJ. But it was Reese, the lawyer and most businesslike member, who likened the experience to the divine.

The feedback only validated Holly's decision to use dual psychedelics for the first time in her practice. But her excitement is now tempered by the sight of Elaine. Her color is slightly off. And her bloodshot eyes hold a haunted look, reminiscent of a victim of domestic assault or other recent trauma.

"You went through a lot yesterday," Holly says, after Elaine sits down across from her. "I'm sorry for that."

"Me, too," Elaine mutters, avoiding eye contact.

"No question, the experience can be overwhelming. Not at all easy to process. Particularly after such a traumatic trip."

Elaine shrugs but still refuses to look up.

"Can we talk about it?"

Her shoulders twitch again. "I don't remember much."

"That must be the midazolam."

"The sedative?"

"Yes. You were having a severe dysphoric reaction. A bad trip. You dropped into the 'hell realm,' as some people call it. When the hallucinations turn nightmarish. I had no choice but to sedate you. And midazolam often causes amnesia for part or all of its duration."

"Oh."

"You don't remember anything from the experience?"

"I remember a meadow. Lots of flowers. Vivid colors . . ."

Holly nods. "That's a good start. You did cry out, though. It sounded as if someone else was with you in the vision. You were screaming at him to go away."

"I . . . I don't remember that."

Holly waits a few seconds before asking, "Was it the wolf?"

Elaine buries her face in her hands and begins to rock in her chair.

Holly knows better than to push too hard, but she also can't ignore it. Elaine has arguably made the most progress of anyone in the group. Early on, she confided to Holly that despite being a leading voice in the fight against the opioid crisis, she was still abusing prescription painkillers such as Vicodin and Percocet. She just hid it better than most. But a month into therapy with ketamine, Elaine found sobriety. A fact Holly has confirmed every week since, with Elaine's permission, through urine drug screening.

Elaine's abstinence coincided with one of her earliest ketamine trips. In the subsequent debrief, she recounted to Holly her powerful hallucination about being chased through a forest by a hungry wolf. By the next session, Elaine had recognized the wolf for what he was: the anthropomorphic representation of her uncle.

From the age of six to nine, Elaine and her little brother had gone on an annual summer fishing trip with their paternal uncle. She hated those excursions and came to despise her uncle, refusing to go back by the time

she turned ten. But it wasn't until she began working with Holly that the
suppressed memories of those nights spent alone in her uncle's cramped
cabin, while her brother slept next door, flooded back to her. Elaine remembered the encounters in harrowing detail: the claustrophobic sense
of being swallowed in her uncle's arms, the stale beer on his breath, the
way his whiskers scratched her face, and the panicky, gut-churning sensation of his pudgy fingers probing between her legs.

It was hard for Holly to stomach the details, but she recognized that
Elaine's devastating molestation had contributed to, or likely caused, her
severe anxiety, her inability to sustain romantic relationships, and ulti-
mately her opioid addiction. Holly is convinced that for Elaine to heal
from her PTSD and remain sober, she needs to confront those horrific
memories.

"After yesterday's session, Elaine, did you . . . relapse?"

"No!" Elaine snaps, her face still covered by her fingers. "Want me to
pee in a cup right now to prove it?"

"No. It's just that you seem so shaken."

Elaine pulls her hands from her face. "Because I am!"

Holly reaches for her wrist, but Elaine recoils from her touch.

I moved too fast. I pushed too hard.

Holly had predicted Elaine would be the most vulnerable member to
compounding doses of psychedelics. And she silently berates herself for
not listening to the inner voice that told her to slow down, to begin with
smaller doses. But what was done was done. "Aside from the flowers,
Elaine, do you remember anything else from yesterday's session?"

"No." She pauses. "Except . . ."

"Except what?"

Elaine's eyes narrow. "When I woke up. Or came to. Or whatever. I
was in your . . . arms."

"Yes. Right after I injected the midazolam, you reached out and clung
to me. And you asked me—pleaded with me—to keep holding you."

Elaine's chin drops, and her gaze falls to the floor.

Holly suppresses a sigh. She has no idea how far yesterday's experience might have set her client back.

Though there are twenty minutes still left in their session, Elaine rises abruptly to her feet. Turning away, she murmurs something Holly can't decipher.

"I didn't catch that," Holly says.

Elaine looks back over her shoulder. "I said it didn't feel right."

"What didn't?"

"That hug. The way you touched me. It didn't feel right at all."

CHAPTER 7

Dr. Aaron Laing watches his wife cross the deck to the table where he sits overlooking what feels like the entire Pacific Ocean on this cloudless spring morning. Holly strides toward him in leggings and a simple gray top, with that combination of purpose and grace that Aaron has always found so appealing. After ten years of marriage, he feels more attracted to his wife than ever. Her angular, almost androgynous features have aged well, and she's even more striking now than she was as his resident, over a decade earlier. But he understands that part of his response is due to her absence from his life. And he's more determined than ever to win her back.

He stands up to greet her, and they repeat their awkward dance of separation, where he leans in to kiss her, and she quickly pulls out of the hug. His lips brush over her ear instead of her cheek.

"I've missed this, Holl," Aaron says once they're both seated.

She tilts her head. "You missed brunch?"

"Well, that goes without saying." They had their second date here, also brunch, eleven years before. Nestled two stories above Laguna Beach's rolling shoreline, the restaurant has been popular forever with tourists and locals for its basic but consistently good food, bustling ambience, and spectacular view. "What I meant is dining with you."

"Oh, yeah, me too," she says distractedly. "Look, Aaron, what I really need right now is your advice."

"Anytime. You know that."

It comes as no surprise to him that's why she asked him to meet. Their relationship began as a teacher-student dynamic, which, after a decade of marriage, is still at the core of their connection. Holly has always been most drawn to him when she's vulnerable. And he has always accepted that and, when necessary, capitalized on it.

Aaron beckons a server with a wave, but when the young man with the sleeves of tattoos arrives to take Holly's order, she declines, explaining that she doesn't have time to stay for a meal.

Aaron swallows his disappointment. He can tell from the way his wife keeps looking at the table how troubled she is. "What's wrong, Holl?"

"This client of mine." She clears her throat. "She didn't respond well to our last session."

Aaron raises an eyebrow. "Under ketamine?"

She hesitates. "Yes."

Aaron has to bite his tongue. While he isn't as vehemently opposed to the use of psychedelics in therapy as some of his colleagues, he has never remotely considered them to be the panacea—the Holy Grail of psychotherapeutics—that Holly and her grandfather do. And he certainly doesn't trust them to be free of risk. "What happened in the session?"

"My client had a serious dysphoric reaction. I had to sedate her with midazolam. She clung to me afterwards. Trembling like a leaf. She wouldn't let go. Now her memories are all jumbled." Holly swallows. "She's misinterpreting that embrace, Aaron."

"Misinterpreting? As in, she thinks it was inappropriate?"

"Yes."

They had argued before over Holly's clinical use of these potent drugs with patients, which Aaron has always viewed as too aggressive, verging on cavalier. Holly has never been willing to accept the obvious—that she is playing with fire. He has to restrain himself from saying, *I told you so*. What she needs most now is his unconditional support. And besides, he might not get another opportunity like this anytime soon. "Does your client have a history of being sexually abused?"

Holly nods. "In her childhood, yes. She exhibits classic PTSD symptoms. But her specific memories of that abuse only surfaced during our work together."

"Which would make her particularly susceptible." His gaze drifts off toward the ocean. "Was her abuser female?"

"No. But my client identifies as gay. And she has consistently struggled with physical intimacy issues in her relationships."

"Makes sense." Aaron looks back to his wife. He can't help noticing how her fragility softens the sharpest of her features, the angle of her jawline and the ridges above her copper-brown eyes. "Obviously, you explained to your client what really did happen?"

"I tried."

"But she wasn't convinced?"

"No."

"And you're worried she's going to do something . . . rash?"

"That's one of my concerns."

"What else?"

"We've been making real progress over the past three months," Holly says. "Elaine was . . . emerging from that shell of childhood wounds. But she has other issues, too. Namely, addiction."

"To?"

"Opioids."

"And you're worried she might relapse?"

Holly exhales. "She walked out of our session. I'm not convinced she's coming back."

"That's her decision, Holl. Sounds to me like you reached her in a way no one else has."

"But what good did it do her?"

"I bet her response—her misremembering of what happened with you two—is at least in part attributable to transference," Aaron says, using the psychological term to describe when a client misinterprets a therapeutic connection and empathy for a romantic attachment to their therapist.

She squints. "Are you wondering if I have feelings of countertransference for Elaine?"

"Do you?"

"No," she says without a trace of defensiveness.

"Then, no. I'm not. You're experienced enough to recognize if you did."

"What would you do if this happened with one of your clients?"

Aaron is tempted to tell her that it wouldn't have happened with his patients. That he would never have toyed with psychedelics in the first place. But instead, he says, "I suspect that with a little time and reflection, she'll want to come back to your care. But in the meantime, there's only one thing you can do."

"Which is?"

"Protect yourself."

Holly's face falls. "You think she might launch a complaint?"

"Or go public in some other way."

"Jesus . . ."

"Hopefully not, but you have to do everything you can to prevent that."

"And how do I do that?"

He reaches across the table and places his hand over hers, relieved that she doesn't pull away. "Talk to her, Holly. Make her see the light."

"And if she doesn't?"

"She'll come around," he says, though he's more focused on the feeling of her warm knuckles in his hand.

They sit quietly for a while, as the briny scent of calamari wafts to them from a nearby table. Finally, Holly smiles and says, "Thank you." She pats the back of his wrist with her other hand and then gently slips free of his grip.

He hides his frustration behind a smile. "Don't you miss this?"

"Of course, I do," she says. "And I appreciate how you're always there for me."

"Not enough to come home though?"

"That's different."

"Why?"

"Please, Aaron. Not now. It's not the time."

"Graham's doing better," he says. "He really is. Especially since we started him on the new combination of mood stabilizers."

"*We?* You mean you prescribed medication for your own son?"

"Someone had to."

She sighs. "This isn't about Graham."

But Aaron believes otherwise.

His sons, Nate and Graham, were twelve when Aaron and Holly married. She tried to bond with both of her new stepsons, but the fraternal twins responded entirely differently. One welcomed her, the other resented her. Holly and Nate have always been close. But everything comes easy to Nate: sports, academics, and relationships. A first-year med student on scholarship at Columbia, Nate is on track to follow his father's career path. Graham, on the other hand, takes more after his mother, an expert in self-sabotage who finds conflict where it doesn't exist. When Graham was eighteen, another psychiatrist diagnosed him with a borderline personality disorder. But Aaron disagreed with his colleague, believing Graham was too functional in his life and his relationships to fit the criteria. While Aaron appreciates that Graham is still adrift, to his mind it's because his son is a deeply sensitive soul who needs a lot more support than his twin brother.

But even Aaron can't ignore the damage Graham's volatility has inflicted on his marriage. And Holly sometimes mistakes Aaron's protectiveness over his flawed, vulnerable son for siding with him against her. Especially since that online trolling incident.

"You're right," Aaron says. "It's not the time to discuss this. I'm only here to offer my advice. To help you however I can. But . . ."

"But what?"

"These days, it seems impossible for us to find time to talk."

Holly stares at him with a look of affection, maybe even love, but that doesn't diminish the growing distance he senses between them. "The last few months have been out of control," she says. "I've barely had a minute to myself."

"Not easy being a celebrity, is it?"

"Hardly," she snorts. "But ever since Simon Lowry—an actual

celebrity—publicized my involvement in his treatment, my practice has gone wild. It's too much. I'm pulled in a hundred directions. I never asked for that, Aaron."

"And I never asked you to leave," he blurts, regretting the words as soon as they pass his lips.

Holly brushes her hand over his arm again. "Thank you, Aaron, for your support and your wisdom," she says as she rises to her feet.

CHAPTER 8

Friday, April 5

Seven recliners, but only six occupants. Sitting across from her clients, Holly scans the semicircle of chairs and bites back her disappointment over the one empty seat, the second-last from the right, where Elaine usually sits.

JJ is dressed, as always, to the nines, in a colorful spring dress, with multiple gold bracelets that jangle every time she moves her arm, her glow no doubt a result of high-end Korean skin care. Baljit looks uncharacteristically casual in jeans and sneakers, although Holly assumes the CEO is wearing designer labels. Liisa wears one of her typical neutral, shapeless maxi dresses. Reese has on her usual lawyer uniform—dark blazer and slacks—complemented by that familiar no-time-to-waste expression of hers. Salvador has paired his ubiquitous ball cap with a chunky silver chain today. And Simon wears tight white pants and a black T-shirt which strains to hold in his gut.

"Can we talk about the elephant in the room?" Reese asks, as she sits up in her chair. "Or, more specifically, the one *not* in the room."

"Elephant? Elaine?" Baljit grunts. "More like an emaciated gazelle, if you ask me."

"Elaine isn't feeling well," Holly says, misleading with the truth.

Liisa turns to Holly with a knowing look. "She had a serious reaction to the dual psychedelics, didn't she?"

There it is again. But Holly takes a breath and pushes away the reflex defensiveness. She's never certain whether she reads more skepticism into Liisa's comments than the psychologist intends. After all, if Holly were in group therapy, she would probably also question her therapist's approach more than anyone else in the room. Ignoring the question, Holly says, "While we are a group—"

"A tribe!" Salvador cries.

"Hey, colonizer," Baljit says, "you sure that whole cultural appropriation thing still holds water?"

"Colonizer?" Salvador rolls his wrists over to expose his forearms. "Check your prescription, *chica*. No one this brown ever colonized squat! At least not on this continent."

"Look, it's wonderful you see each other as a community," Holly says. "But I still have to respect your individual privacy. Elaine isn't here today. We'll just have to leave it at that and move on."

"Actually, she's more like a sight hound," Baljit says.

"What are you talking about?" Reese asks, frowning.

"If we're coming up with animal metaphors for Elaine, then I'm going with a whippet or a greyhound."

"No one is doing that." Reese's tone signals that she has had it.

"How about we focus on each of your experiences under dual therapy instead?" Holly asks, ending the speculation. "I've had a chance to discuss it with you individually. But who's willing to share their experience with the group?"

"I used to read tons of sci-fi when I was a kid," JJ pipes up, beaming with a look of wonderment. "Books about traveling to new dimensions. That kind of stuff. And to me, that's exactly what it felt like! A new dimension. Lights I'd never seen before with colors that made their own sounds. Both eerie and beautiful at the same time."

Reese shakes her head. "For me, it was more like . . . I don't know . . . the afterlife."

JJ's eyes go wide. "As in heaven?"

"Heaven, hell, purgatory . . . all at once." Reese frowns again, as though skeptical of the words coming from her own mouth. "I was in the presence of spirits. Too many to even comprehend. As if I was with the entire human collective at once. Not so much with, but a part of. If that makes any sense?"

Holly is pleased to hear Reese volunteer such intimate details. She might be the most emotionally balanced member of the group, but when it comes to sharing feelings, Reese is the most tight-lipped, too. Aside from a passing mention of a mother with early onset dementia, Holly has not yet penetrated the web of past traumas that led Reese into addiction, but she knows better than to try to delve now in front of the others.

"I only saw one spirit," Liisa murmurs. "My mother's ghost."

"When did she pass?" Holly asks.

"When I was four."

JJ leans toward her, mouth agape. "Did you speak to her?"

Liisa nods.

"What did she say to you?" JJ's voice squeaks with excitement.

Holly wants to tell JJ to back off, but Liisa is already answering. "She kept telling me it was OK."

"What was?"

"My life." Liisa's voice thickens. "That I didn't need to feel guilty. That I was doing as well as I could."

"And you are, Liisa." Holly nods encouragingly. "This is exactly the kind of response I was hoping you'd experience."

Liisa's face scrunches. "Hallucinations?"

"No." Holly smiles. "Acceptance. We all live in heaven, hell, and purgatory. Often simultaneously. We're all part of the human collective. And it's not until we shed the shackles of our own egos that we connect to something much larger than ourselves. It's in *that* place where we find unconditional love and acceptance." More than anything, Holly wants her clients to experience the same kind of epiphany as she did on her ayahuasca retreat in Peru.

"Holy crap, Dr. D!" Simon bellows. "I lived through some serious love-ins when I first broke through in the seventies, but you make those hippie-dippies sound like a bunch of Young Republicans."

Holly chuckles. "OK, maybe that was a tad enthusiastic? Maybe I'm projecting? As a part of my training, I've journeyed on psychedelics, too, and I've experienced the same release and feeling of connection some of you are describing. So, why don't you tell us about your experience then, Simon?"

"I don't know about acceptance," he says. "But it was fucking brilliant. Magical. I danced with a sunflower and sang with crows."

Holly nods encouragingly. "Peaceful, right?"

"Utterly."

"Mine, too," Salvador chimes in. "Exactly like the dreams I used to have when I was a child. All those brilliant shapes and colors."

Holly recalls him telling her in a private session how he would sometimes escape the bullying he experienced as a teenager for being different—too eccentric, too effeminate—into a world of his own imagination. "Excellent, Salvador. Peace and acceptance, they go hand in hand. Now, what I'd love to hear—if any of you are willing to share—is how the experience affected your cravings." She resists the urge to turn to Liisa, whose sobriety is most on her mind.

Baljit holds out her palm. "I haven't even thought about going to a casino since I came to. Probably the longest stretch I can remember without feeling that itch."

Reese nods vehemently. "Exactly! I haven't felt tempted by the bottle in days, and I've been in mergers and acquisitions hell all week."

"Me neither!" JJ says, beaming at Reese. Lately, the two of them have begun to arrive at the office together, and Holly assumes that their friendship has blossomed outside of therapy, though what a lawyer and an heiress have in common is anyone's guess.

The others speak up almost at once, each eager to confirm that they, too, haven't felt any urges to indulge their specific addictions since they underwent dual psychedelic therapy. Even Liisa nods enthusiastically, but Holly can't tell if she's only doing it for the sake of appearances.

Holly feels deeply satisfied as the clients file out of the room after the session. It's as if they have collectively knocked down another wall in their path to sobriety.

Except Elaine.

Elaine hadn't even called to say she wasn't coming today. Usually, she was the first one there. She often showed up early to try to squeeze in any extra minutes for counseling, but of course Holly's assistant and gatekeeper, Tanya, wouldn't allow it. Tanya protects her time and schedule like a hawk.

As Holly carefully documents her detailed notes on their group session, quoting her clients as accurately as she can remember, she can't shake the thought that Aaron is right. She does have to be proactive. Holly clicks open Elaine's record, finds her mobile number, and dials, but it rings directly to voicemail.

Over the next hour, Holly tries the line two more times, without getting an answer. Finally, with the worry gnawing at her, and in spite of her better instincts, Holly copies Elaine's address into her phone's navigation app and heads down to her car.

Outside, it's a mild and sunny spring day that could've fallen in almost any month of the relatively seasonless weather pattern of coastal Southern California. The short drive takes Holly from her office in the center of the business district, along the highway, and then up to a modest neighborhood on Ocean Vista Drive in the hills above the heart of Laguna Beach.

Holly's heart is already pounding as she pulls into the driveway of the nondescript, three-story condo building and parks in the one available guest spot. Two spaces over, she recognizes Elaine's car, a light-blue compact Nissan. Glancing through the back window, Holly spots posters rolled up on the back seat along with a few placards, facedown, in the gap between the seats.

Holly walks up to Elaine's ground-floor unit and raps on the door. Just as she is about to knock again, the door opens a crack. Elaine stares at Holly through the gap without opening the door much wider. "What are you doing here?" she demands.

"Sorry to just drop in on you, Elaine. But after you didn't show for the group session, I was . . . concerned."

"Don't worry about me."

"Can we talk about it?"

"There's nothing to talk about."

"Can I come in?"

"I don't think so, no."

Holly's not ready to give up. "Can you come out, then, Elaine? Please. I won't bother you again."

After a moment of hesitation, Elaine opens the door just wide enough to slip out through the space. Standing a few steps back from Holly, she folds her arms across her chest. Her long-sleeved shirt and loose sweats hang off her gaunt frame. Her face looks older than a thirty-year-old's should. "I'm not coming back to the group," she says. "Or to you."

"All right." Holly studies her eyes, searching for the telltale signs of opioid toxicity, such as the pinpoint pupils or the vacant gaze.

"I'm not high, in case you're wondering."

"I'm happy to hear that."

"I'm done using. Guess I have to credit the ketamine for that much, at least." Elaine huffs. "Not that it was worth the hell you put me through."

Holly takes a small step forward, and Elaine immediately backs away. "I feel terrible about that last session. It was my fault. You weren't ready."

Elaine's eyes blaze. "I'll never be ready for that."

"No, no." Holly feels her face flushing. "I meant not ready for using dual psychedelics. I should've gone slower. Used smaller doses."

Elaine stares at her feet. "You shouldn't have *touched* me."

"I didn't touch you," Holly says. "I mean I did, but only after you threw your arms around me. You begged me to hold you. You were terrified. Obviously, knowing what I know, I shouldn't have let that happen. But your memories—at least about my intentions—are faulty. They've been affected by that medication, midazolam, that I had to give you."

Elaine shakes her head slightly. "I'm done with all that," she says barely above a whisper.

"With what?"

Elaine's eyes bore into Holly's. "My whole life I knew my uncle had done something terrible to me. But I suppressed those memories. Instead, I blamed myself. Hated myself. Numbed myself. No more. I'm not going to victim-shame myself any longer. I know what you did."

"What your uncle did to you was beyond traumatic. Evil. And I can't imagine how triggering it would be to wake up from the midazolam and find yourself in my arms. But nothing happened." Holly tries to control her voice as she feels herself growing more frantic. "I swear to you."

"I've been a fraud." Elaine sounds as if she's talking to herself now.

"Selling myself as some champion for the victims of the opioid crisis when all along I was still secretly using myself."

"What does that have to do with—"

Elaine's chin snaps up, and her blazing eyes cut Holly off in mid-question. "I'm done being a hypocrite! I've dedicated my life to speaking up for victims. To being their voice. I can't stay silent now. Not after how you took advantage of me when I was most vulnerable! I know what you did. Soon everyone else will, too."

CHAPTER 9

Saturday, April 6

It's the oldest and possibly smallest of Simon's four homes—the others being in New York, Paris, and Mallorca (if he is to count his summer retreat)—but it's still his favorite. The four-bedroom house is nestled right on Victoria Beach. And aside from the nuisance of being approached by random fans in swimwear, Simon never tires of lounging on the deck that's merely yards from the breaking surf, especially at sunset with a vodka soda in hand.

This is his first protracted solo stay in his beach home. In the past, Simon would have always brought one or, just as often, multiple female houseguests. And if he couldn't find anyone to invite, he would just hire professionals. The parties he used to throw here were legendary but, by necessity, extremely discreet. He'd even designed his own kink room, complete with wall-mounted restraints, padded tables, and a cage.

It wasn't age that limited his activities recently. At sixty-seven, his voracious sexual appetite has shown little sign of diminishing. And after his physical performance could no longer keep up with his vibrant imagination, he started to supplement it with increasing doses of Viagra and other pharmaceuticals. Even the suicide of his best friend—after Jeremy found his wife willingly bound and gagged in Simon's bed—hadn't been enough to deter his sexploits. That took the #MeToo movement, which put the fear of God into Simon. Especially after the incident with that nineteen-year-old groupie, Brianna. The bruising around her neck was an accident. But it still cost him three million dollars in hush money and forced him into treatment for his sex addiction. The whole unpleasant episode eventually led him to Holly and her psychedelic therapy. And finally, perhaps, a cure.

But at this moment, Simon isn't lazing on his deck or reminiscing about his red room. Instead, he's sitting in his living room along with five other members of his tribe on the blue velvet chairs which cost thousands of dollars each and took six months to arrive from Italy. Simon hadn't called this clients-only meeting, but he did offer to host after Reese suggested it. After all, he feels closer to the tribe than he does to his own family, although it's not much of a comparison since he is estranged from his few remaining relatives.

Judging by the glum faces surrounding him, the others are as distressed as he is by the bombshell JJ has just dropped on the group.

A scowl is screwed onto Baljit's lip. Simon has always found her facial features too severe for his taste, but it hasn't stopped him from fantasizing about how she might look in a leather mask with only chains wrapped around those generous breasts and hips of hers. He drops his gaze to the ground, as Dr. Danvers taught him, to avoid sexualizing the woman again.

"What do you mean Elaine is planning to go public?" Baljit demands of JJ. "How?"

"How does anybody go public these days?" JJ cries. "Through social media. Plaster it across multiple sites."

Even without JJ's thick eyeliner, fake breasts, and designer outfits, Simon would still have been attracted to the tiny heiress. He has always been a sucker for petite Asians. But it doesn't make up for the way she treated him last month after she came over to his beach house for dinner. To storm out like she did, over a few harmless comments he had made about the pleasure of being chained? And then to completely ghost him afterwards? It was a total overreaction. He was a little surprised she'd returned to his home today for the group meeting. Maybe she thought there would be safety in numbers.

"Why would Elaine do that?" Salvador's voice cracks.

JJ glances at the others with an almost conspiratorial air. "Elaine told me that Dr. Danvers touched her inappropriately while she was under," she says in a hushed voice.

Reese grimaces. "In the middle of a group session? Elaine actually believes that?"

It seems to Simon that the no-nonsense attorney lives in genderless business wear, but he has often picked up on an unconsciously sensual vibe—a repressed sexuality in her that he would love to set free. Again, he looks away. But it's not necessary. He's focused solely on her arguments today.

"Elaine thinks Dr. Danvers touched her another time, too," JJ says. "During a previous ketamine session, when she apparently gave Elaine that valium-like medicine."

"Midazolam," Liisa offers.

"That's the one."

"Why does that matter?" Baljit demands.

"Midazolam often induces brief memory loss," Liisa says in the know-it-all tone that Simon finds so irritating. "Sometimes even for the time period right before it was administered."

"And we're supposed to believe what?" Reese points a finger at JJ. "That Dr. Danvers is so desperate to molest Elaine that she uses psychedelics to take advantage of her in the *middle* of group therapy and then wipes her memory clean afterwards?"

Simon imagines being cross-examined by Reese on the stand. He doesn't know what kind of lawyer she is but bets she would be a formidable opponent in the courtroom.

JJ taps her chest, her bracelets zooming down her arm. "Hey, I'm just the messenger," she says with a laugh.

"Why did Elaine confide in you?" Baljit asks.

JJ shrugs. "Maybe because I'm the only one who called her after she no-showed for group therapy?"

Baljit turns to Liisa. "You're still a therapist, aren't you? How do you reach someone with those kinds of paranoid delusions?"

Simon finds Liisa tough to read. The middle-aged psychologist is arguably the quietest member of the group. He doesn't know many Finns, but he has heard they are a stoic bunch. Liisa usually speaks up only to establish her intellectual superiority or to question Dr. Danvers's approach. Simon realizes he might be biased against Liisa because she comes across as so asexual. But he has softened to her after she shared her trippy conversation with her dead mother. Maybe she is more human than he assumed?

"How do we know that nothing happened between them?" Liisa asks.

"Come on!" Salvador groans. "You can't actually believe something did?"

"It's happened before."

Simon whips his head toward her. "*With Dr. D?*"

"No, not that I know of," Liisa says. "But a few years ago, a renowned research group in Canada was doing a major study on using psychedelics in PTSD. Some of the subjects in the study later came forward with claims of inappropriate touching, sexual harassment, and even sexual relationships with the research therapists. Some of the allegations were proven to be true. A few were even caught on tape."

"No way," says Simon, who's no stranger to using substances to help set the mood in the bedroom. "There's not a fucking chance that Dr. D is molesting Elaine or anyone else. With or without roofies."

Baljit glances at him with a biting grin. "And you of all people should know."

"Absolutely." Simon forces a laugh. "Trust the sex addict. I mean . . . not always, of course . . . just in this case."

"I don't believe it, either. Not a single word of it," says Salvador, and the others all nod.

"When is Elaine planning to post this accusation?" Reese asks JJ, who simply shrugs in response.

"Doesn't she understand this isn't only about her?" Baljit snaps.

"Yeah, why now?" Salvador pulls his ball cap down lower on his forehead. "For the first time in eons I'm finally in control of my life again. Free from the pills and the blow."

"Can you imagine what will happen once Elaine does post?" Reese asks.

"Especially if she names the rest of us," JJ says.

"That's the least of my worries," Simon says.

"Really?" Baljit folds her arms. "You're the only household name here. And also, the one who shone a glaring spotlight on our group."

"Without consent from any of us," Reese adds.

"I didn't name any of you," Simon says, bristling under the scrutiny of the two alpha females of the group. "Besides, I could fill a warehouse with all the dirt printed about me over the years. What's a little more bad publicity at this point? What I care about is what happens to us. Our tribe. And the progress we've all made."

"That'll be over in a heartbeat," Reese says, straightening her French cuffs, and looking more like a lawyer with every passing minute.

Liisa nods. "The state's Medical Board would have to investigate. At the very least, the group therapy would be put on hold."

"Forget hold," JJ says. "The tribe would be disbanded. Finished. As dead as Dr. Danvers's career will be."

"We can't let that happen," Salvador moans. "We just can't. I'll never keep it together. Not with the deadline for my new athletic line only weeks away. Do you have any idea how much focus it takes to design and plan that kind of show?"

Baljit shrugs. "Someone better talk to Elaine."

"I tried, trust me." JJ clutches her chest again. "Like talking to a wall."

"We need to go see her," Baljit says, standing up.

"All of us?" Salvador asks.

"Yup, as a group," Baljit says. "Make her feel like she's outnumbered and overpowered. Maybe then she'll see the light and cut the bullshit."

CHAPTER 10

Holly finds herself driving the Coastal Highway without a destination in mind.

After she left Elaine's home, Holly repeatedly tried Aaron's phone but couldn't reach him. As she drove back toward her office, her pulse hammered in her ears and her breathing sped up. She could sense the first panic attack in years creeping up on her. As she saw it, she had two choices: return to her office and self-medicate or get the hell out of Laguna. She opted for the latter.

After fifteen minutes of aimless driving, her phone rings. She taps the button on the steering wheel to answer, and Aaron's first words are "Three missed calls, Holl? What's wrong?"

"It backfired, Aaron! Elaine is going public."

"She can't do that."

"There's no way to stop her."

"There must be," he says flatly.

"There's no dissuading her. Her delusion is fixed. It's her new cause célèbre. Her hill to die on."

"Let me try."

"God no!" Holly punches her steering wheel. "That would be way over the line."

"Surely, we've moved a little beyond ethical concerns by this point, Holl?"

She isn't sure if he's implying that her ethics have been questionable all along or that it's too late to worry about them now. "OK, forget about ethics, Aaron. Practically speaking, it could make everything so much worse if you were to go see her."

"Don't take this wrong, Holl, but how could things get much worse?"

"Elaine would know I betrayed her confidentiality. Or worse, she could legitimately accuse me of trying to intimidate her into silence. The optics are beyond horrible."

Aaron's sigh reverberates through the speakers. "Then you need to lawyer up. Immediately."

"What can an attorney do at this point?"

"He can send a cease-and-desist letter. Let her know just how much she would be risking by libeling you. How it could ruin her financially and destroy her reputation. After all, who would take her seriously as an advocate after crying wolf like that?"

Holly knows he's right. She has already thought about talking to a lawyer. For a fleeting moment, she even considered reaching out to Reese, wondering if her preexisting relationship with Elaine might be advantageous. But Holly dismisses the thought as desperate and wildly inappropriate. Still, even though she's convinced she didn't cross any professional lines with Elaine, the thought of muzzling her vulnerable and hurting client through a lawyer makes Holly feel slimy. Like one of those weasels before #MeToo who used NDAs and other legal threats to silence their victims.

"I know just the guy," Aaron goes on. "I'll reach out to him. He'll straighten it out."

Holly ignores the slight doubt in his voice, focusing instead on her gratitude. Despite her ambivalence about their marriage and the gravitational life forces that have been pulling them apart for years, her husband is always there when she needs him most. "Thank you, Aaron. You have no idea . . ." Only the lump in her throat stops her from adding, "I love you."

After Holly disconnects, she spots the signs for the turnoff to Dana

Point and decides to drop in on her grandfather again. She parks in front of the house and lets herself inside, where she finds Walter in the kitchen, boiling water for his afternoon tea.

"Hello, Koala," he says with a big smile.

"It's all gone to crap, Papa," she says as she plops down on a chair at the kitchen table. She hugs her knees to her chest, like she did when she was a teenager, as she pukes out the story of her confrontation with Elaine.

Walter doesn't comment. Instead, he turns to the cupboard and pulls down another mug. He opens a packet and dissolves it in hot water before placing it in front of her. The hot chocolate is too sweet and far too processed for her taste. But it reminds her of childhood, which is exactly what she needs right now. "I'm sorry, Papa," she murmurs into her cup.

He sits down across from her. "For what, my darling?"

"The harm I might've done. To the whole psychedelic therapy movement."

Walter dismisses it with a small wave. "This isn't your fault, Koala."

And Holly knows she has come to the right place. "The waiting is the worst. Like being trapped in a glass house with a hurricane barreling down on you."

He chuckles. "Someone's got a flair for the dramatic."

"You know how these things go."

"You didn't do anything inappropriate. Frankly, the whole thing is ludicrous."

"Doesn't matter. My client is a professional victims' advocate. She knows how to make a splash."

"With such a flimsy allegation?"

"Once it gets out, it will be impossible to stuff that genie back into the bottle. Even if the allegations are discredited, the damage will be done. My practice—what's left of it, anyway—will never be the same."

"About the MDMA, Holly. You protected yourself, right? Your clients procured their own medicine and signed waivers?"

"Of course."

"This client, she hasn't spoken out yet, has she?"

Holly shakes her head.

"Maybe she's having second thoughts?"

"If you'd seen her eyes, you'd know better."

"Have you spoken to a lawyer?"

"Aaron's working on that."

Walter lays a tremulous hand on her wrist. "You've weathered worse, Koala."

Holly's eyes fill with tears, but she blinks them away. "Even if I have, I'm not sure I can do it again."

"You're stronger than you think. Always have been."

"And you're blind when it comes to me."

He lets go of her wrist. "That's what macular degeneration will do."

"Not funny." Holly hates it when her grandfather jokes about his frailty. She can't bear the thought of losing him, though she realizes he won't be able to live on his own for much longer. And she knows that for Walter, losing his independence would be worse than death.

They sip their drinks in silence. Finally, Walter uses both hands to push himself up from the table. "You know what might help?"

"What's that?" Holly asks, although she already has an inkling of what he has in mind.

"I'm too old and feeble to take you back to Peru. But maybe I can get you there in spirit?"

The comment confirms her suspicions. "Really, Papa?"

"Come," Walter says as he shuffles out of the room, heading toward the solarium at the back of the house.

She follows him into the bright sunroom and, after he points to the black beanbag chair in the corner, drops down onto it.

Walter slides an LP out of its sleeve and places it on the turntable. Soon, the sweep of orchestral strings fills the room, and Holly recognizes the soothing melody for the first movement of Beethoven's Sixth Symphony, one of their favorites.

Walter opens a decorative black box near the turntable and extracts a long, slim silver canister.

She laughs out loud. "Since when do you vape?"

"My eyesight's not good enough to pack a pipe. Besides, the fingers are too arthritic. This wouldn't be my first choice, but these vape pens come preloaded with predictable doses."

She nods to the pen. "DMT, right?"

"Yes, dimethyltryptamine. The active ingredient of ayahuasca."

She exhales. "The God Molecule."

"Nonsense. What a loopy term for a neuroactive biochemical," Walter grumbles. "Then again, it's not solely hippies and psychonauts who are prone to such hyperbole. The Incans used to call ayahuasca the 'spirit vine.'"

"Speaks to its potency, doesn't it?"

"I'd brew you a tea like we used to drink in Peru, but that would take hours and hours to have any effect."

"But smoking DMT is so intense. Way more powerful than LSD or ketamine."

"True. But it has a very quick onset and then offset. The whole trip will last thirty minutes or less. With any luck it will reboot your mind. Reframe your thoughts. Perhaps it's exactly what you need right now?"

Holly can practically see herself as an eighteen-year-old, sitting cross-legged on a patch of dirt under a dense canopy of leaves across from her *curandero*, her trip guide, who wore the same traditional Peruvian chullo hat and alpaca-wool sweater every day. She vividly recalls the brilliant visions that swirled inside her head soon after she drank the earthy, bitter ayahuasca tea. Her father was central to those visions. She remembers how her chest warmed at the glowing sight of him. And how he repeatedly told her, in the most loving and conciliatory tone, that she wasn't responsible for the car crash that killed him.

At the time, the visions felt so real that Holly accepted her dad's reassurances as fact. They freed her from the spiral of self-recrimination and suicidal thoughts. She returned home from Peru a different person. Almost whole. But since the ayahuasca had never conjured specific memories of the accident itself, in time doubt began to creep back in. More and more, Holly wondered if the exoneration her dad offered her in those visions was simply the product of her wishful imagination. And she coped the only way she knew how: by avoiding thoughts of the accident and never seeking out details of what actually happened that day.

Walter now holds the vape pen out to her, and Holly hesitates a moment before she takes it between her fingers. He digs in a drawer behind him and pulls out a black blindfold, which Holly also accepts and then slips over her forehead.

He eases himself down into the chair across from her. "I'll be here for you, Koala."

"My *curandero*?"

"I wish I were as qualified." He chuckles. "No. I'll simply be your trip sitter."

Holly holds the pen near her lips, feeling unexpectedly nervous all of a sudden. "Two long inhales, right?"

"Yes." Walter smiles. "Find your safe and happy place."

Holly can only smile to herself. Being here with her grandfather is one of her happiest—and safest—places.

She exhales and then brings the pen to her lips, tasting the cool tip. She sucks in fully, feeling the burn of the smoke as it snakes down her windpipe. Fighting off a cough, she holds her breath, keeping the chemicals trapped in her lungs for as long as possible. She blows out a white puff of smoke and then launches into a coughing fit. The unexpectedly acrid stench makes her eyes water.

"Stinks, doesn't it?" Walter chuckles.

As soon as Holly catches her breath, she inhales a second long puff. Then she lowers the mask over her eyes. Everything goes dark around her.

"Go back to the forest, Koala."

Holly can't tell if it's her imagination, but her grandfather's voice already sounds distorted. "Remember how the branches were everywhere?" he asks. "So thick you couldn't see the sun or the sky above."

A vision begins to take shape. But it's not a forest. Lights of every color surround her. Like a tunnel made from a prism. At first, the lights weave and bend in synchrony with the strings and horns of the orchestra. And then they turn into streaks as Holly suddenly shoots down a tunnel past them, as if fired out of a cannon. But the movement feels so calm and tranquil, more like floating in a warm bath than rocketing through space.

Suddenly, the lights explode above her, and she's standing under the crescendo of fireworks. For a moment, there's only darkness again. Then something slowly materializes out of the blackness, as though the individual molecules are bonding right in front of her eyes to take the shape of something. No, not something. *Someone.* But the form isn't entirely human. His whole body is translucent. And while Holly can make out his facial features, she can also somehow see his brain behind it. And his beating heart inside his chest.

He takes a step toward her. As he flexes his knees, she can see the muscles under the skin of his legs contract against the bones. But she feels no fear. Only love. She opens her arms to welcome him.

Hollycopter.

Even if he hadn't uttered the nickname that he alone used for her, she would have recognized him. She can feel his presence as strongly as a warm breeze against her cheek.

Daddy!

I'm here, Holly.

Where is here?

With you. Wherever you are. Wherever you go.

Joy overwhelms her. An ecstasy which is almost painful in its intensity. *You are, Dad?*

Always, Hollycopter.

She feels the wet warmth of her own tears soaking the bottom of her blindfold, and remembers that she has a body, anchored to the earth by gravity. *The accident, Dad . . . was it my fault?*

No, Hollycopter.

Tell me what happened, Daddy! I can't remember.

Something else appears beside her father's ethereal form, and he turns toward it. It's made entirely of light, and yet also looks familiar. Then she places it. The old family station wagon! Suddenly, the vehicle bursts into flames, and Holly recoils from the intense heat of the blaze.

But the raging fire doesn't deter her father. He approaches it. Holly lunges to try to stop him, but her feet won't budge. All she can do is wave her hands frantically.

No, no, no, Daddy. Don't!

He flashes her a smile that is love incarnate.

And then he slowly lowers himself inside the flaming vehicle.

CHAPTER 11

What a dump! Simon thinks as Salvador's knee digs into his thigh. They sit together with Reese, all three of them squeezed onto a lumpy fabric sofa in front of a cheap wooden coffee table. The rest of the chairs don't even match, and the walls are lined with framed posters. Simon only recognizes a few of the faces captured on the wall, including those of Sinéad O'Connor and Patti Smith. To his eye, the place has all the sophistication and charm of a college dorm room.

Clearly social activism doesn't pay top dollar.

Simon can't remember a time when he had to worry about money. He was twenty-two when his debut album rocketed to the top of the *Billboard* charts and stayed there for twelve weeks, going double platinum. It earned him two Grammys and, as it turned out, a lifelong celebrity status with all its trappings. No one ever warned him about the downsides of fame and recognizability—the excesses, the enablers, the sycophants, the parasites, and that sense of living your life in a glass box—but even if they had, he still wouldn't have walked away from it then. Or now.

Simon repositions his leg to free it from Salvador's. The other man is sitting way too close, and besides, Simon's hip aches from having to wedge himself onto the sofa. As annoying as Salvador can be, Simon has a soft spot for the insecure designer. He reminds Simon of many of his artistic friends who live with the same endless quest for validation, which they can never find within themselves. Behind his pudgy, androgynous features, and despite his artistic pretentiousness, Salvador gives off the vibe of someone who was deeply wounded as a child. In that way, he reminds Simon of himself.

Elaine sits motionless on a plastic chair in the corner with a water glass in hand, which JJ had insisted on getting her. She has hardly said two words since the rest of the group ambushed her at her door. She looks particularly gaunt today, as if she could just recede into her chair. Simon has never gone for that heroin-chic look, which in Elaine's case might actually be authentic.

"We know you've been through hell, Elaine," says Baljit, who assumed control of this intervention from the outset. "But we're also certain that Dr. Danvers would never do anything to harm you."

"It's true," Salvador says. "She's been our guardian angel."

"You don't know what I went through," Elaine murmurs, pulling her knees to her chest and folding her thin arms around them.

"It's disgusting what your uncle did," JJ says, leaning in.

Elaine's gaze drops to her lap. "I meant with Dr. Danvers."

"I was convinced I saw my dead relatives," Reese says, without specifying which ones. "They were so real to me that I didn't think it could possibly be a hallucination. In some ways, I still believe I did see them."

"It's not the same thing," Elaine says in a small voice.

Baljit's face creases with frustration. "We were under such heavy medication. We all saw things that appeared totally real to us."

Elaine shakes her head. "It was afterwards. When I woke up. She was swallowing me in her arms. Her hot breath on my cheek. It felt exactly like being back on my uncle's boat."

Simon suppresses a sigh, recognizing the futility of this exercise. Elaine's expression is resolute, verging on zealous. He saw a similar look in the eyes of his nineteen-year-old accuser and, even more so, her trashy mother, as he sat across the table from them in the deposition. He knew immediately that their silence was going to cost him millions, just as he can tell now that they're not going to be able to persuade Elaine to stand down.

But it doesn't stop Reese from trying. "Think about it, Elaine. Even if Dr. Danvers had the most twisted designs on you, why would she take advantage of you in the middle of group therapy? With a half dozen witnesses present?"

Simon enjoys watching Reese soft-pedal her cross-examination, like lawyers do with unhinged but sympathetic complainants.

"Maybe she gets off on that?" Elaine says.

"Gets off on what?"

"The risk? The exposure? The danger? Who knows?"

"Oh, come on!" Baljit snaps. "You can't actually believe that! That she would risk her entire career to what? Cop a quick feel?"

Elaine's cheeks flush. "Says the woman who keeps risking her family's financial future at the craps table."

"My odds are still a hell of a lot better than molesting someone in the middle of group therapy and expecting no one to notice. Besides, you get off on being a fucking victim, don't you?" Baljit glares at her. "Oh, great. Cue the white woman waterworks."

Elaine's enormous eyes have filled with tears, but she doesn't respond.

"It does seem like a helluva stretch," Simon says, growing weary of all the bickering. "And I've spent most of my life flirting with risk and impulsivity."

"Elaine, you've got it all wrong," Salvador cries. "I saw the whole thing. I'd already come to from the ketamine. Right after I pulled my mask off, I saw her holding you. She was *comforting* you. There was nothing sexual in the hug. You've got to believe me."

Simon flashes him a questioning glance. No one contradicts Salvador, but if he actually witnessed the embrace, then why hadn't he spoken up before? Salvador seems unable to maintain eye contact.

"We want to support you, Elaine," JJ says, pressing her hand to her heart. "We really, really do."

Reese turns to Elaine. "Isn't it possible you relived your past trauma so intensely—in such a real way to you—that under influence of multiple drugs, you projected that unforgivable abuse into the present. And onto Dr. Danvers?"

"No," Elaine mutters without making eye contact with her.

Reese catches Simon's eye, and he can tell that she's longing to treat Elaine like a hostile witness. He watches Liisa, expecting the psychologist to weigh in with some kind of wisdom, but she remains as silent and impassive as she has been for the rest of the intervention.

"What if you're wrong, Elaine?" Baljit demands.

JJ nods solemnly. "When this comes to light, our group won't survive. It just won't."

"And it might set all of us back," Reese adds. "Back to that dark place where our addictions controlled us. You're an advocate, right? You care about the sobriety of addicts?"

Elaine won't even look at Reese anymore.

Simon's hip aches and his stomach turns. "I'm too old for this shit," he mumbles to himself. Louder, he says, "Don't be so fucking selfish, Elaine."

She looks around the room at each of them, her gaze unwavering, and then she rises to her feet. "Thank you all for coming. But there's no point in discussing it anymore."

CHAPTER 12

Monday, April 8

Holly sits behind her white concrete desk, a minimalist rectangle without drawers that the clinic's designer badgered her into ordering. She has yet to hear back from Aaron's attorney. Bracing for the worst, she googles her own name again and, after finding no new links, rechecks her social media. Still nothing. She's amazed it hasn't all blown up since she left Elaine's place on Friday. Holly read somewhere that social media posts get more attention on Mondays. She wonders if Elaine deliberately waited for the weekend to pass to target a wider audience.

Patients with terminal illnesses report how the time spent waiting for the diagnosis to be confirmed—the biopsy to come back or the scan to be interpreted—can be the most unnerving period, worse even than the certainty of a medical death sentence. Waiting now for Elaine's accusations to go viral is Holly's closest comparable experience, and yet she is remarkably calm. Ever since she vaped DMT in her grandfather's solarium, she has felt almost detached. As if the potential career-ending fallout from Elaine's allegations will affect someone other than herself. As if the price she will pay for being a pioneer of psychedelic therapy will be worth the cost if her patients are freed of their addictions. As a psychiatrist, she's impressed by the grounding power of DMT. And, as a diehard psychedelic therapy advocate, she feels vindicated.

But Holly hasn't been able to shake the thoughts of the fatal crash since she saw her dad again in her visions after vaping DMT. It reminds her of Peru. Despite the profound healing power of that ayahuasca retreat, Holly had forgotten the main downside of those visions: the niggling sense of incompleteness. She could sense essential details from the car accident lying just below the surface of her consciousness but refusing to bubble up to it. The frustration of not remembering has returned now like an itch she can't quite reach.

Holly glances down at her open handbag and sees the tip of the vape pen, which her grandfather insisted she take home with her, poking out of the inner pouch. She resists the temptation to take a few puffs now to see if she can conjure her father again. To fill in that vital memory gap.

A light knock at the partially open door pulls Holly from those thoughts. She gently nudges her bag closed with the toe of her shoe. Tanya, her sweet but overwhelmed office assistant, opens the door wider.

"That, uh, reporter called again," Tanya says, bobbing from foot to foot.

Holly nods. She doesn't need to ask her assistant which reporter. It could only be Katy Armstrong, who writes for the *Orange County Register*.

After Simon went public, admitting to his battles with addiction and glorifying Holly's therapy, she was inundated with media requests. She did a handful of select interviews, from the *New York Times* to NBC. She only agreed to speak to Katy because she represented the most-read local newspaper.

Holly can still picture their conversation, which they held in this office.

Petite, with black hair tied in a tight ponytail and wearing throwback, round wire glasses, Katy looked innocuous enough. But from the moment Holly sat down across from her, she could tell by the young reporter's body language—elbows dug into the armrest, back arched, and shoulders tilted forward as if ready to pounce—that this interview would be different from the others.

After a couple of softball questions, Katy launched right into it. "At the end of the day, Dr. Danvers, aren't you basically replacing one addiction for another?"

Holly shook her head. "Psychedelics don't work that way. They're not addicting in the traditional sense."

"Can you elaborate?"

"Most psychedelics, like ketamine, activate serotonin receptors inside the brain. They reduce the energy needed to switch between different activity states and help reprogram the pathways. We call it neuroplasticity. In other words, they stimulate regions of the brain that aren't normally active. And those effects last long after the drug wears off. Unlike other medications, antidepressants for example, we don't keep clients on psychedelics indefinitely."

Katy leaned farther forward, her eyes probing. "Just how long do you keep your patients on them?"

"Depends on the indication. But in general, it's one treatment with ketamine per week for three to six months."

"And in that time, patients come to your office every week to get high?"

"No," Holly said, focusing on her breathing, refusing to let herself be provoked. "Once a week, they come in for administration of ketamine under carefully monitored and controlled conditions. Those are followed by two more sessions—in one-on-one and group settings—to debrief and cognitively deconstruct the experience."

"And this method of yours cured Simon Lowry?"

"You know I can't comment on individual clients, Katy."

"But he already said it did. I was just hoping to hear your perspective."

Holly only smiled and shook her head.

"All right," Katy said. "Can we talk about the risks associated with psychedelics?"

"Like all medications, they have side effects. But compared to most other psychiatric medications, they're relatively safe and well tolerated."

"What about the deaths? Like the stories of people jumping out of buildings because they thought they could fly?"

"There are very few deaths attributable to ketamine. Most of those occurred among recreational users who co-ingested multiple other substances like alcohol, GHB, or opioids."

Katy eyed her skeptically. "And what about the potential for sexual violation?"

"Violation?"

"Like with that large study in Canada where some therapists were caught on video surveillance molesting patients who were drugged."

"Unfortunately, rare as they are, cases of unethical therapists abusing their clients' trust and vulnerability do occur. But the overwhelming majority happen without the use of any psychoactive medication."

At the time of the interview, which was well before Elaine's allegation, Holly had thought the reporter was just reaching for sensational claims to disparage her therapy. She was tempted to ask Katy if she or someone close to her had suffered a traumatic experience involving psychedelics, but Holly bit her tongue. In the end, she felt as if she had held her own in the interview and, to the reporter's credit, the article was less biased or negative than what she had expected. Since the story ran, Katy has reached out regularly for follow-up, but Holly hasn't replied.

Now, as she imagines how Katy might respond to Elaine's allegations, Holly fights off a shudder and pushes the thought away. "You know the drill, Tanya."

"You'll call her back when you have a free moment?" her assistant asks.

Holly nods. They both understand it to mean she will ignore the call. "Can you please bring in the next client?"

A minute or two later, Tanya ushers in the last client of the day, Liisa Koskinen.

The fiftyish psychologist wears another loose-fitting, shapeless dress, this one a dull green. But as Holly sits down across from her, the first thing she notices is her colleague's posture. Unlike previous sessions, when Liisa would sit ramrod straight, today she leans back in her seat with her hands resting loosely on her lap. Even her expression is free of the usual tension across her square jaw and through the frown lines at the corners of her eyes.

"Liisa, you look—"

"Less defensive?" she ventures with a wry smile. It transforms her face.

"I was going to say relaxed."

"I'm not the easiest client, am I?" Liisa is grinning now, and the rare smile makes her look younger.

"It can be tough for those of us in this field."

"To be a patient?"

"Exactly."

"And you know this from personal experience?"

Holly shows her a small smile but doesn't take the bait. She has no intention of sharing the details of her own mental health history. That would be crossing a line.

"There I go again, don't I?" Liisa laughs. "Always trying to analyze the analyst."

"Hard to turn it off, isn't it?"

"A real job hazard. But it's not like this is my first time in therapy. I can't quite figure it out."

"Figure what out, Liisa?"

"Self-care is one of the basic principles in psychology. The non-aviation equivalent of putting your own oxygen mask on before trying to help anyone else. I've worked with a few therapists before you, but I've always resisted letting them in beyond a certain point. This time . . . it's turned out different."

"Different good or different bad?"

"Good," Liisa says. "I must admit I was very skeptical of the whole idea of using psychedelics in therapy. I wasn't a believer."

"But you came here anyway," Holly says.

"I was desperate. I'd tried everything else. From hypnosis to anesthetic detox. But I was still a slave to Xanax. I couldn't sleep without one. Or, for that matter, get through a day without a pill or two." Liisa shakes her head. "Who am I kidding? I couldn't make it to lunchtime."

"And now?"

"I haven't swallowed a single pill since you put us under dual therapy."

Holly flushes with satisfaction. Validation, too. All the risk she assumed in pushing the envelope with dual therapy seems worthwhile knowing that the last holdout in the group has reached sobriety. But all Holly says is "Does that make you more of a believer in psychedelics, Liisa?"

"I'm getting there, yes."

Holly can tell from her frown that there has to be a caveat. "But?"

"When something seems to be too good to be true . . ."

"I've thought the same, too. Psychedelics do have side effects. Plenty of them. You've seen the dysphoric reactions in our group." Holly can't help but think of Elaine, and it dampens her mood. "And some of those experiences . . . the trips . . . they can't be unseen."

"I guess nothing is perfect. In truth, all drugs are poisons."

For the first time since meeting her, Holly feels a real connection with her colleague. And she senses the opportunity to dig deeper. "Can we talk a bit more about your mother?"

Liisa sighs. "All roads lead back to childhood, huh?"

"Not always, no. But as we both know, childhood trauma is the single biggest risk factor for adulthood addiction."

"True."

"Do you remember much about her?"

Liisa looks down. "Hardly anything. She died a few weeks after I turned four. A massive blood clot during childbirth. Technically, the day after. I never saw her again after she went to the hospital." Her voice drops. "I lost a mother and gained a baby sister."

"That must have turned your world upside down."

Liisa shakes her head. "I don't really remember any of it."

"Your sister's arrival?"

"My mother," Liisa says. "I've seen photos, of course. But it wasn't until I took the dual psychedelics that I recalled any real memories of her."

"How did you respond to those memories?"

"They were . . ." Liisa clears her throat. "Kind of liberating."

"You felt her love?"

Liisa only shrugs.

"OK. What about your dad?"

"It was tough for him. Freshly widowed with a baby and a toddler at home. And still working long hours in the physics lab at UC Santa Cruz. With an hour commute each way from our home in Monterey. Being Finnish to the core, my father just ignored the grief. To this day, he still doesn't speak of my mother's death."

"How would you describe childhood without a mom?"

Liisa considers it for a moment. "My father always provided for my sister and me, but he didn't know how to express his feelings. Not even sure he was capable of it. And then, after he remarried, our stepmother, Helmi, tried, in her way. But she wasn't much better."

Holly leans toward her. "You didn't feel loved as a child?"

Liisa's cheeks redden. "So what? With or without a mother, countless children grow up feeling the same. And they don't wind up as Xanax addicts."

Holly smiles patiently. "If one of your clients said the same to you, you might call it deflection."

"Maybe so." Liisa clears her throat again. "But my trauma still pales compared to what, say, someone like Elaine went through."

"Everyone's trauma is unique," Holly says, but Liisa's comment resonates. "What about your daughter? She's in college now, isn't she?"

"She's a senior," Liisa shifts in her seat. "What does this have to do with her?"

"Your experience growing up without a mother . . . did that affect your own approach to parenting?"

"I never knew any different." She shrugs. "Besides, Kimberly is strong."

Liisa has been evasive about her homelife from the outset. Holly still doesn't know what happened between Liisa and her ex-husband, only that he lives on the East Coast now. Recognizing her client's rising defensiveness, Holly veers the conversation elsewhere, focusing on abstinence strategies until the end of their session.

After Liisa leaves, Holly finishes her charting. Just as she is about to pack up for the day, her assistant appears in her doorway, shifting from one foot to the other. "What's up, Tanya?"

"There's a Tyler Golding on the phone," she says. "He wants to talk to you about his sister."

Holly's heart thuds as she connects the surname. "Elaine's brother?"

Tanya nods. "He says it's important."

Holly suppresses a groan. *Is this how it begins?* "Put him through, please."

Seconds later her phone rings and, after taking a deep breath, Holly answers. "Dr. Danvers."

There's a long pause. "I'm Tyler Golding. I think you know my sister, Elaine."

"I'm sorry, but I'm not at liberty to discuss my clients." Holly braces for the expected verbal tirade.

He hesitates. "I'm kinda worried about Elaine."

She sits up straighter. "Why?"

"I can't reach her."

"I don't mean to pry, Tyler, but I thought you and your sister were estranged?"

"I haven't spoken to Elaine in almost three years." Before Holly can ask anything further, Tyler adds, "Growing up, we were tight. But then the drugs. Nonstop. Elaine put our family through hell. The lies, the stealing, the revolving-door rehab visits . . . My dad died of a heart attack before he was fifty. Mom followed him a couple years later. They called it cancer, but I'm pretty sure she just gave up."

"That must have been hard for you to see," Holly says, still wondering as to the purpose of his call.

"I never bought any of my sister's bullshit about being some kind of opioid victims' champion. She might've fooled the others, but last time I saw Elaine, she was higher than a kite. I could see it in her tiny pupils. And I wasn't about to let her put me in an early grave, too."

"I get it, Tyler." Holly thinks of the times Elaine mentioned her sadness over her estrangement from her little brother, without ever explaining the reason behind it. "So why are you trying to reach your sister now?"

"Elaine called me a couple days back. A bunch of times. Then she blew up my phone with texts. She left this rambling voicemail. Some weird stuff about childhood trips on our uncle's boat and how she'd never let anything like that happen again."

Holly's breathing picks up, and her grip tightens on the receiver. "Did Elaine explain what she meant by that?"

"Nope. All the other messages were about how she'd turned over a new leaf. How she found a cure for her addiction. Psychedelics or some-thing? Not that I believed a word of it." He snorts. "But Elaine told me that if I didn't get back to her, she was going to drive up to San Jose to track me down."

"Did you call her back?"

"I tried. Last night. Even followed up with a couple of texts. But she hasn't responded. Even though she made it sound urgent." He sighs heavily. "You know how it is with opioid addicts. When they stop answering your calls . . ."

Holly knows exactly how it is, but she still can't slow her breathing. "How did you find me, Tyler?"

"I don't know any of Elaine's friends down there. But she mentioned your name in a couple of texts. And I found your office online."

"I see."

"Look, I'm four hundred miles away. I thought, maybe . . ."

"Yes, Tyler." Holly rubs her temples. "I'll check on your sister."

"Thank you, Dr. Danvers." He pauses. "And if . . . if you do find my sister, please tell her not to come looking for me. I'm not ready to see her yet."

After she disconnects, Holly cradles the phone in her hand, wavering. The last time she attempted to intervene with Elaine, she only made the situation worse. But how can she leave things as they stand? Particularly after what she just learned from Tyler.

Holly takes another deep breath and then tries Elaine's phone, but it goes to voicemail.

"Screw it," she mutters under her breath as she hops up from her desk.

Holly drives over to Elaine's building, fighting what passes for rush hour traffic in Laguna Beach, and parks in the same spot as she did two days ago, beside the blue Nissan. She steps up to the ground-floor door and knocks. Her mouth goes dry, and her palms dampen. After their run-in, she never expected to find herself at this door again, let alone so soon. No answer. She knocks harder. Still nothing.

"Elaine!" Holly calls, pounding on the door with the side of her fist.

A minute or more passes without a reply.

Holly reaches for the doorknob. It turns freely. Pushing the door open slightly, Holly calls out again. "Elaine? Are you home?"

When there's still no answer, Holly opens the door wider and takes a tentative step inside. Just as she's about to call out again, something in the corner of the living room catches her eye.

Across the room, Elaine is slumped on the chair, her head angled back, her ear pressed to her shoulder. Her vacant eyes are wide open. Her skin is the color of slate. A single trickle of blood has dried from the crease of her left elbow down the inside of her forearm.

An empty syringe lies beside her bare foot.

CHAPTER 13

Tuesday, April 9

The sun has barely risen, and despite the cloudless skies, the cool breeze off the water still carries a bite. But Simon, who wears only a T-shirt and board shorts, doesn't mind. It's one of his favorite times of day: sitting on his deck and savoring his morning coffee, an oat milk cappuccino. While Victoria Beach is still deserted. Before the lapping of the waves and the crooning of the gulls are drowned out by a cacophony of children, boom boxes, volleyball players, and countless other invaders of his beach.

As Simon leans back and peruses the e-version of *Rolling Stone* on his tablet, a pop-up notification labeled "The Tribe" appears in the corner of the screen. He immediately taps on the group chat icon and sees two new messages from Salvador.

The first reads: *HOLY FUCK!!*

The second is a hyperlink.

As soon as Simon clicks it, a web page from some news site that he doesn't recognize fills his screen. His jaw drops the moment he sees the headline: "Opioid Crisis Activist Dead."

As Simon reads the story, he experiences more déjà vu than shock. Too often, he has learned of the death of a friend or an acquaintance through a similar type of media report. While the post offers some details about Elaine's history of addiction, recovery, and activism, including a

well-attended march she organized to city hall last year, it lacks any specifics about her death. It says only that Elaine was found in her home and
that officials have not yet confirmed a cause of death. But that doesn't
stop the writer from speculating. He even tracked down a friend of hers
in the movement who bemoaned her loss and cited her death as a cau-
tionary tale for the ever-present risk of relapse among recovering addicts.

Simon hasn't even finished reading when his tablet pings with multiple texts from other group members.

Baljit: Elaine died after we saw her? The same day??

Salvador: OMG, SHE MUST HAVE!!

Liisa: Do we know for certain she overdosed?

Baljit: You think it was killer bees?

Salvador: TOO SOON!!

Reese: What else could it have been?

Baljit: What becomes of the group now?

Simon: We carry on, right?

Salvador (finally releasing the caps lock key): We have to! It's what
Elaine would have wanted.

Baljit: Really?? The one who was going to detonate the group from the
inside?

Salvador: I meant she'd want us to stay clean. 😒

Baljit: On the plus side, at least her allegations won't go viral now.

Salvador: JESUS CHRIST, BALJIT!

Baljit: Can't bring her back from the dead. 🙍

Reese: We've all thought it, Salvador.

Simon finds himself nodding in agreement. His life would be less complicated and less expensive if his own accuser had gone a similar route.

Reese: JJ? You out there?

Simon realizes that JJ is the only member who hasn't yet weighed in on the group chat.

JJ: This is fucking awful. I'm devastated. How can we go on?

No new texts appear in the chain for a few seconds, and then another pops up.

Baljit: And then there were six.

CHAPTER 14

Wednesday, April 10

Aaron and Holly have already hiked or walked—it's an ongoing debate between them how to label their favorite four-mile loop, the Dartmoor Boat Canyon Trail—two miles and climbed over seven hundred vertical feet. But they haven't shared more than a few words in that time.

Since Holly first informed him of Elaine's death, two days earlier, Aaron hasn't pressed for details, sensing his wife needed time to digest it. But as they pause now at a scenic lookout to sip their waters and admire the endless expanse of the Pacific below them, he decides the moment is right. "Two days," he says.

"Huh?" she asks without looking up from her bottle.

"Is that enough time to process what happened to your client?"

"It took me one second to process what happened to her. An opioid overdose."

Aaron chuckles. "End of story?"

Holly shrugs. "What am I supposed to do?"

"Grieve her?"

She studies the label on her water bottle before replying. "Do you know that twenty Californians die every single day from opioid over-doses?"

"I did not. At least, not so specifically."

After another long sip, she finally says to him, "I never knew the exact number either. Not until Elaine shared that depressing stat with me."

"No shortage of irony there," he says. "Dying from the illness she dedicated her life to combating?"

"What's so unusual about that?" Holly asks. "Advocates die all the time from diseases they're crusading against."

Aaron stares hard at her. "You're not fooling anyone, Holl."

"Is that what I'm trying to do?" Her voice sounds almost playful, but he knows better.

"You can be as stoic as a statue for the rest of the world, but I can tell this is eating you up."

She meets his gaze for a few seconds and then looks back out to the rolling Laguna shoreline below them as it snakes alongside the cyan-colored ocean. "She was terrified of needles, you know?"

"An opioid addict?"

"Her addiction was to pills. Vicodin, Percocet, et cetera. She once told me that her needle phobia was the only reason she hadn't overdosed years ago like so many others."

"But this time she injected?"

Holly starts to walk again. "The evidence was lying right there by her foot."

Aaron follows after. "What are you thinking, Holly?"

"I don't know. But it's so hard to imagine her injecting herself. Maybe she wasn't looking for just another high?"

"Wait. Suicide? Is that you what you believe?"

"I have no fucking idea what to think!" Holly snaps and then glances at him with a conciliatory grin. "Sorry, Aaron. You don't deserve that. I'm only venting."

"Vent away." He waves to the dirt trail and the barren hills surrounding them. "This is our safe space."

"At the end of the day, it doesn't really matter whether her death was an accidental overdose or something else," she says.

"Why not?"

She shakes her head. "Either way, I failed her."

"Come on, Holl."

"I took her on pro bono, Aaron. My charity case. Now she's dead. Some charity, huh?"

"Holly . . ."

She surges forward, breaking into a jog.

Aaron hurries to catch up with her, breathing heavier and feeling a slight burn in his thighs. "Let's say you were an oncologist instead of a psychiatrist," he says.

"Sure. Why not?"

"Would you blame yourself for every patient you lost to cancer?"

"Not exactly a fair comparison."

"Why not? Like cancer, opioid addiction is extremely lethal. The world's best doctor isn't going to be able to prevent all overdoses in her practice. Or all suicides, for that matter. You know this, Holly."

"But how many oncologists cause cancer in their own patients?"

Aaron throws his hands up in the air and has to catch himself as he stumbles over a small rock. "You caused her to misinterpret her own memory, is that it? Is it your fault she confused you for her childhood abuser?"

Holly slows to a gentle trot. "I gave her unproven therapy, Aaron. I combined two powerful psychedelics. And I did it as much for my own gain as for hers. Clearly, Elaine wasn't ready."

Aaron doesn't entirely disagree, but it's the last thing Holly needs to hear at this moment. "You helped her to unlock the lifelong secret that had been suffocating her like quicksand. You gave her her first real chance at recovery."

"I pushed her too far, too quickly."

"It's always so easy in retrospect," Aaron says. "Accidental or deliberate, she was always going to be at huge risk. You can look back and try to make all the sense out of her death as you want to, but it will still be just as senseless."

Holly stops, and so does Aaron. "You'd feel differently if she'd been your patient."

"Maybe." He lays a hand gently on her shoulder. "I've lost five patients—that I know of—to suicide. The last one hurt just as much as the first. But I don't blame myself for any of them."

She eyes him dolefully. "Lucky you."

"I look at it another way, Holl."

"Which is?"

"How many people have I saved from suicide? How many deaths have I prevented? How many loved ones have I spared the agony of suffering that kind of loss? No way of knowing, but one thing I am certain of is that it's a hell of a lot more than the ones who died."

"A win-loss column?" She snorts. "That's a rosy way of looking at it."

"It's not rosy, it's realistic. Look at you. How many of your clients—those recalcitrant addicts—have become sober thanks to you and your innovative methods? How many overdoses have you prevented?"

"You're really pulling out all the stops, aren't you?" Holly groans. "It's odd, though."

"What is?"

"The last time I saw Elaine—the day before she died—she told me she was done with drugs. The way she said it, too, made me believe her."

"I don't need to tell you that relapse is the rule not the exception among addicts."

"True. But there was something different about her. A real focus. A passion for self-agency."

"Sure. In the moment. Then something changed. Maybe she was triggered? A text? A call? God only knows. In a crisis, people usually revert to what they know best, where they find most comfort."

"Maybe." Holly is silent for a long moment. "But you want to hear the worst part? What really makes me hate myself?"

He squeezes her shoulder. "I do."

Holly's eyes redden and tears begin to pool above her lower lids. "I'm relieved."

"Because of the accusations she was going to make?"

"Yes!" Holly cries. "They won't see the light of day now."

"That's understandable. Natural, even. No matter how her allegations might have landed, the whole ordeal was going to be an absolute nightmare for you."

"Do you know how guilty that makes me feel?" She wipes her eyes with the sleeve of her shirt. "A woman died, maybe because of the therapy I gave her. And now I'm relieved she's dead? What kind of monster am I?"

Aaron looks deeply into her eyes. "How else are you supposed to respond? After escaping an existential threat like that? Relief is inevitable."

Holly's face crumples, and she embraces him, squeezing him tight enough that he can feel every sob that racks her body.

Aaron hates to see his wife in such pain and distress. But he loves the feeling of her in his arms. And he realizes that, at some level, the two are inseparable.

CHAPTER 15

Thursday, April 11

Holly wakes up feeling slightly disoriented. Technically, she is in her own bed, but she hasn't lived in Aaron's house for almost six months. And lying there with her old comforter wrapped around her, she can't help second-guessing her decision to have slept over. But she didn't want to be alone last night. And after dinner, where she and Aaron split a bottle of pinot noir, it seemed the most natural thing in the world to crawl into bed with him.

Holly doesn't regret their sex. In fact, she initiated it. Physically, they have always been in sync. Ten years into their marriage, she still loves the way he kisses her. And in spite of their generational age gap—he's the only lover she's ever had who is more than three years older than her, let alone twenty—she has never felt as comfortable with anyone else in bed.

But good sex alone has never been enough. Their relationship was much easier when she was his resident, his protégée. Back then, he was fiercely protective and supportive of her. That ended when she began to make a name for herself at the university level. Whether overshadowed by her success or frustrated by his perception that her career took precedence over their relationship, Aaron hasn't always been able to hide his professional jealousy, which sometimes manifests as pettiness or dismissiveness of her work with psychedelics. And for her part, Holly recognizes she has been too blinded by her own ambition to always be sympathetic to his.

Lying beside her husband now, his shoulders rising and falling with each light snore, she feels just as ambivalent as she had before climbing into bed with him. Only last week she had been looking for the right moment to raise the idea of formalizing their separation. She had even tentatively accepted a date with the cute Swiss architect who lives two floors below her in her condo building.

Holly eases out of bed, careful not to wake Aaron. She collects her clothes from the chair, changes, and then tiptoes out of the room. As she heads down the stairs, the scent of brewed coffee wafts up to her, and she wonders if Aaron got up before her and brewed a pot before going back to bed. Tempted as she is to grab a cup on the way out, she decides against it.

Holly is only a few feet from the front door when the last voice in the world she wants to hear calls out to her. "G'morning. Bet you could use a coffee, huh?"

Suppressing a sigh, she turns to see Aaron's son Graham standing in the kitchen doorway and holding up a carafe, tilting it from side to side. "Oh, hi, Graham. I didn't realize you were staying here."

"I have my own place. But Dad lets me come and go as I please. Y'know," he says with an ugly laugh, "kinda like you."

Holly only smiles, refusing to rise to the bait.

Graham's face and neck look fuller than the last time she saw him, and his shirt can't hold back the bulge of his belly. He resembles his fraternal twin, Nate, even less than before. Nate is sweet, active, fit, and studious. Graham is none of those things. Lazy and directionless, his sense of entitlement knows no bounds. But the last thing Holly needs is to get into another altercation with Graham. "Your dad told me you started a new job," she says.

"Yup. A start-up specializing in cutting-edge consumer surveillance products. Very *Mission: Impossible*-ish, y'know? Six-figure salary right out of the gate. This one is a can't-lose proposition."

Holly has serious doubts, but says, "That's wonderful. Congrats."

He shrugs. "Oh, and by the way, I was sorry to hear about your patient."

A chill runs up the back of Holly's neck. "My patient?"

"The one who OD'd. Must be tough losing someone that way."

"Your dad told you about her?"

"Nah," Graham says. "I was in the car when you called him. On speaker phone."

Why the fuck wouldn't Aaron have mentioned that? "I can't really discuss it, Graham. I'm sure you understand."

"Probably wasn't your fault, right? And I bet if I was in your position, I wouldn't want to talk about it, either." He exhales noisily. "Something like that must really shake your belief in yourself, huh? Or do you just get used to it after a while?"

"I meant that it's privileged information," Holly says, biting down on her back teeth. "Patient-doctor confidentiality."

"Even if she's dead?"

"Even then."

"That blows." Graham shrugs. "I was super-curious to hear what she was accusing you of. Sounded major."

"I think you might be taking what you overheard out of context."

"Maybe." Graham laughs again. "Or maybe I'm just touching a nerve? You seem kinda jumpy, Holly. Real stressed."

Holly's jaw aches from grinding. "Good to see you, Graham," she says as she takes a step toward the door. "But I have to get to work."

He raises the carafe again. "No coffee to go?"

"I'm good. Thanks."

"Holly?" Aaron calls from upstairs. "Who are you talking to?"

She could scream. "Just down here with Graham," she says.

Graham chuckles again as he deposits the pot on the nearest counter. "Would love to chat more, but duty calls. The new gig and all." He brushes past her on his way out the door. "Tell Dad I'll drop by later when you're gone. I'm assuming you *will* be gone again? That's usually how this works with you two, isn't it?"

Graham disappears out the door without waiting for a response, which Holly wasn't about to provide anyway.

Moments later, Aaron appears in a house robe and slippers. "Did I miss Graham?"

Lucky you. "He had to run to work."

"Ah. Glad to hear he's prioritizing appropriately."

"Why didn't you mention he was listening in on our phone call?"

"Our call?" Aaron frowns. "Oh! When you first called to tell me about the overdose?"

"Yes!" Holly takes a slow breath to keep her voice in check. "When I shared highly confidential client information with you. Only because you're my colleague."

"I was driving Graham to work. And you sounded so distraught. I didn't want to make you wait."

"No one else was supposed to hear that."

Aaron taps his chest. "Honestly, I didn't even think Graham was listening. He had his headphones on."

"You should've told me."

"No, of course." He hangs his head. "You're right. I'm sorry."

Holly only nods, realizing there's nothing to be done about it now.

"Graham's a different person these days," Aaron says. "Between the change in medications and the new job, I think he's finally maturing. For real this time, Holly."

She bites her tongue. Aaron has a huge blind spot when it comes to his son. He never accepted Graham's diagnosis of a borderline personality disorder. Instead, he has always excused his son's manipulative behavior as either the symptoms of a mood disorder or a reflection of his sensitive nature. But Holly is convinced that Graham does have serious personality issues. And his dad is Graham's ultimate enabler, going so far as to insert himself into his son's psychiatric care.

The moment Holly met Graham, she recognized him as a deeply wounded child. One who was still mourning his parents' divorce while feeling trapped in the shadow of his far more gifted twin brother. She felt genuine pity for Graham. And despite the boy's challenging nature and tendency to lash out, she tried, with varying degrees of success, to take the higher road: to show him nothing but love, support, and patience.

Until the trolling began.

Six years ago, a friend and colleague of hers called Holly to alert her that her scores on the most popular rate-your-therapist website had plummeted. Soon after, the negative and hurtful reviews began to pile up.

Like the two-star review which read: *Dr. Danvers is nice enough, but she is distant and uninterested. She stared at the wall behind me the whole session.*

Another one-star review followed. *Me and the missus went to her for couples' therapy. The doc tried to hit on me. We're divorced now. Thanks for nothing, "Doctor" Danvers!*

Hate to say it, because she's smart and all, but the woman needs a shower. Two stars.

I urge you to look elsewhere to have your mental health treated. I'm no better after seeing her for five years. One star.

Then came the review that pushed Holly over the edge. It didn't even have a star rating, only a text narrative. *Wish I could give zero stars here. But nothing will bring Dad back. If his depression was cured, Dr. Danvers, how do you explain the shotgun blast?*

Holly, who already had her suspicions, turned to a cyber investigator. He tracked the IP address of the troll to Graham's high school. When she confronted Graham, the then fifteen-year-old not only denied any involvement but tried to frame his own brother. As always, Aaron attempted to smooth things over. The incident led to their first separation. Even after Aaron and Holly reconciled, her relationship with his son was permanently fractured.

She shakes off the unpleasant memory as Aaron steps closer. "I missed you, Holl," he says. "Six months is too long to wait for a night like that."

"Agreed."

He kisses her cheek. "How'd you sleep?"

"Pretty well. I've being missing that comforter."

"There's an easy fix for that."

"You don't mind if I take it back to my place?"

His pinched smile betrays his annoyance. "Even easier than that."

"Last night was lovely, Aaron. But it doesn't change anything."

He eyes her incredulously. "Do you have any idea how many married couples would kill for what we still have after ten years? That kind of connection and passion?"

Unshaven, his salt-and-pepper hair ruffled, and his housecoat worn, he looks a little haggard to her. Older, too. But Holly still finds Aaron attractive in that same nerdy intellectual way that originally caught her eye. She has always been a sucker for that look. "Passion has never been our problem," she says.

He strokes her cheek lightly. "Graham's doing better. He won't be an issue for us."

Not only will he always be an issue for us, he's proof of your fallibility as a father and a therapist. But she sees no point in arguing. "It's not only him."

"We have other challenges. Of course. What couple doesn't ten years into a marriage? But we always do better as a team. Take, for example, what you've gone through this past week. Hasn't it helped to have me around?"

"You know it has, Aaron. And I hope I've been clear how appreciative I am."

"You have," he says. "OK, enough about that. How are you feeling?"

"Confused," she admits.

He cups her chin. "It's been a while."

"I meant about Elaine."

"Oh." He takes his hand from her face. "You're still not willing to give yourself a break?"

"More than willing. Believe me, if I could just switch off the guilt, I would." Holly pauses. She still can't fathom how Elaine could have injected herself. It doesn't make sense. But she doesn't have the energy to rehash it with him. "You did make an excellent point yesterday, though. About the other patients. The ones that psychedelic therapy has helped."

"Me?" he asks in mock surprise. "What's that old saying? Give an infinite number of monkeys a typewriter and eventually one of them will write a Shakespearean sonnet."

"Well, Curious George, I think you might've typed one yesterday." She chuckles. "I do have other clients. As a matter of fact, six of them alone in Elaine's group. They're all doing better on psychedelic therapy. All of them still sober or abstinent."

"What becomes of that group now?"

Holly has been pondering that very question. After Elaine's death, Holly canceled the group's weekly ketamine infusion, but she didn't call off the one-on-one sessions, which are scheduled for tomorrow. She wonders how many of them, if any, will show up. And will they still see themselves as a tribe after losing one of their own?

CHAPTER 16

It's been thirty-two years since Simon last registered a song on the *Bill-board* top twenty, or hit any other significant list, but his concerts still sell out stadiums. And he is recognized almost anywhere he goes, which is the one thing Simon would change about celebrity. It's also why he usually has his meals, especially ones involving business, in private. But JJ insisted on meeting at this trendy café, no doubt, he suspects, because of their misunderstanding last month inside his home.

Simon now finds himself wearing sunglasses indoors in a corner booth, pretending not to notice the people noticing him. Especially the balding guy two tables over with the chunky, blue-framed glasses, who keeps glancing his way as if witnessing an epiphany.

JJ didn't tell Simon why she wanted to meet. Nor did she mention that Salvador would be joining them. But after she sits down between the two men, JJ makes it clear that she tried to convene the whole tribe. "Reese is stuck in LA with a deposition," she says. "Baljit had to go to the desert on business. And Liisa went to San Diego to visit her daughter."

Salvador grimaces. "Liisa has a daughter?"

"One big happy family," JJ says.

"You'd think she might have mentioned that in group session." Salvador huffs. "The rest of us are here bearing our messy souls. And this superior Scandi bitch hides a daughter from us?"

"Technically, Finns are Nordic, not Scandinavian," JJ says.

"Now you sound like her!"

Simon turns to Salvador. "What does Liisa ever share in group? Aside from constantly reminding us how in the know she is. Shit, I have no idea what the woman is even hooked on."

"Xanax." Salvador eyes him knowingly. "As in downers."

Simon grunts a laugh. "That figures, doesn't it?"

"It can't be easy for Liisa," JJ mutters, staring at the tabletop. "My calling is to throw fabulous parties and raise a fortune for charity. People expect me to be a raging alcoholic. 'Real Housewives of Laguna.' But a therapist in therapy? And for addiction, no less. That must suck."

"Coming clean on my sex addiction hasn't exactly been my crowning glory," Simon says. As soon as the words leave his lips, he's inspired by an idea for a song. But the thought fizzles almost as quickly as it formed. Jeremy would have known how to work the concept into beautifully ironic lyrics, and Simon would have found a complementary melody. But since Simon lost his songwriting partner, his own creative output has dried up. Worse, he knows in his heart that more recent compositions have become derivative and clichéd. He's a caricature of the talent he once was.

Salvador motions from Simon to JJ. "Lovely as it is to see you two darlings, I have final fittings for my show all week. Five of me couldn't get everything done that I need to." He turns to JJ. "What's with the urgent rendezvous?"

JJ shakes her head as if confused by the question. "Elaine is *dead*."

Salvador giggles in that anxious way of his. "Not exactly a news flash, love."

"Doesn't it worry you?"

His nose wrinkles. "That needle wasn't in my arm."

Before JJ can respond, the bald guy in the blue glasses steps up to their table. "Sorry to interrupt," he says. "But I'm such a fan! I can't even tell you!"

"Thank you," Simon says. "But we're in the middle of a meeting here."

"Of course," the man says, looking over to Salvador with starry eyes.

"I'm a buyer for Saks. And I just have to tell you, Salvador, that your spring collection absolutely blew my mind!"

"Jesus," Simon grumbles. *I'm now overshadowed by this second-rate Vera Wang?*

Salvador lays a hand on his chest. "How sweet. Just what I needed to hear today. I'm touched. And you are . . . ?"

"Brody . . . Brody Stevens." He extends his hand toward Salvador.

Simon pushes the man's arm down. "We're busy here, Brody. Would you be an absolute dear and fuck off?"

Brody spins on his heels and mutters something as he walks off, but the only words Simon can make out are "overrated has-been."

Salvador frowns at him. "Was that necessary?"

"Maybe not necessary, but quite satisfying."

Salvador turns to JJ again. "We're all saddened by Elaine's loss. But she was an addict."

"We're all addicts," JJ points out.

"Yes, but her crutch was opioids. That's night-and-day different."

"Is it though?"

"Absolutely!" Simon interjects. "Say you fell off the wagon, JJ . . ."

"What if I did?"

"Then you'd get blackout drunk and likely end up God knows where after some poor decision." Simon motions to Salvador. "And if *he* did, he'd go on some all-night pill and powder bender. And if I did, I'd get laid. Repeatedly. We'd all wake up the next day full of shame and self-loathing. But the key difference is that we *would* wake up."

"It's true." Salvador nods. "With downers—and let's face it, it's basically nothing but fentanyl these days—it's Russian roulette every single time. Especially if you use alone."

"It's like an occupational hazard in my world," Simon says. "I couldn't tell you how many friends I've lost over the years to heroin and now fentanyl."

Salvador shudders. "I lost my Misha to the needle only last year. My absolute fave. Nobody—I mean nobody—could rock a runway like her. But that same attitude put her underground at just twenty-two." He raises a palm skyward. "Misha might've been the love of my life."

"Hang on." Simon grimaces. "You're straight?"

"I don't do labels, Simon."

JJ rolls her eyes, showing no patience for their digression. "Elaine didn't use needles!"

"She did last week," Salvador says.

"And don't you find that . . . strange?"

"Should I?"

"You saw her that day when we all went over there."

"We all did," Simon says. "What's your point, JJ?"

"Elaine believed that Dr. Danvers violated her," JJ says. "And she was absolutely determined to expose her. Obsessed! And that's the day she chooses to switch to needles?"

"Makes perfect sense to me," Salvador says.

"How?" JJ demands.

"The stress must've gotten to her. Triggered her. Made her fall back on the opioids. Maybe, Elaine couldn't get her hands on any pills and had no choice but to inject?"

JJ shakes her head obstinately, like a child refusing to obey a parent. "And where would she get the fentanyl if she couldn't find pills?"

"Any street corner?" Salvador says. "Fentanyl is everywhere."

JJ squints at Salvador. "Does that make sense to you? Elaine buys fentanyl—for the first time ever—on the same day she was planning to expose Dr. Danvers?"

Simon has never seen JJ looking this out of sorts. Not even the evening she stormed out of his home, red-faced and indignant. It's as if she's scared. "Hang on!" He slaps the table. "Are you suggesting Dr. D *silenced* Elaine?"

"No, no, no. Not at all!" JJ looks frantically from Simon to Salvador and back. "But don't you think Elaine's death looks suspicious?"

Simon bristles. "No. It looks fucking pathetic and predictable."

CHAPTER 17

Friday, April 12

"One point six million," Baljit says. "That's the most I've ever lost in one sitting."

"At a *casino*?" Holly asks incredulously.

Baljit nods. Wearing a gray blazer, skirt, and Jimmy Choo pumps, she sits in the matching chair across from Holly with her legs crossed, the epitome of a chic executive. "A craps table. In fucking Macau, of all places!"

"But it didn't wipe you out, did it?"

"Nope. Neither did the other ten or twelve mill I've shit away over the past few years in casinos. Then again, business is good," Baljit says in embarrassment. "And my father has deep pockets."

"Your dad covered your losses?"

Baljit fingers the pendant on her necklace. "A few times. When I wasn't quite liquid enough."

"Your father sounds devoted."

Baljit snorts.

"What does that mean?"

Baljit rubs the slight crease between her eyebrows as if trying to flatten it. "Sikhism is a relatively progressive culture and religion. All about egalitarianism. There isn't supposed to be a distinction between men and women within the *gurdwara*—the community."

"But your father isn't so egalitarian?"

"My father puts the capital T in toxic masculinity."

Holly tilts her head. "Sounds like he's there for when you need him, though?"

"With money? Sure. But those loans always come with a smug 'I told you so' attached. Which I think makes it almost worthwhile for him. Besides, I've made a fortune for him and the others since I took over the family business five years ago."

"If he's such a chauvinist, then why let a woman take over?"

"Because he didn't have a son. And at eighty-four, he was too frail to keep running the company himself. Trust me, it kills him to have a woman in charge."

Holly can't resist a smile. "Not yet, apparently."

Baljit laughs. "Hey, that's my line."

"You're an only child, right?"

"Yup. And I didn't come easily. Dad was fifty and Mom almost forty when they met. They had to go through the whole fertility rigamarole. Back then, it was harder. And Mom had to have a hysterectomy soon after I was born. Dad never forgave me for being born without a Y chromosome. The one thing life never gave him. A son."

"Do you think all of those emotions played into your gambling addiction?"

"You figure, Dr. Freud?" Baljit shoots up a hand in apology. "Sorry. Look. You're the one who's paid to do the analyzing. But as I see it, money has always been a surrogate for love for me. No wonder I got addicted to chasing it."

Holly nods, pleased Baljit has made the connection for herself. "Have you stayed away from the casino since I last saw you?"

Baljit grins. "Not so much as a scratch-and-win ticket in over four weeks."

"Are you still being triggered by your father?"

"Constantly. But I'm taking out my rage at the gym. On the spin bike, the elliptical, and especially any dipshit who looks at me twice while I'm working out."

"Good." Holly smiles. "And the cravings to gamble?"

"Honestly? Since that last session with ketamine and MDMA, there's been nothing. It's the weirdest thing. It's as if I haven't eaten in days, but I'm still not hungry."

This is music to Holly's ears. She makes a mental note to document Baljit's quote verbatim in the meticulous file she's keeping on the group. But she saves the most delicate conversation for last. "I'd like to talk about what happened with Elaine."

Baljit shrugs. "What more is there to say?"

"A lot, for some."

"Not me."

"Under the circumstances, I'm not sure we'll be able to continue with our group therapy."

Baljit's head snaps back in surprise. "Why not?"

"The whole point of the group was to help support one another through your struggles with addiction."

"How has that changed? If anything, we need even more support now."

Holly resists the urge to tell her that group therapy failed Elaine in the worst way imaginable. That she, personally, failed Elaine. All she says is "Ours is innovative therapy. Unproven, some would argue. Certainly not mainstream. And there's a lot more scrutiny. On me, at least. Ever since the media learned about us—"

"Simon! That foolish lech should have never outed our group like that." Baljit wags a finger. "But this isn't really about the media. It's about Elaine, isn't it?"

Not only her. Holly thinks of Katy Armstrong and how the reporter would pounce were she to learn of Elaine and her association with the ketamine group. But Baljit is essentially right. And she's far too smart to be misdirected. Still, Holly isn't willing to share her guilt with another client. It wouldn't be appropriate. Instead, she says, "Regardless, I think we have to take a break. At a minimum, from using psychedelics in our therapy."

"No!" Baljit cries. She smooths her skirt before speaking in a calmer tone. "What happened to Elaine was unfortunate. But when you think about it, kind of inevitable."

"Inevitable?"

"A lifelong opioid addict who just found out she'd been sexually abused as a kid?" Baljit shakes her head. "Might as well have locked a pyromaniac in a room full of rags, gasoline, and matches."

Despite the hyperbole, Holly sees Baljit's point. Moreover, she's relieved to hear that Baljit—the first of the tribe she has interviewed since Elaine's death—is eager to proceed with therapy. But "We'll see" is all Holly is willing to say.

Fifteen minutes after Baljit leaves, Reese occupies the same chair, dressed in a navy suit and wearing minimal makeup. The similarities between Reese and Baljit are hard to overlook. Both in their late thirties, educated, successful, ambitious, blunt, and impenetrably self-assured. Holly realizes the same description could apply to her, as well. And yet the two women don't remind Holly of each other, and she certainly doesn't see herself in either of them. Racial differences aside, Baljit is married with a seven-year-old daughter, although as best Holly can tell, her husband spends most of his time in Asia. Reese, on the other hand, is single. More significantly, the two women give off wholly different vibes. Baljit seems driven by unbridled determination to prove herself—in essence, to win—while Reese, despite her intolerance for inefficiency, is far more contemplative and practical. In some ways, Holly sees her as the rock of the group.

"How are things?" Holly asks.

"Six weeks without a drop," Reese says matter-of-factly.

"And how are you feeling about it?"

Reese considers the question for a moment. "I've been through rehab three times and gone to God knows how many AA meetings. I was beginning to think I'd never be able to stay on the wagon."

"No?"

"I used to go to bed drunk. Even if I blacked out, I'd still get up the next morning and be at work on time. I've always done my job well and risen steadily up the corporate ladder. I'm a top-earning partner at thirty-eight, despite the drinking. But I'd basically resigned myself to the idea that I would live my whole life as a functional alcoholic and then die alone." She sighs. "It's not an uncommon fate for lawyers."

"You're not resigned anymore?"

Reese sweeps her hand around the room. "This changed everything. The ketamine. Our group. You. A few months ago, I didn't think sobriety would ever be in my future, and now it feels . . . easy."

"I'm glad, Reese."

"Me, too. Because while I could drink my way through my career, I couldn't do the same with the rest of my life."

"You mean with your family?"

"I don't have a family. I was an only child. And my parents are dead."

Reese has always resisted discussing her childhood, but Holly senses an opening. "How old were you when your parents died?"

"Mom passed about fifteen years ago. But it was a blessing. She had early onset Alzheimer's."

Holly offers a sympathetic smile. "And your father?"

"I was eight." Reese snorts. "They told me he died of cancer."

"He didn't?"

"When I was in ninth grade, one of my cousins broke it to me that Dad actually died of cirrhosis. I think he called it a 'shot liver.' Because as my loveable cousin stressed—in front of a bunch of my classmates, mind you—Dad was a fall-down drunk."

"That's awful."

Reese shrugs. "Like father, like daughter, huh?"

"I meant finding out that way."

"Not the best way to hear it. Then again, I like to think my cousin came to regret humiliating me. Especially after his prized dirt bike blew up. Well, caught fire." A small smile tugs at the corner of Reese's mouth.

Holly arches an eyebrow. "How?"

"A loose wire and a leak in the gas tank." Reese eyes her knowingly. "He wasn't hurt, but I don't think his motorbike was ever rideable again."

"I see." Holly maintains a neutral expression, but she's surprised to hear that her most unflappable client acted out to that degree. Even as a teenager.

As if reading her mind, Reese says, "I know it's not really an excuse, but I was young and stupid and going through one of the worst periods of my life."

"Why's that?"

"My mom had just been put into a home."

Holly frowns. "When you were in high school?"

"Her dementia spiraled quickly. She was only in her forties, but she didn't even recognize me anymore." Reese swallows. "My aunt and uncle took me in when I was thirteen."

"That must have been hard."

Reese shrugs. "They did their best, but they had three young kids of their own to cope with. Last thing they needed was a teenager sulking around. And, as you can probably tell, I wasn't the easiest kid."

"Firestarter with a sass mouth?"

Reese laughs softly. "Little bit."

Nodding, Holly considers how the trauma of being effectively orphaned in her adolescence, coupled with a genetic predisposition, could easily have triggered Reese's descent into alcoholism.

"Lucky for me, the DNA tests say that I'm not at increased risk for early onset Alzheimer's," Reese says. "And so far, my liver has handled everything I've thrown at it like a champ."

"Still . . ."

"It's life, Dr. Danvers." Reese's smile is almost serene. "The point is, I never thought marriage . . . or kids were even on the table for me. But now—for the first time ever—I'm thinking I might be able to actually have a family of my own."

"That's beautiful, Reese."

"No. It's simply a fact."

Holly hesitates. "The last thing I want to do is dampen your optimism. But things are going to have to change in our therapy. At least in the short term."

"Because of Elaine?"

"Yes."

"Change how?"

"I'm not sure if we'll be able to continue with the psychedelics in the same way." Holly repeats the same rationale she shared with Baljit.

"It's such a waste," Reese mutters. "All of it."

"I agree."

"How Elaine ever managed to convince herself that you'd be stupid enough to molest her in the middle of a group session . . ."

Holly can feel her cheeks flush. "You knew about that?"

"We all did."

"The whole group?"

Reese nods. "She told JJ."

"JJ? Why her?"

"JJ called Elaine after she skipped our last group session."

Holly's skin crawls. "There was no substance to Elaine's allegations!"

"Obviously," Reese says, as if Holly is having a hard time keeping up. "That's what we all tried to tell her."

"*We all?*" Holly's jaw drops. "You discussed it with Elaine? All of you?"

"We went to see her. The whole group. To try to talk some sense into her."

"When?"

"The day she overdosed."

Holly closes her eyes and sees Elaine slumped in the chair again, the needle at her feet. She must have overdosed shortly after the tribe's visit. A question, unbidden, comes to mind: *Could one of you have been involved?*

CHAPTER 18

JJ, who is the last appointment of the day, sits uncharacteristically still in the chair across from Holly. Unlike previous visits, JJ is dressed plainly in jeans and a simple black top. Her bracelets are gone. And her mood is as subdued as her outfit. Usually, the animated socialite is painfully forthcoming on everything from her alcoholism to her multiple failed marriages. Normally, she laughs freely and often. She cries openly whenever she discusses the series of devastating miscarriages that crushed her dreams of motherhood. And JJ usually shows up to her appointments with food or other small gifts—candles, potpourri, and assorted bric-a-brac—for Holly and Tanya, despite Holly's attempts to dissuade her.

Not only did JJ show up empty-handed today, but she has kept her eyes fixed to the floor and hardly uttered more than a few words since sitting down.

Unable to engage JJ on anything else, Holly finally raises the topic of Elaine. "I understand the whole group visited Elaine the day she died."

JJ shoots forward in her seat. "Who told you?"

"Does it matter?"

JJ shakes her head adamantly. "It wasn't my idea to go!"

"I didn't mean it like that. I'm just curious why you went as a group."

JJ's gaze falls to her lap. "It was a mistake."

"A mistake?"

"I mean . . . look what ended up happening."

"I'm not following, JJ," Holly says. "Are you suggesting Elaine's overdose was somehow related to the group's visit?"

"No, no." JJ shifts in her chair. "But Elaine was beside herself. And us being there wasn't helping one bit. Plus . . ."

Holly waits for her to finish the thought.

JJ shakes her head. "The optics are bad."

"Bad how?"

"Just plain bad."

"Why? Because it would look like you were all acting in your own self-interest? Pressuring Elaine into silence?"

"All of it!" JJ stares at Holly with eyes that border on frantic. "Just terrible."

After the comment, JJ retreats back into near silence. She appears to be relieved as the session ends, and she hurries out of the office without so much as a goodbye.

As soon as JJ is gone, Holly leans back in her chair and stares at the ceiling fixture, barely conscious of the soft thrum of the central AC in the background. Aside from waving goodbye to Tanya, who tentatively pokes her head into the office to say she is going home, Holly barely moves a muscle in the next fifteen minutes. She realizes she should be documenting the group's response to Elaine's death or working on a chapter for her book, which her publisher wants to take to market as soon as possible, but she feels absolutely drained. Not so much from the long office day, but rather from the relentless swirl of recent events.

Holly is relieved that five of the six remaining group members are eager to resume their ketamine therapy. JJ was less committal, probably because she seems to have taken Elaine's death so much harder than any of the others.

Elaine continues to weigh heavily on Holly's mind, too. She can't believe how many people are aware of Elaine's accusations. It's bad enough that Graham found out, but it bothers Holly even more that the whole tribe knows. She can't believe they went to see Elaine en masse. Had they really thought they could talk her out of those allegations? Did their visit help push her to overdose? Or did one of them actually lend a hand?

Holly's phone buzzes on her desk. She can tell from the distinct staccato pattern that Aaron is calling, but she doesn't reach for it. She has already ignored two of his previous calls and only responded to his texts with a single, deliberately terse reply: *Sorry, tied up for the day.*

Her charged conversation with Graham aside, Holly regrets having slept with Aaron. It was the wrong message to send him when she is still so doubtful about their future.

"At least you're consistent," she mutters to herself, thinking of how screwed up her personal *and* professional lives are.

Holly's eyes drift to the slot under her desk where her purse sits. Even though its clasp is closed, she can sense the DMT pen inside. She thinks again of the peace it brought her the last time she vaped. Holly knows how unprofessional it would be to vape in her own office but, unable to resist the temptation, she digs the pen out of the purse. Clutching it tightly in her palm, she heads over to the group therapy room. After closing the door behind her, she lowers herself onto the same chair where Elaine used to sit.

After putting on headphones, Holly chooses a classic folk-rock playlist from her phone and hits shuffle. Immediately, the melodic guitar riff of James Taylor's intro to "Fire and Rain" fills her ears, and it's impossible for Holly to overlook the irony of opening with a song about suicide.

After lowering her blindfold over her eyes, she brings the cool tip of the vape to her lips and inhales the acrid vapor, fighting off the cough and holding her breath for as long as she can. She exhales, and the stench stings her nostrils. She catches her breath and immediately takes another long drag.

Holly has barely exhaled again when a light show explodes behind her mask. The dazzling dance of colors is more beautiful than the northern lights and more intense than a mid-August meteor shower.

Holly is overcome by the oddest sensation. It's like her skin is peeling away from her body. And yet, there is nothing distressing about it. On the contrary, the feeling is comforting. It's as if her soul is being freed from the rest of her, like a butterfly emerging from its cocoon.

She feels herself morphing into a form of pure light. She watches in awe as her spirit melds with the infinite luminescence enshrouding her. She no longer feels like a distinct entity, but rather a miniscule fragment of a much greater being.

A nearby cluster of lights suddenly coalesces into the shape of a face, which shatters her sense of tranquility the moment Holly recognizes it.

Elaine? She gasps.

Elaine's disembodied face stares back, free of the anger and blame that burned in her eyes on their last encounter. Instead, she radiates profound sadness. *Why?* she whimpers. Sorrow and confusion tumble over her lips in a dark stream that cools the air around them.

Holly's mind races with assumptions, all of them useless. *Why what, Elaine?*

Why am I here?

Holly looks around at an immense cedar forest, cool and green. Occasionally, shafts of sunlight penetrate the gloom. The earth is black and damp. *I . . . I don't know.*

The face glows brighter. *You do! You must.*

I don't! Holly feels guilt flutter in her heart. *You overdosed, Elaine. But I don't understand it. You told me you were done forever. No more opioids.*

I was done.

But I saw you, Elaine. In the chair. The needle by your foot. Did somebody do this to you?

Needles terrify me. Elaine's eyes are black pools. Something ripples in their depths.

A drifting sensation sweeps over Holly. As if she can feel herself dissolving. *Tell me, Elaine. Please! What happened to you?*

A rustling in the underbrush nearby makes Holly spin around. But all is quiet and still, save the dust motes in the sunbeams. When she turns back, Elaine is gone.

Holly's terror deepens. She looks down at her hands to see her fingers disappearing into wisps of smoke, and struggles to keep herself whole, having no idea how to accomplish it.

Another voice from somewhere in the forest: *Hollycopter.*

The release is immediate, an outpouring of love. *Daddy!*

She cannot see her father, but she senses that he is there beside her. She feels his roots supporting her and his boughs shading her. She is filled with the certainty that he is the towering cedar to her left. He is light, soft, resinous, and durable; he is connected to every other tree in this forest in a vast network of vibrational energies.

It's all right, Hollycopter. Everything will be OK.

No, Daddy. Nothing will ever be okay again. Elaine . . .

Her father's voice comes from underground, through a thousand vibrating rootlets. *It's not your fault. Not Elaine's death, and not mine.*

She feels deep inside that this is true, that all is well, and she lies down on the damp black earth to look up between the branches to the blue sky beyond. *As above, so below*, she thinks, and wonders where the thought comes from.

Her teeth begin to chatter, and her arms and legs tremble violently, evaporating into curls and wisps of smoke that mix with the motes in the sunbeams. Unable to control her body, Holly decides to surrender, allowing the energy to dissipate of its own accord, flowing out into the forest around her.

Holly gathers her bearings. She feels the soft leather of the chair against her back and the cloth over her eyes. Over the soft strumming of an acoustic guitar, Holly hears a click. Then footsteps. She reaches up and yanks the mask away from her eyes, suddenly alert and sober.

She glances urgently around the room, but it appears the same as when she had first sat down.

Then she notices. The door is ajar.

CHAPTER 19

Long before Holly bought herself a watch that tracked her daily steps, she loved to walk. Sometimes she wonders if it's built into her DNA. Even as a young child, she used to trek miles with her parents and grandparents. And ever since she moved into her fourth-floor rental unit in the condo building off Cliff Road, she often leaves her car in the garage and walks the one-and-a-half miles to and from work.

As she approaches the entrance to her building now, she sees the stooped form of an elderly man sitting on the bench under the front light.

"Papa!" she says, hurrying up to the door to greet him. "Is everything OK?"

"Everything is fine, Koala."

"How did you get here?"

Walter rises stiffly from the seat. "How does anyone get anywhere these days? Uber."

"Hope you haven't been waiting too long."

"Ten minutes? Maybe fifteen. At my age, who keeps time?"

She kisses him on the cheek, inhaling the reassuringly familiar scent of his cologne, a mix of sage and mint. "Why didn't you call first?"

"I took a chance." He shrugs. "Thought I'd surprise you."

Holly grins. "You're a sight for sore eyes. Come on in." She links elbows with him and leads him through the door and up the elevator, forgoing the staircase this once.

As soon as they're inside her condo, Holly puts on the kettle and steeps two cups of jasmine tea. She brings one over to him on the living room couch. "I can't remember the last time you dropped in on me."

"And I can't remember what I had for lunch or breakfast." He chuckles. "I don't get out much since this macular degeneration set in. But I do miss being able to drive myself. Matter of fact, after your grandmother, it's the thing I miss the very most about my eighties." He laughs. "Ah, how youth is wasted on the young."

"And yet you're here now?"

"I can't visit my own granddaughter? When did you become so suspicious?"

"Papa . . ."

"I had to pick up a prescription in town." His blue eyes are paler than they used to be but just as penetrating. "I wanted to see you, all right? I've been concerned. After the way you lost your patient . . ."

Holly can't stop herself from wrapping him in another hug. It occurs to her that his love is the only unconditional thing she has in her life.

"Is it that bad, Koala?" he asks with his rough face still pressed to her cheek.

"I don't know," she says, releasing him. "So much has happened in the past few days."

"My Uber ride wasn't cheap. Make it worth my while. Tell your papa."

And she does. Holly describes how she reconnected with Aaron, despite her ongoing ambivalence about their relationship, and her subsequent confrontation with his son. She admits to her gnawing guilt over Elaine's death, which is compounded by her relief that Elaine's allegations will never see the light of day. And then Holly tells Walter about her mixed feelings over continuing psychedelic therapy with the remaining group members.

Walter studies her quizzically. "The others in this group? They want to continue with psychedelics?"

"They do, yes."

He nods. "Losing a patient to suicide or an overdose . . . it happens to all psychiatrists, no?"

"To most. And I get it. If my client had been on some well-established antidepressant, of course, I wouldn't stop that same medication on all the other patients it was helping."

Walter reaches for his cup without commenting.

"But as we've discussed, Papa, I'm pushing the boundary of mainstream medicine and psychiatry. *We* know how effective psychedelics are, but there are so many doubters. A lot of people are watching, some of whom want us to fail. Especially since Simon went public. If that reporter from the *Orange County Register* ever found out about Elaine . . ." She whistles.

"Has anyone linked your patient's death to psychedelics?"

"No." She hesitates. "At least, not yet."

"Not yet? I don't understand."

"I'm not sure how long it can stay a secret. Too many people know about Elaine's allegations."

Walter tilts his head. "Who knows?"

"The whole group. Graham knows, too. He overheard us on Aaron's car phone."

Walter's wordless sigh is enough to convey his understanding.

"I saw Elaine again today. In a vision."

The creases around Walter's eyes deepen. "A vision? On DMT?"

"Yes. Just before I left the office. I thought another trip might help . . . clarify things."

"Did it?"

"No. But the hallucination, it was so vivid. Elaine was demanding to know why she overdosed."

"Oh, Koala, you know these visions are merely projections of our own thoughts and emotions. They're the embodiment of our musings and hopes. Self-fulfilling hallucinations, if you will. You can't read too much into them." He chuckles. "Not that I haven't been guilty of doing the same myself too many times."

"But in this case, they're also a projection of my doubt and suspicions."

"Suspicions?"

"What happened to Elaine doesn't add up."

"What doesn't add up?"

"I'm trained to recognize the signs of suicidality. But the last time I saw her—the day before her death—Elaine didn't show a flicker of intent."

"But her overdose could have been accidental, no?"

"I suppose, but she was terrified of needles. I wonder if someone else might have been there." Holly sighs. "Especially since I just found out that the rest of the group went to her home to confront her. To talk her out of posting her accusations. On the very day she died."

"Maybe that was the straw that broke the camel's back?"

"Yeah, maybe," she mutters, but she is unconvinced. "There's something else, too."

"Tell me."

"When I came to after vaping the DMT this afternoon, the door to my office was open."

He frowns. "I don't understand."

"My office was locked. Everyone was gone for the day. And . . . Papa, I was careful to shut the door before I vaped."

"Do you not have cleaners?"

"We do, yes. But they usually come later."

Walter stares at her. "Holly, these growing suspicions of yours . . ."

She realizes that she must sound a little paranoid and wonders if it could be a lingering effect from the DMT. "You're right. It was probably just the cleaners."

They lapse into brief silence as they both sip their tea. "I had a second vision on that DMT trip," she says.

"What else did you see?"

"Dad. I didn't really see him. I felt him."

Walter stares down into his cup. "Oh."

"He told me it wasn't my fault."

"What wasn't?"

"Elaine's death." She hesitates. "The car accident, too. It was just like those visions I had of Dad in Peru. But maybe it's always just been wishful thinking? Like you said, self-fulfilling hallucinations. Projecting what I wanted to hear because I've never been able to remember what happened."

Walter says nothing. He won't even look at her. Her grandfather is never someone to shy away from difficult conversations or emotions. Except when it comes to the memory of his only son. Especially the circumstances of his death.

CHAPTER 20

Saturday, April 13

There was a time when, after a call like the one he had had with his lawyer the previous evening, Simon would have trashed his own room, smashing the artwork off the walls and destroying the furniture along with one or more of his own guitars.

Not anymore. The new Simon—*more like the very old one*—sits quietly in the waiting room of the law firm in downtown Newport Beach, waiting on a second opinion.

He has been at the office for almost twenty minutes, and without looking up, he senses the eyes of the receptionist on him. She doesn't look old enough to recognize him or his music. But he finds her attention distressing. At this point, he's afraid that if he as much as makes eye contact with her, it might lead to another complaint.

Reese finally steps into the waiting room in another dark business suit. Despite her deep-set hazel eyes and almost triangular shaped face, Simon finds her distinctive look attractive, intriguing even. But she also intimidates him. Those keen eyes give him the sense that she sees right through him.

Also, Simon finds it disorienting to see a tribe member in another office, outside of Dr. Danvers's clinic. Especially when Reese extends her hand and greets him as if they're meeting for the first time. "Good morning, Simon," she says and then turns back the way she came.

He follows her down a hallway to a spacious corner office with floor-to-ceiling views of the marina. "Someone's a big shooter," he says with a whistle as he sits down across the desk from her.

"Your call made it sound urgent."

"Right to business, huh?"

"I don't have long," she says unapologetically. "I have an urgent closing today."

"On a Saturday?"

She snorts. "As if that matters to my clients."

His gaze falls to her marble desktop. "Someone else has come forward."

"Come forward?"

"Another complainant." He clears his throat as he looks back up at her. "Allegations and such."

She squints at him. "About Dr. Danvers?"

"What? No. Not her. *Me.*"

She looks skyward. "I'm not following you, Simon."

"Earlier this year, I had to settle out of court with this woman. She made certain claims that I—"

Reese shoots up a hand. "Whoa, let me stop you right there. I'm not that kind of attorney, Simon. I practice corporate law. Primarily M&As. Mergers and acquisitions."

"I get that. I'm not an idiot. I just wanted to get your opinion. As a friend."

"A friend?"

"OK. As a member of the tribe, then."

She rolls her eyes. "I think that term has already been claimed."

"Oh, yeah." Simon chuckles. "Member of the Tribe. A MOT. My manager, David Hirschberg, describes himself as that all the time."

"Honestly, Simon," she says, as she steals a glance at her watch, "my opinion is going to be as good as useless to you."

"I've seen how sharp your mind is in group, Reese. Just hear me out. Please. It won't take long."

She leans back in her chair. "All right."

"Earlier this year, I settled out of court with this person. For a stupid amount of money, even though her claims were bullshit. But in light of the current . . . climate . . . everyone thought it was in my best interest to make the deal."

"I assume the other party signed an NDA?"

"Exactly."

"Let me guess. Someone else has come forward with a similar claim?"

"That's the thing!" Simon cries. "It's not just anyone else. It's Brianna's best friend!"

"Her friend is accusing you, too?"

Simon slumps in his chair. "I met them at the same time. In Portland. They approached me after a concert. Invited themselves back to my hotel suite. Sure, I partied with them. But nothing much happened. At least, not that night. They came on tour with me for a few weeks. I thought we all had a blast. We even kept in touch after." He knows better than to mention the accidental bruising around Brianna's neck, still not convinced he was responsible for it.

Reese's expression remains blank, but he senses the disdain behind her impassive eyes. "Here's my opinion, Simon. Save yourself some legal fees and settle with the second one using the exact same contract as you did with the first."

"But Brianna signed an NDA."

"And?"

"She must have told her friend! It's way too coincidental otherwise."

"Can you prove that?"

"No. But where will it end? If I settle every time one talks—clearly breaking the terms of the NDA—then it will only encourage others. It's like negotiating with terrorists."

"Negotiating with terrorists? Are you fucking serious, Simon? You had sex with these women!"

"Totally consensual! I'm not a neanderthal. I never so much as smile at a woman without confirming consent."

Reese rubs her eyes. "I'm assuming they're not in your . . . age group?"

Simon shakes his head.

"And neither of them are pop stars or record executives or in any other position of wealth or authority?"

"No."

"So there's a massive power differential between your position and theirs. And therefore, no real distinction between consent and coercion."

"It's not like that," Simon mutters.

"That's exactly what it is." Her tone is matter-of-fact. "I assume you have enough available funds to pay for a second settlement?"

"I could manage it, I suppose."

"Compare that to the cost to your reputation if the second claimant were to make her claims public. Or worse, she decided to file a criminal complaint."

"There weren't any crimes!"

"You want to talk about encouraging others? Wait till this gets out."

Simon feels himself shrinking in his seat. More than the expense, he dreads the thought of going through the settlement process again. He can still picture the hateful glare of Brianna's mother at the deposition. It wasn't too different from the withering looks his own mother gave him when he disappointed her. Which was often. And he suspects Reese is now hiding a similar degree of scorn for him behind her poker face.

All those millions of adoring fans—all that anonymous love—and yet anyone who knows me despises me.

Reese stands up from her seat. "I'm late for my conference call."

"Sure," Simon says as he pushes himself to his feet, his hip aching. "Thank you for the time."

"Best of luck with it," she says as she leads him toward the door.

Though Simon knows Reese is right, he regrets having come. Now another tribe member is as disgusted with him as JJ is. "Too bad you missed the meeting that JJ called," he says, because he can't think of anything else to fill the silence.

"I was up against the deadline on a major contract," she says. "Never enough time."

He hesitates at the door. "She's really thrown off, huh?"

"Who is?" Reese frowns. "JJ?"

"Yeah. She's totally freaked out about Elaine."

"How so?"

He shrugs. "JJ thinks it looks suspicious or something."

Reese stops. "Suspicious? Why? Everyone knows how Elaine died."

"That's what I told her." He taps his chest. "But JJ kept rambling on. Panic-stricken about how we went to see Elaine together. And how we tried to convince her to keep quiet. She figures we were the last ones to see her alive."

"So what?"

"People might assume we went there to silence her."

Reese eyes him stonily for a moment before her expression relaxes. "What is it with this group? First Elaine's wild claims about Dr. Danvers. And now JJ and this wacky theory."

"I fucking hate unfounded accusations," Simon grumbles, thinking of his own latest accuser. "Who knows? Maybe it's the psychedelics? Apparently, not everyone can handle them like a rock star."

CHAPTER 21

Graham's office is in the opposite direction from the hospital where Aaron is headed to do his weekend rounds, but relieved that his son is gainfully employed, he doesn't mind giving him a ride to work. This morning, however, Aaron is slightly alarmed by his son's tone.

"Because he's a complete asshole, Dad!" Graham says of Hassan, the colleague whom he has been griping about for the entire drive.

Aaron keeps his eyes on the road, focusing on the passing oaks and sycamores planted along the median. "Then don't engage with him."

"He sits in the cubicle right beside mine! What am I supposed to do?"

"The higher road, Graham. How many times have we discussed this?"

"I never start it! But Hassan is so fucking passive-aggressive. Like yesterday, he says to me: 'Oh, because you left early, I had to present the proposal on my own.'"

"Did you leave early?"

"I'm a grown-ass man, Dad! I don't clock in and clock out like some tollbooth attendant."

Aaron suppresses a sigh. It's as if his son goes out of his way to be self-defeating. But unlike Holly, Aaron doesn't believe it's because Graham has a personality disorder. He has had to live his whole life in his twin brother's shadow. And what a shadow Nate casts. His teachers and coaches have always reached the same conclusion: Nate is exceptional. Consequently, Aaron has had to be more protective of Graham, who struggles with life as much as his twin brother breezes through it. How could it not affect Graham's mood and temperament? Or contribute to his oppositional nature?

"So, Elaine Golding, huh?" Graham says out of the blue.

Aaron turns to him. "What about her?"

"She's the one you two were talking about, right? On the speaker phone with you-know-who?"

Aaron tightens his grip on the steering wheel. "What does any of that have to do with Hassan?"

"Nothing. But I'm guessing she has a lot to do with Holly. I did a little online search. Elaine Golding—noted opioid activist—OD'd in Laguna on the same day as that patient you two were discussing. She had to be the one who was threatening to expose Holly, right?"

"This is none of your concern."

"What are the chances they weren't the same person?"

"What's the matter with you?" Aaron snaps. "Don't you understand that I can't talk about this even if I wanted to? And trust me, I don't."

"God, you're as touchy as she is about this."

Aaron can feel his cheeks burning. "Don't . . ."

"I didn't ask to be pulled in on that phone call, did I, Dad? But now I'm pretty freakin' curious."

"Let it go, Graham."

"You got to admit, Dad. It's kind of convenient. This woman is threatening to destroy Holly's career with some bombshell . . . and then poof." He snaps his fingers. "She ODs before she can reveal anything?"

"Leave it the fuck alone!" Aaron yells.

The shout startles Graham into silence. Aaron rarely raises his voice, and he can't remember the last time he dropped an F-bomb, let alone in front of his son. But it's a nerve Graham should have known better than to touch.

After dropping Graham off without so much as a look or a word exchanged between them, Aaron has to focus on his breathing to settle his raging emotions. Even before his son decided to meddle in Holly's business, Aaron had been obsessing over his wife's recent lack of responsiveness. After she slept over, he had begun to think they might be back on the path toward reconciliation. But since then, she has avoided his calls and his texts, and he can feel his optimism seeping away.

The last thing Holly needs is Graham poking around Elaine's death and escalating her distress. But Aaron is also painfully aware that Holly connects best to him when she's at her most vulnerable. The more he calms, the more opportunity he recognizes in her predicament.

Rather than turn north along the Coastal Highway toward his office, Aaron instead heads south. Twenty minutes later, he pulls up to the familiar old rancher in Dana Point.

Aaron hasn't shown up alone at Walter's house in years, if ever. As soon as the old man sees him at the door, he demands, "Did something happen to Holly?"

"No, no." Aaron waves off the idea. "I was just in the neighborhood. Thought I'd drop in."

"Ah." Walter eyes him skeptically. "Well, I was just brewing tea. Care for a cuppa, as the Brits say?"

"I'd love one, thanks."

Aaron can't help but notice the new hobble in Walter's step, but the old man still moves at a good clip as he leads Aaron into the kitchen.

"In the neighborhood, were you?" Walter asks as he fills a second teacup from the kettle.

Aaron considers making up a cover story, but he suspects Walter would see straight through it. "I'm worried about your granddaughter," he admits.

Walter passes him the cup with the teabag still in it and then sits down across from him at the table. "Worried about what, specifically?"

"After her client died . . ." Aaron holds up a hand. "She must've told you about that, right?"

Walter nods.

"It devastated her."

"Wouldn't any psychiatrist be devastated to lose a patient that way?"

"Of course. The guilt and self-recrimination, that's to be expected. But there's more to it."

"Oh? What else?"

"It's rocked her confidence, Walter. In a way that I've never seen in her before. Frankly, I think she's a little lost."

Walter sips his tea without commenting. Even at ninety, his silence is still intimidating. And few people intimidate Aaron.

Finally, the old man lowers his cup. "How does you coming here to see me help Holly?"

"Who's more influential in your granddaughter's life than you?"

"Not you?"

"Not at the moment, no."

Walter nods. "Do you think that's possibly related to how skeptical . . . how unsupportive . . . you've been of her work?"

Her work or yours? Aaron wants to ask. He has always believed that Holly's relentless focus on psychedelics was driven by the legacy of her grandfather's lifelong, and failed, ambition to establish them as a mental health cure-all. But Aaron also appreciates that it would be a mistake to antagonize the one person he needs as an ally. "You're right," he says. "I was blinded by my own bias. I should have been more supportive."

"I'm sorry. My eyesight's really failing me these days. For a while there, I mistook you for Aaron."

Aaron laughs politely at the dig. "No, Walter, even I have to admit that Holly's work has been groundbreaking. Particularly, in this group. Apparently, the remaining six members have shown a remarkable response. All of them sober. Like that rock star said: Holly's method has worked where everything else failed."

"That man should have kept his mouth shut."

"I want to support her, Walter."

He raises an eyebrow. "Is that all you want?"

Aaron hesitates. "Maybe not all. But right now, it's my priority. It's what Holly needs."

"Hmm."

"Help me help her, Walter."

"And how do I do that?"

"Well, for the past two days, she hasn't been taking my calls."

"And you think I can change her mind?" Walter chuckles. "How well do you know my granddaughter?"

"Fair point." Aaron smiles. "But if anyone could convince her to, it's you."

"I've always stayed out of your relationship. Even when I've had strong feelings on the matter." Walter glances at him sidelong. "It's not my place to intervene."

Aaron realizes he has to play his trump card. "It's not only about her feelings."

Walter frowns. "It's not?"

"Like it or not, that rock star has put Holly's work in the limelight. If she loses faith and gives up now with so many people watching? Think how far that could set back the whole psychedelic movement."

Walter's blue eyes give away little, but Aaron senses that he has planted enough of a seed. He doesn't try to expand on it. To do so would just be cruel. Besides, Walter can't last forever. And once he is gone, Holly will need her husband more than ever.

CHAPTER 22

Sunday, April 14

Every time Holly drives Route 73, she thinks of her father. He died somewhere along this stretch of freeway. She was in the car when it flipped, but she has no memory of the accident, let alone where it occurred. Ever since that retreat to Peru, where she found enough peace and acceptance to move forward with her life, Holly has avoided looking into the crash. But that is changing. Haunted by her DMT-induced visions, she decided this morning that she couldn't hide from the accident any longer.

Shortly after she woke up, she sat down at her laptop and typed "Route 73" and "Martin Danvers" into the search bar. A list of articles immediately popped up. Holly was relieved to learn that her dad had been pronounced dead at the scene. That he hadn't suffered. And it was surreal to read the stories about her unconscious, sixteen-year-old self being extracted from the car and rushed to a local trauma center. More disturbing were the photos of the wreckage: the family's wood-paneled station wagon, overturned off the side of the freeway with the driver's side hood crushed in. But those horrible images also gave Holly a vital clue. In the background of one of them, she spotted a sign for the Pacific Ridge Trailhead and used it to pinpoint the location of the crash site.

Now, as her GPS informs her that the spot is two hundred fifty feet ahead on her right, Holly feels queasy. There are no markers of any kind, but based on the nearby trail sign, she knows she's at the right place. Her palms are slick on the steering wheel and her pulse pounds in her ears as she slows to a stop on the side of the freeway and forces herself to climb out of the car.

Holly glances around at the uninspiring shrubs, trees, and dirt lining both sides of the freeway and the median itself. Cars fly by, and she can feel the ground shake whenever a truck roars past. The road is bone-straight with clear sightlines for miles. The reports never mentioned any weather issues on the evening of the accident. In fact, none of them gave a reason for the single car accident beyond "authorities believe speed or reckless driving might have contributed."

But that makes no sense to Holly. She remembers her father as a safe driver. It was her mom who used to terrify her behind the wheel. Perpetually late, her mother made up time by speeding and running stale yellow lights.

It has been at least two or three months since Holly's last conversation with her mom. They don't speak often, which was true even before her mother moved to South Carolina with her new husband. They weren't especially close before the accident—Holly was always a daddy's girl—and afterwards, her mom just shut down. She wasn't emotionally available for her daughter. But in retrospect, Holly understands. Her mom lacked the capacity to deal with that kind of trauma and instead soon lost herself in a relationship with a new man. To have expected otherwise from her mother would have been like expecting a tone-deaf person to sing an aria. Still, Holly doubts she would have survived losing the most important person in her life were it not for the steadfast support of her grandparents, especially Walter.

Holly forces herself to focus on the day of the accident. She has a flickering recollection—not for the first time—of being upset about something, but she can't summon anything specific.

Where the hell were we going that evening, Dad?

She stares down at the ditch beside her, wondering if this patch of dirt is the spot where the car ended up after flipping three times. Where her father's heart stopped beating.

Holly has the vaguest recollection of screaming. Something tells her that she was in tears before impact. *Were we fighting?*

She squeezes her eyes shut to block out other distractions. But hard as she concentrates, nothing more surfaces.

As Holly opens her eyes again, she wonders if she is doing what she did after Elaine's death. Maybe Aaron is right. Maybe she is just desperate to make sense of the senseless.

The mental image of Elaine slumped in her chair, blood on her arm and syringe at her foot, comes to mind. It still doesn't add up for Holly. Elaine was an activist. One who had found a new cause to champion in her delusional belief that she was being abused by her therapist. What happened after the tribe confronted her? Why would the needle-phobic Elaine choose that evening of all times to start injecting opioids? And why is bubbly and ebullient JJ the only one so troubled by the group's intervention?

Holly kicks at the dirt in frustration. Lately, all she seems to do is generate questions without answers.

She takes one final look around the hills before getting back into her car.

Before she drives away, she asks aloud, "What happened here, Dad?"

CHAPTER 23

Monday, April 15

"When do we get another session, Doc?" Salvador asks. The brim of his ball cap is twisted to the right, and he leans back in his chair with his arm dangling over its back.

"What do you call this?" Holly asks from the seat across from him.

"You know what I mean!" Salvador giggles. "With ketamine! And maybe Ecstasy, too?"

"What's the rush, Salvador?"

"I'm getting that itch again."

"For cocaine?"

"And Adderall, too. Maybe that even more. I'm under such pressure at work. God, I need my focus back."

"As I explained last time, Salvador, after Elaine—"

"Fuck Elaine!"

"Excuse me?"

He sits up straighter. "Look, I'm sorry she's gone. But she is. Why should that derail a good treatment—maybe the best one—for the rest of us?"

Holly finds his point hard to argue. "Today is for counseling only, Salvador. We can revisit psychedelic therapy at another session."

"When?" he demands.

"Soon, I hope."

"Fine." Salvador pouts and slumps lower in his chair.

Holly rolls her hand in a tell-me-more gesture. "Describe this itch."

"My show." He shakes his head. "It's shit, right now. I'm stuck. At the worst possible moment."

"I thought you were putting the final touches on it?"

"Those are the most important ones!" he cries. "All the subtle little modifications. The fits and the accessories. They make or break the designs! It's hopeless! I'm desperate for inspiration."

"And you think you'll find it in Adderall?"

"I'm sure as hell not finding it in espresso."

She nods. "You're struggling with your fear of failure again, aren't you?"

"It's no fear!" he cries. "Right now, it's a foregone conclusion."

"This is what we talked about, Salvador. You know that's not rational. Look where you are in your professional life. What you've accomplished. By the age of thirty."

"Thirty!" His laugh is frantic. "You want to me list all the designers who were *the* shit at thirty and nonexistent by forty? A designer's life span is shorter than a hamster's."

"Any form of celebrity can be fleeting."

"Don't you get it, Doc? I can't afford one wrong turn. There are no second chances in my business."

"Is that it? Or are you really afraid of being exposed for the impostor you think you are?"

"I've been an impostor my whole miserable life," he grumbles.

Holly has heard this before, but she senses that he needs to get it off his chest again. "Tell me about that."

"Growing up in East LA and being all this?" He sweeps his hand along his torso and groans. "All the other boys obsessed with basketball, cars, and *chicas*. And little *fifí* me, who'd rather stay home watching *Project Runway*."

"You never felt accepted."

"*Accepted?*" His laughter is brittle. "I had to be an impostor just to stay alive! At school, I faked machismo. At least, my version of it. But the bullies, they saw right through me."

Holly's heart goes out to him. But she stays quiet, permitting him the time and space to express himself on his own terms.

"From day one, I knew how different I was," he says. "How *fluid*."

"Sexually?"

"That, too. Most people don't believe me, but I actually prefer women. For company and sex. Who knows? If I'd heard of nonbinary when I was growing up, I might have identified as that. Instead of the freak the other kids saw me as." His voice cracks. "Accepted? At fourteen, I would've killed to have just been left alone to my dreams and my designs."

"I'm sorry, Salvador," Holly says. "What about your family?"

"My sisters didn't get me. Even Papi. He tried, but I was like an alien to him. I just embarrassed him." He swallows. "Only Mamá. She always got me. We're alike that way. We both live for beauty."

"I admire you, Salvador. I do. The strength it took to get where you are." Holly extends her hand to him. "But this fear of being exposed. After all you had to go through. It seems to be a huge trigger for you."

Sitting up straighter, he stares helplessly at her. "How does that help me? Trigger or not, I've got a gun to my head. This new show. What I need now is another ketamine trip. Either that or to go back to the street stuff."

"Don't do that, Salvador."

"Will you help me?"

"I will. Soon." She sighs, hoping it's a promise she will be able to keep. "Meantime, resist the urges. Give me a little more time. OK?"

"Yeah. I'll try." He hesitates. "Dr. Danvers?"

"Yes?"

"If ketamine really isn't addictive, then how come I'm craving it so much?"

Holly smiles. "Because your therapy is incomplete. Once your sobriety is stable, and we've finished our counseling work, you won't need ketamine anymore. You probably won't even want it. Or any substance."

A relieved look crosses Salvador's face. "That'd be nice."

After the session ends and Salvador has left, Holly summarizes the visit in his electronic record and then opens the detailed notes she is keeping on the group. She records his comment about craving ketamine, and she is about to add more when a soft rap at the door draws her attention. She looks up to see Tanya's worried face in the doorway. "What's up?"

"*She* just called again," Tanya says. "The reporter."

Holly's stomach plummets. "About Elaine?"

Tanya grimaces. "I . . . I don't think so. She said she was following up from last week."

Holly sighs with relief. "You know what to tell her, Tanya."

"You'll get back to her as soon as you're free?"

Holly grins. "You're a quick study, Tanya."

"But even putting all those media requests aside, your stack of new client requests is huge since Simon's interview." She hesitates. "We're going to have to respond at some point."

"In good time."

"All right," Tanya says uncertainly, before she turns away from the door. "I'll go get your next appointment."

A minute or two later, Tanya ushers Liisa into the seat Salvador just vacated.

"Hello, Liisa. How are you?" Holly asks.

Liisa utters a little laugh. "I always struggle with that, too."

"With pleasantries?"

"With opening a therapeutic conversation," Liisa says. "I sometimes start with . . . 'Why don't you bring me up to speed?' That allows clients to launch into whatever is foremost on their mind."

Holly smiles. "Why don't you bring me up to speed then?"

"It feels like we're in limbo."

"Do you mean the group as a whole or you and me, specifically?"

"Both," Liisa says. "As you know, I came into this group very skeptical. And only because I'd tried everything else. But I've been off the Xanax for almost two weeks now. Ever since you tried us on dual therapy. And I'm sold."

"You can get to the *but* now . . ."

"Since Elaine's death, we've stalled. And I think we both know that talk therapy alone will not suffice."

"I would've thought you, of all people, would understand why we had to suspend the ketamine infusions."

"Yes and no."

"Can you elaborate?"

"Of course you'd have reason for trepidation after Elaine's overdose. But I think we can agree that, as an opioid addict, she was in an entirely different stratosphere of risk from the rest of us."

Not if her overdose was intentional. Or it wasn't self-administered.

"None of the rest of our relapses would likely be fatal," Liisa continues. "Not to be too flippant, but Simon's not going to OD on rough sex, and Baljit isn't going to die from gambling."

"What's your point, Liisa?"

"Your therapy has gotten us to this stage. Six long-term addicts who are all presently abstinent. But we're still susceptible. Fragile. And each of us is far more likely to relapse if you stop the psychedelics cold turkey."

Holly finds it impossible to argue with her point. "I am considering restarting."

Liisa's shoulders dip with relief. "With ketamine?" Then she adds hopefully, "Or dual therapy?"

"Only ketamine. At least for now. And it would have to be in a more controlled setting."

"What does that look like?"

"Administering it individually. In sessions like these. Not as a group. But obviously, we could still continue with the group debriefs."

"Makes sense to me," Liisa says with a satisfied nod.

Holly decides the time is as right as it ever will be to raise the question that has been troubling her. "Can I ask you something unrelated to psychedelics?"

"All right."

"When you and the rest of the group went to see Elaine . . ."

Liisa crosses her arms. "What about it?"

"You were the only mental health expert in the group. Did you think it was a good idea to go?"

Her eyes narrow. "It wasn't my idea."

"That wasn't the question."

Liisa shrugs. "I went along with the will of the group. To show solidarity. As a fellow client, not as a counselor."

"Of course." Holly is tempted to ask Liisa what distressed JJ so much about that intervention, but she knows it would be a flagrant ethical transgression to discuss one client's issues with another. That doesn't apply to the dead though. "How did Elaine seem to you?"

"We caught her by surprise, obviously." Liisa pauses. "She was quiet. Withdrawn even. Defensive, too."

"But did your therapeutic instincts tell you she was on the verge of a relapse?"

Liisa considers it for a moment. "Not really, no."

"Or suicidal?"

Liisa's face scrunches. "You think Elaine deliberately overdosed?"

"Not necessarily. I just wondered what you thought."

Liisa shakes her head. "I didn't remotely get that sense from her."

"I see."

"In fact, her defensiveness aside, the one other word I would've used to describe Elaine that day might have been: determined." Liisa stares at her so intently that Holly has to look away.

CHAPTER 24

Tuesday, April 16

Holly has to remind JJ to hold her arm still so she can secure the IV into the vein at the crease of the elbow. Even then, JJ still relentlessly taps the floor with her purple-and-white Dolce & Gabbana sneaker, which Holly remembers seeing priced online at over a thousand dollars a pair.

After Holly had acquiesced to the will of the group, Tanya found time to schedule all of the clients in for ketamine infusions on the very next day, which was supposed to have been set aside for Holly's research and writing. She has started to dodge emails from her editor, requesting chapters. Her literary agent is hounding her, too, wanting a sample to try to sell the foreign rights. But Holly finds it all too much in the aftermath of Elaine's overdose.

JJ was the last of the group to show up for the first ketamine infusion following Elaine's death. The other five clients sailed through their sessions, but JJ appears far more anxious than any of the others. She can't sit still. Her finger won't stop drumming the armrest. And her eyes dart around the room.

"Are you sure you're up for this?" Holly asks as she tapes the IV into place.

"I need this," JJ says flatly. "Yesterday, I caught myself scouring the pantry for a bottle of vodka I'd hidden in there a few months ago. Luckily my housekeeper had sniffed it out on her big booze purge. Don't know what would've happened if I'd found it."

"All right."

JJ glances around at the empty recliners in the room. "It's weird not to have the others here during the ketamine drip."

After her experience with Elaine, Holly has second thoughts herself. She even considered asking Tanya to stay in the room as a chaperone to witness the infusions but dismissed the idea as an unnecessary invasion of her clients' privacy.

"In light of the circumstances, this is the only way we can proceed after . . . Elaine." Holly clears her throat. "With one-on-one supervision."

A pained look crosses JJ's face, but all she says is "I guess that makes sense."

"I know you normally listen to your music on headphones, but since you're the only one here, do you mind if I put the music over the speakers instead?"

"Sure."

"Your usual playlist? The jazz?"

"Yes, please."

Holly taps a button on her laptop, launching the instrumental music. Holly doesn't recognize the first tune—jazz has never been her thing—but she does find something soothing in the gentle blend of instruments, which seem to follow their own beat.

Without being asked, JJ lowers the blindfold over her eyes.

"Ready?" Holly asks.

JJ nods.

"Set and setting, remember?" Holly says. "Go to your happy place, JJ."

She knows JJ's happy place is on that lanai in Hawaii in that moment when she revealed her first positive pregnancy test to her husband. Holly can't help but think how bittersweet the memory must be for JJ. How the pregnancy failed, as did the others that followed, and her marriages with them. And how JJ's drinking steadily worsened as her hopes of motherhood faded.

Holly connects the syringe of ketamine to the IV and slowly depresses the plunger, administering the same dose she gave JJ on her previous infusion. Once the medication has emptied into the vein, Holly disconnects the syringe and reaches for the other one that she has preloaded with midazolam to have ready in case JJ were to have a dysphoric reaction.

After a minute or two, JJ's foot stills. Her breathing slows, and her whole body appears to relax. "Beautiful," she mumbles.

"What do you see?" Holly asks.

"No, not see, hear," JJ says dreamily. "The music. I feel it all over my body."

"How so?"

"The drumbeats, they vibrate in my fingertips. The sax and trumpet are like a warm rush through my chest. And the piano . . . the piano feels like heat across my shoulders. Like walking the beach in the morning with the sun on my neck."

"Lovely," Holly says. "Just go with it."

JJ is quiet for a minute or two. And Holly focuses on the music, trying and failing to perceive its tactile qualities the way JJ does. Anything to resist the urge to question her client. But it's futile. "What's troubling you so much, JJ?"

"Nothing," she murmurs.

"Not now. Before the infusion. Since Elaine died, you just haven't been yourself. At least not with me."

"I spoke to her."

"I heard," Holly says. "Along with the rest of the tribe, right?"

JJ shakes her head lazily from side to side. "Not that time."

"Oh, yeah. You spoke to Elaine before, didn't you? That was why the group went to see her."

"No, not then . . . later."

"Later?" Holly's neck stiffens. "Are you saying you spoke to Elaine again *after* the tribe confronted her?"

"Yes." JJ shifts on the recliner. Her legs twist from side to side, and she repositions herself as if trying to find a comfortable spot and failing. "I should've told her. I really should have. I feel awful about what happened."

Holly sits up bone straight. "Told Elaine what?"

JJ's voice rises. "Is it getting louder?"

"I'll turn it down." Holly lowers the volume. She realizes she probably shouldn't persist in questioning her client under the influence, but she can't resist. "Why do you feel awful, JJ? What didn't you tell her?"

JJ doesn't reply for several seconds as her breathing quickens and she continues to shuffle in her seat. Finally, she says, "I saw you, too."

"Focus on the last time you spoke to Elaine. What should you have told her?"

"You were here!"

"What are you talking about?"

"I forgot my jacket. The cleaner downstairs, she let me back into the office to get it. I heard noises. And that smell!"

Holly feels panic swirling in her gut. "What smell? When?"

"That stink. Like burnt plastic. I thought there was a fire. I had to check." Despite the blindfold she is wearing, JJ points somewhere across the room. "You were right here."

The foreboding grips Holly like a hand to her throat. *The office door!* JJ was the one who had opened it.

"That stink! I searched it online," JJ says, her voice rising. "It was DMT, wasn't it?"

"This isn't about me . . ." Holly sputters.

"Turn it down!" JJ cries, grabbing at her ears.

Holly turns off the music. But it doesn't help to calm JJ.

"I can't breathe." She pulls her right arm back, stretching the IV tubing that runs from it.

Holly lurches forward. She fumbles to attach the syringe to the IV port and, as soon as it's connected, plunges the whole dose of midazolam into JJ's arm.

"Make it stop!" JJ cries, rocking in the recliner while grabbing her ears.

Holly can barely breathe herself, but she forces calm into her voice. "Everything will be all right, JJ. I'm here."

After a minute or two, JJ's rocking slows, and her respiration lessens. Soon, she is still again.

"JJ?"

Her only response is an unintelligible whimper. And then she begins to snore.

Holly clings to the belief that the hefty dose of midazolam she gave JJ will probably blur her memory of this session. But it won't touch her earlier recollection of having walked in on Holly while she was tripping on an illegal psychedelic inside her own office.

Holly's heart hammers. *Did I just interrogate a client under the influence of psychedelics for my own benefit?* It's another in a series of self-inflicted wounds. She doesn't recognize her own motivations anymore. And what kind of therapist loses insight into herself?

Besides, even if Holly can achieve the results she hopes for through psychedelic therapy, how can the ends still justify the means?

CHAPTER 25

Aaron has never before been invited to the condo that Holly rented after their separation. And when he received her text asking him to come, he assumed Walter must have interceded on his behalf. Aaron even rushed out after work to catch his favorite flower shop before closing, where the florist assembled a colorful bouquet of Holly's favorites, including peonies, roses, calla lilies, and hydrangeas. The sweet floral scent filled his car on the drive over and only heightened his anticipation and excitement.

But the moment Holly opens the door, Aaron sees that she is not right. Her face is pale, her eyes forlorn. He reflexively drops the hand that holds the bouquet, wishing he could tuck it behind his leg.

Holly glances down at them. "They're beautiful," she mumbles. "Thank you."

He hands her the flowers and follows her inside. The condo is bright and modern, with high-end cabinetry, granite countertops, and top-of-the-line appliances, but it's also smaller than he expected.

"What's going on, Holl?" he asks.

Without answering, she pulls down a vase from a cabinet, fills it with water, and arranges the flowers inside. "Glass of wine?" she asks.

"For both of us, from the looks of it."

After pouring two generous glasses of a Spanish Syrah, Holly leads him to the couch and sits down beside him but far enough away to leave a gap between their legs.

"I fucked up, Aaron," she says, blank-faced.

Much as he wishes she were talking about her distancing herself from him since the night they slept together, he knows better. "What happened?"

"I . . ." Her cheeks redden. "I vaped DMT."

"That's the active compound in ayahuasca, right?"

She nods.

"What's the big deal? As long as I've known you, you've used psychedelics intermittently. Self-care. Isn't that how you describe it?"

"But never in my office."

His head twitches involuntarily. "Holly, please don't tell me you indulged in psychedelics with your patients?"

She waves her hand. "No! Nothing like that. It was a couple of days ago. After the office closed. I thought I was alone."

"But you weren't?"

"One of my clients came back for her jacket, and the cleaners let her in. But she only told me today." She hangs her head. "She saw me, Aaron. JJ saw me vaping."

Her angst makes sudden sense. "But you didn't see her?"

"I had a blindfold on. I heard the door open, but I assumed it was the cleaners." She sighs. "DMT has this very pungent stench. JJ figured out exactly what I was vaping."

He squeezes his temples between his thumb and forefinger. "Why did she wait to tell you?"

"She blurted it out under ketamine therapy."

"Jesus! Your practice is like Woodstock or something. Nonstop psychedelics."

Holly's shoulders sag and her chin drops lower as she reaches for her wineglass.

"I'm sorry," he says and gently lays a hand on her other wrist. "That wasn't fair. You caught me by surprise."

"I can relate," she murmurs.

"Are you worried your patient is going to report you?"

"Or tell others."

"Who?"

"Members of the group? Friends?" She shrugs. "JJ seems to know everyone."

"It would be her word against yours," Aaron says, struggling to find a kernel of reassurance to offer.

Holly flashes him a look that tells him just how little she thinks of that defense.

"She shouldn't mention it to anyone else," he says, stating the obvious. "I hope you made that clear to her."

Holly looks away. "I didn't have the chance. She had a dysphoric reaction to the ketamine. Totally flipped out. I had to sedate her with midazolam. I doubt she even remembers telling me."

"But she won't have forgotten seeing you with the vape pen."

"No. She definitely will not."

Aaron squeezes Holly's wrist and is pleased that she doesn't pull away from his grip.

She closes her eyes for a moment. "That wasn't even the only bombshell JJ dropped on me during our session."

He frowns. "What else?"

"She told me she spoke to Elaine. The night of her overdose. *After* the group had already gone to confront her."

"What did they talk about?"

"I don't know. All JJ would say is that she 'should've told her.'"

"Told Elaine what?"

"That's the thing, Aaron! JJ kept digressing. Focusing on my DMT use. And then she had a massive panic attack. I couldn't get the rest of it out of her."

"Does it really matter now?"

"Maybe. Maybe not. Who knows?" Holly's voice cracks. "I can't believe this is happening again."

"After Elaine?"

"Yes. With Elaine, I was terrified of what her allegations could do to me and my practice. But at least they were unfounded. But this? Vaping an illicit substance in my own office? That's indefensible. If the Medical Board were to get wind of that . . ."

It might be career-ending, Aaron thinks. But rather than state the obvious, he says, "JJ only spoke of it under the influence. Do you really think she intends to pursue it?"

"I have no idea. None at all." Holly looks back up at him, and her misty eyes fill with raw vulnerability. "What should I do?"

"You really want my advice?" Aaron pauses, wanting Holly to be aware of how much she needs him. "Even after the last time? When I was the one who told you to talk to your patient?"

She nods. "It wouldn't have made a difference with Elaine whether I spoke to her or not. She was so single-minded."

"Then my advice is going to be the same this time."

"Speak to JJ?"

"You have a good therapeutic relationship with her, right?"

"I think she trusts me, yes."

"Then make her understand what she saw occurred in a private moment. It just happened to have been at your office but had nothing to do with your practice. No different than if she had run into you at a bar after you'd had a few cocktails."

Holly nods. "I like that. Yes. It's almost an accurate analogy."

Aaron winks. "Accurate enough."

Holly shuffles nearer to him, closing the gap between their legs and nestling her head in the crook of his neck. He slides a hand over her far shoulder and pulls her in tighter, drinking in the lavender scent of her shampoo.

"Don't know if I could do this without you," she says.

CHAPTER 26

Wednesday, April 17

Walter nods toward the cup of hot chocolate, which Holly hasn't touched since he placed it in front of her. "This must be serious, Koala."

She sighs a laugh. "I'm not thirsty. I just felt like some company."

"Now that, I can provide," Walter says from where he sits across the kitchen table.

She fingers the handle of her cup without lifting it. "I keep making things worse, Papa."

"Worse how?"

Holly tells Walter about the incident where JJ walked in on her while she was vaping DMT, and then says, "Honestly, I don't know if I could get through this without Aaron's support. He has been such a stalwart lately."

"You're speaking to him again, I assume."

"Again?" She frowns. "When wasn't I?"

"Did he mention that he came to see me?"

"No. When?"

"A few days ago. He said he was in the neighborhood."

She can't hide her skepticism. "What business would Aaron have in Dana Point?"

"Exactly." Walter grins. "He came because he couldn't reach you."

"Oh." Holly thinks of the calls and texts that she ignored on the day or two after she slept with him. Indebted as she feels to Aaron, the idea of him airing their domestic issues to her grandfather irks her. "What did you tell him?"

"To take it up with you."

"It was no big deal. Aaron overreacted. I was just tied up for a couple of days."

Walter shrugs. "I will give the man this. He cares deeply for you. But for him to think he could enlist my help to influence you by trying to make it about the cause . . ."

Holly sits up. "What are you talking about?"

"Aaron insinuated that if I helped to mend the communication breakdown between the two of you, somehow that might save the psychedelic movement."

"That's ridiculous."

"Utterly. But even if it were true, I wouldn't have raised a finger. Who does he think I am? That I would barter my granddaughter's feelings like that?"

She stares at him for a helpless moment. "I'm so sorry, Papa. For everything."

"*You're* sorry?" Walter cries. "What the hell, Holly?"

She can't remember the last time she heard her grandfather raise his voice. "I . . . don't understand."

He holds his trembling palms out to her. "I am the one who gave you that stupid DMT pen."

"You didn't tell me to vape it in my office."

"You wouldn't have vaped it anywhere if it weren't for me."

"Oh, Papa. I just keep screwing up."

"No, Koala. No." He drops his hands. His face falls. "This is my fault. I've been so shortsighted. And so unfair to you. Loading my tired old hopes and aspirations on your shoulders. I've been very selfish."

Holly leans forward and squeezes his bony elbow. "Hardly. You inspired me. I'm every bit as committed to establishing the value of psychedelic therapy as you are. Maybe more so! After all, psychedelics saved my life in Peru." She sighs. "And if you've been shortsighted, then I've been blind."

Walter says nothing for a few seconds. Finally, he pats the back of her hand and smiles. "Is it possible that I might have passed some of my pigheaded genes along to my favorite granddaughter?"

"Your *only* granddaughter. And we don't need a DNA test to know that you did."

They sit in silence. Walter's touch is comforting, but his remorse only makes her feel more responsible. "I went to the site of the accident," she finally says, needing to get it off her chest.

Walter cocks his head. "Which accident?"

"Dad's."

He pulls his arm free of her hand. "That was a waste of gas."

"I wanted to see it."

Walter shrinks in his seat, withdrawing the way he always does at the mention of his son's death. "Don't you have enough on your plate right now?"

"I do. But lately, I can't stop thinking about it."

"It's those hallucinations, isn't it?" He shakes his head miserably. "The damn DMT again . . . What a mistake it was to lead you back down that road."

"The DMT isn't to blame. Neither are you, Papa. I've been avoiding memories of the accident ever since we came back from Peru. When I thought I was healed. But I think the stress of everything that's been going on keeps pushing that piece of unfinished emotional business to the surface." *Or maybe my guilt about Elaine is forcing me to face my guilt about Dad?* "I can't hide from it any longer. I need to know."

"What?" Walter grunts. "What is it you think you need to know?"

"It makes no sense. That stretch of freeway is straight as an arrow. And the weather was good that day. What could've made Dad crash the car like he did?"

"We'll never know."

"The police must have investigated."

He nods slightly. "They interviewed you. Don't you remember?"

She shakes her head. "In the hospital?"

"The day after. The doctors kept you in for observation. You were still concussed, but otherwise physically all right."

"Were you there?"

"Of course."

Holly's chest flutters. "What did I tell them?"

He looks away. "That you couldn't remember anything about the accident."

"Were there witnesses?"

He shakes his head. "None that came forward. The Good Samaritans who pulled you out of the car arrived after the crash."

"But the authorities must have blamed it on something?"

"Reckless driving."

"Dad? I remember him as such a good driver."

"Not that day," Walter mutters.

"What are you keeping from me, Papa?"

"You think I haven't thought about this a million times?" His voice is thick. "Maybe your father had some kind of medical emergency? Maybe he fell asleep at the wheel? Why does it matter? Nothing will bring him back. How does it help to talk about it?" He pauses to swallow, and she sees a trembling in his throat. "Who does it help?"

CHAPTER 27

Thursday, April 18

All the recliners are full this morning. But it's not because of any new tribe members. Tanya had wheeled the seventh chair out of the room earlier, arguing that it wasn't needed since Holly had no groups of more than six. Holly saw right through her assistant's excuse, appreciating that Tanya was only trying to protect her from reminders of Elaine.

Aside from JJ, the others had cruised through their first infusion after Elaine's death. Holly can already sense the difference in the group. There's less tension in their faces. The overall vibe in the room is much more relaxed. Except, of course, for JJ. She's sitting in her usual chair this morning, but she has barely said a word and has avoided all eye contact since arriving. With her eyes glued to the floor, JJ's glossy black hair is a curtain concealing her face.

"Not to be too graphic or anything." Salvador giggles. "But it feels like the laxative finally kicked in after days and days of holding all that crap inside. Like poor JoJo."

"Who's JoJo?" Simon asks.

"One of my models. She was, anyway. Until the day she miscalculated her dose of laxatives before my show. Trust me, she wasn't the *only* thing gliding down that catwalk."

Baljit groans. "That's gross, Sal. A literal shit show. But I got to admit it does make such a difference to get that little ketamine top-up."

"Difference how?" Holly asks.

Baljit shrugs. "I can't even put it into words."

"It's like a release," Reese offers. "A circuit breaker in the cycle of craving."

Simon jabs a finger in Reese's direction "That's exactly right! A circuit breaker. I love it!"

"But it's nowhere near as intense as the dual therapy with ketamine and MDMA," Liisa points out.

"That's a good point." Holly nods at her. "We wouldn't expect to have such intense sensory-perceptual distortions using only a single psychedelic agent."

"No idea what that mumbo jumbo means," Salvador says. "But I'll tell you this: that kitty flipping was wild! Totally OTT!"

"Did anyone have any visions on the ketamine alone?" Holly asks.

"No visions," Simon says. "But I could feel everything super-intensely. The blindfold across my eyes, the pad of the chair against my back, and especially the music! Oh my god, the music! It was like it was coming from inside me. As if the whole band was playing inside my chest."

Holly notices that JJ glances over to Simon, but she doesn't remark on the similarities to what she described during her infusion.

"For me, it was more like a feeling," Baljit says. "This sense of floating away from myself."

"They call that depersonalization," Liisa explains.

Baljit scoffs. "Whatever, Professor. But it didn't feel like I was losing myself. It was more like I belonged to something else. Something bigger. Like the universe was giving me this giant bear hug."

"Good," Holly says. "That's what we're striving for."

Liisa frowns. "Being part of some collective?"

Holly shakes her head, but before she can say anything, Baljit says, "Acceptance, right?"

"Exactly," Holly says, wondering if Baljit is thinking of her father. "And after the ketamine, did you notice an effect on your compulsions? Your cravings?"

"Totally," Simon says with a deferential nod to Reese. "Like she said, it kind of settled the urges. Took away that hunger."

"Yes!" Salvador cries. "The horrible itch is gone. Or at least, manageable. Thank goddess! I can finally focus on work again. And just in time!"

"I fell off the wagon," Reese blurts.

All eyes in the room dart to her. "After the ketamine?" Holly asks.

"No, right before." Reese studies her hands. "The night before the infusion, of all days. I had some intense deadlines at work and I just . . . I bought a bottle of vodka on the way home. The guy at my local liquor store greeted me like some returning war hero. I had three—no, four—shots before I went to bed."

Holly leans toward her. "It's OK, Reese. There's nothing short about this journey."

"Totally." Simon thumps his armrest. "When we started this, I doubt any of us expected to make it as long as you did."

"It's true." Salvador nods vehemently. "Especially after we had to pause the psychedelics."

"I must've driven past the casino ten times in the past week," Baljit admits. "I even parked in the lot for ten minutes the other night and just stared at the entrance. If it wasn't for my kid's stupid ballet practice, I'd have fallen off the wagon, too. Guaranteed."

Reese nods her appreciation without looking up. "I'm just . . . I'd hoped for better, is all."

"Have you drunk again since our ketamine session?" Holly asks.

Reese shakes her head.

"See!" Salvador says. "It's all you needed. A reset. Like the rest of us."

Simon strums a hand in the air. "Just a speed bump on the journey. Forgotten before you reach home."

Baljit eyes him suspiciously. "Isn't that a line from one of your own songs?"

Simon drops his hand to his side. "Can I help it if I sing the truth?"

Baljit snorts. "Or you did in 1979, anyway."

"I think we're digressing here," Holly says. "Let's focus on how you felt before and after the ketamine infusion."

The energetic discussion continues for another fifteen minutes, until time is up, but the one who's usually the most animated contributes nothing.

Although aware of JJ's silence during the session, Holly never called upon her. But as the others are filing out of the room, she asks, "JJ, can I have a quick word?"

She hesitates at the door. "My day is jam-packed, Dr. Danvers."

With what, foundation lunches and cocktail parties? Holly wonders ungenerously, before catching herself. "Please, JJ. It'll only take a minute or two."

"All right." JJ trudges back to the recliner and sits down, looping her handbag over the armrest.

Holly closes the door behind them and then sits down across from her. "I just wanted to talk to you about our session."

JJ shakes her head. "I don't remember it."

"Nothing?"

"I remember you putting the IV in my arm. And the next thing I know I'm sitting back in the waiting room, feeling kind of groggy and nauseous. And you're telling me I had a bad trip."

"You did."

JJ squints at her. "What does that mean? I don't remember a thing."

"It started off well. You were relaxed." Holly smiles. "Totally absorbed in your playlist."

JJ bites her lip. "And then?"

"You started to get agitated. You told me you couldn't breathe. You became quite . . . frantic. You had a panic attack. That's when I sedated you with the midazolam."

"Which is why I don't remember it?"

Holly nods. She crosses and uncrosses her legs, feeling unsure how to transition into the conversation she wants to have. "Listen, JJ, before the anxiety set in, you were telling me that you spoke to Elaine."

JJ's back straightens and her eyes narrow. "I did?"

"You said that you spoke to her *after* the group had already visited with her. The day she overdosed."

JJ flicks her wrist backhanded as if trying to clear imaginary crumbs. "I was drugged. I didn't know what I was saying."

"You didn't talk to Elaine again?"

JJ rises from her seat. "I really am late."

"You kept telling me that you should have told her something."

JJ grabs her bag. "I have to go."

"It sounded to me as though you were blaming yourself. As if you should've warned her about something?"

JJ's head spins toward Holly. "You don't know what the hell you're talking about!"

"I'm just trying to put the pieces—"

"This is not appropriate!" JJ snaps. "You drugging me! Wiping out my memory with some sedative? And then turning my words against me? None of it!"

Holly brings a hand to her chest. "I'm only trying to understand."

"What the fuck, Dr. Danvers? How many lines are you planning to cross?"

Holly's cheeks heat, but she keeps her tone neutral. "I'm not following."

"First with Elaine. And now this with me? And all these drugs?"

"That's not what—"

"And don't think I didn't see you!"

"See me where?" But Holly already knows, and she braces for the blow.

"Stoned out of your mind in your own office. Vaping DMT, no less. I looked it up. That's hard-core!" Her voice rises with each sentence, and two red blotches appear on her fair cheeks. Her large dark eyes are almost wild. "What kind of doctor does that? Maybe *you're* the one with the real problem."

Ears pounding and face burning, Holly reaches a hand to JJ's arm. "I can explain! It was after work. I thought the building was locked. It would be no different than if you had run into me at a bar after work and—"

JJ shrugs off Holly's hand. "I don't want to hear it. None of it!" She pivots and bolts out of the office.

CHAPTER 28

As Simon sits on his deck, nursing a vodka soda and watching a gaggle of middle-aged men finish their hapless beach volleyball game, his thoughts turn back to this morning's group session.

He's thankful that Dr. Danvers got them back onto the ketamine when she did. Some of the darker fantasies had begun to creep back into the recesses of his brain. And he knows he can't go back there. Not with the sharks circling, and who knows how many others waiting to pounce. He'd rather go Jeremy's way and deliberately overdose on pills and booze than have a new accuser surface.

But Simon was surprised to hear Reese admit that she fell off the wagon. She would have been his last guess for someone in the tribe to slip up. Still, he was impressed that she owned up to it. The more he sees of Reese, the more he likes her. But he knows better than to try anything.

He also noticed how quiet JJ was throughout the session. And those weird glances she would occasionally shoot him. Was there accusation in her eyes? Maybe he's being paranoid, but after the latest lawsuit, he doesn't trust anyone. Absolutely nothing happened with JJ. But what if she decides to make a stink anyway? She is ultra-connected in Southern California. She's got even more money than he does—her grandfather emigrated in 1965, made a fortune importing South Korean delicacies to

California, and now her father runs a venture capital firm—so paying her off wouldn't be an option. If she were to publicize something about that night, he'd be screwed.

Simon checks his phone again to see if JJ had responded to his earlier text that read: *You were quiet today. Everything good?* But there's no reply.

"Fuck it," he says as he taps the button to dial her.

The line rings four or five times, and just when he's about to hang up, JJ answers. "Simon?"

"Oh, hi you," he says injecting a sunniness into his tone that he doesn't feel. "I wanted to check in on you."

"Why?"

"Oh . . . I just thought you seemed a bit out of sorts at our session."

"Out of sorts?"

"Quiet. Not your usual bubbly self." He clears his throat. "Just wanted to make sure nothing was up."

"Nothing is up."

He reads hostility into her tone, and it only makes him feel more anxious. After an awkward pause, he says, "It didn't . . . have anything to do with me—with us—did it?"

"Us? What the hell are you talking about, Simon?"

He doesn't want to remind her of the night she stormed out of his house after his ill-advised comment about chains and bondage. Instead, he says, "You know us musicians, right? The world always revolves around us."

"True enough."

Relieved that he doesn't seem to be the one responsible for her sullenness, Simon tries to end the call. "OK, well, hope you're feeling a bit more chipper at our next group session."

There's a long pause. "Can I ask you something, Simon?"

"Of course."

"Do you think Elaine's death is suspicious?"

"She OD'd herself on opioids. Hard to call that suss these days."

"What if Elaine didn't OD? At least, not by herself."

"What are you talking about, JJ?"

"I think that's what Dr. Danvers believes. She has been poking around a lot. I think she suspects I'm involved."

"*What?* That's nuts!"

"Yeah, yeah, you're right," JJ says in a rush. "I don't even know why I brought it up. Guess I'm still wonky from the ketamine."

Simon grips his phone tighter. "Do you know something about the night Elaine died?"

"No. Not at all. Just off on a tangent again. My brain does that sometimes." Her laugh sounds contrived. "Thanks for checking up on me, Simon. I'll be fine."

"Listen, JJ . . ."

But before he can finish the sentence, the line clicks, and she's gone.

CHAPTER 29

As Holly leans back in her office chair, she checks her phone again. It's almost three p.m., and JJ hasn't responded to any of her three texts. Holly feels trapped. As if her head is already stuck through the hole and she's only waiting for the guillotine blade to drop.

Holly scheduled her day to end early, with the intention of working on her manuscript. Of course, there's no hope for that now. She wonders how she even managed to navigate her other appointments after her run-in with JJ. The rest of her clients certainly didn't get her at her best. But it was helpful, almost calming, to listen to their issues and be distracted by problems other than her own.

Her phone vibrates in her hand and Aaron's name pops up on the screen.

"How are you?" he asks as soon as she answers.

"Not great, Aaron. In fact, not good at all." She goes on to tell him about her disastrous altercation with JJ.

After she finishes, he asks, "No word from her since she took off?"

"She hasn't responded to my texts."

"And you haven't heard from anyone else? No one in the group that she might have talked to about you and the DMT?"

"No. But it's only been a few hours." Holly runs a hand through her hair, resisting the urge to pull out a clump. "It's basically déjà vu."

"How so?"

"Like with Elaine. I can't believe I'm back here in this same mess. Helplessly waiting for a second client to destroy my career with her allegations." She stops to swallow away the lump in her throat. "But this time is even worse because JJ's are true."

"Not really," he says. "She misinterpreted the situation."

"Did she? I was getting stoned in my own office, Aaron."

"For therapeutic purposes, right? Besides, you did it after work. It's not like you were seeing patients while under the influence."

"That kind of hairsplitting won't matter much to the Medical Board."

"Enough with the defeatism!" Aaron says, but his tone is good-natured. "Let me help take your mind off things. Let's grab dinner tonight."

She smiles at the phone. His fierce loyalty might be the best thing she has in her life right now. "Thank you, Aaron. Truly. But I'm not hungry. And I'd be terrible company tonight."

"So what? I'm starving. And I'd be terrific company."

She laughs. "Not tonight. I don't have it in me. How about dinner tomorrow?"

"It's a date!"

"Aaron?"

"Yes?"

"If JJ tells people about the DMT . . ."

"It's going to be OK, Holl. I won't let anything happen to you. I promise."

"Thank you." She pauses. "I love you. You know that, right?"

"I do now," he says with a soft laugh.

Holly heads home right after the call. She sits down to work on a chapter of her book, but failing to put two coherent sentences together, she gives up and lies down on the couch. To distract herself from her negative thoughts, she leafs through a psychiatric journal and ends up nodding off halfway through a particularly dull article on how vegan diets could affect the required dosage of certain mood stabilizers.

Holly wakes up a few minutes after seven o'clock feeling groggy, amazed that she was able to nap, which she almost never does. Feeling like she should eat, she heats up some leftover Thai food she ordered in a few nights before but merely picks at it before eventually throwing most of it away.

She tries to watch an episode of a streaming series on her laptop but loses interest within minutes. She considers opening another bottle of wine but realizes that won't help. As her restlessness crescendos, her sense of inaction makes her feel physically ill. By nine o'clock, she can't take it anymore. She calls JJ, but the line rings through to voicemail, and Holly slams the phone down on the cushion beside her.

I can't leave things like this!

She turns to her laptop and looks up JJ's address in her electronic medical record. She is unsurprised to see that the heiress lives in one of the most luxurious neighborhoods in Newport Beach, which boasts some of the highest priced real estate in the country. Holly assumes JJ must live in the penthouse suite.

Knowing better, and with a sinking feeling in her gut, Holly gets to her feet and grabs her car keys.

It takes less than fifteen minutes in the light evening traffic to reach Lido Park Drive in Newport. A few blocks from her final destination, she hears a siren and sees the flashing lights of a police cruiser in her rear-view mirror. She worries that she is about to be pulled over, but as she slows to the side of the road, the cruiser races past her.

Even before her GPS announces she has reached JJ's home, Holly's heart begins to thump against her ribs. More flashing lights are clustered out front of the building ahead of her. The gnawing in her stomach turns to burning.

She finds a parking spot a block away and hurries toward the entrance on foot. An older, Black police officer with gray hair steps forward to intercept her, waving her back. "Sorry, ma'am. We're not allowing anyone in or out right now."

"What happened?" Holly demands.

"There's been a medical emergency."

Holly notices a group of first responders collected near the far corner of the building. Behind them stands a cluster of civilians, presumably other condo residents. Making a wide sweep around the officer, Holly hurries toward the gathering. "Ma'am!" the officer calls to her back, but fear propels Holly forward.

She reaches the civilians, some of whom are wearing pajamas and nightgowns. A few are chatting in hushed voices, but most stand in silence, staring at the wall of first responders in front of them.

Holly moves toward the uniformed personnel. A tall, broad-shouldered female firefighter steps forward to cut her off. "You can't be here," the young woman says.

"What's happening?" Holly asks.

She motions to the civilians. "You need to step back with the others, ma'am."

Holly stands on her tiptoes to peer over the first responders. She scans the ground behind them and catches a glimpse of what appears to be a tarp thrown over a section of the blacktop.

Right as she feels the firefighter's hand grip her elbow to pull her back, Holly notices an unnaturally twisted leg extending out from under one corner of the tarp.

As shocking as the sight is, it's the purple-and-white sneaker that steals her breath.

CHAPTER 30

At just after ten p.m., Simon sits behind the electronic keyboard in his home studio, aimlessly tapping the B-sharp key. He sat down hours ago determined to write a song, or if not a whole one, then at least a chorus or a few bars. But the longer he stares at the keys, the deeper his resignation grows. Not only does he not have a new song in him today, he doubts he will ever write another. Not one good enough to share with the world, anyway.

Writing hits used to be almost as easy as breathing. Sometimes, when they were recording a new album, and Jeremy handed him a page of scribbled lyrics, Simon would compose a new tune in his head before he'd finished reading the last line. But he's too old and too broken for that kind of inspiration anymore. Besides, Jeremy is too dead.

When his phone dings with a new text, Simon is relieved for the distraction. He looks down to see that Baljit has launched a new group chat with three letters: *OMG*. Below it, she sends a link to a local news story. It was posted only minutes before.

"Oh, fuck," Simon mutters as he reads the headline: "Jang Heiress Found Dead."

The article describes multiple 911 calls from a luxury condo building in Newport at around nine p.m. A woman was pronounced dead at the scene after having presumably jumped from the balcony of her eleventh-floor penthouse. The police haven't released the victim's name, but multiple eyewitnesses confirmed her to be Justine Jang.

New texts roll up the screen.

Salvador: JJ DOVE OFF HER OWN BALCONY? WTF?!?

Baljit: She wasn't right at the group session this morning. Nothing like her chatty self!

Salvador: RIGHT?! Same when I texted her earlier tonight. Could barely squeeze two words out of her.

Baljit: Texted her about what??

Salvador: The after party for my upcoming show. She offered to help.

Reese: JJ and I were supposed to get together tonight. But I had an eleventh-hour crisis on a file at work.

Salvador: Shit happens, Reese.

Reese: But maybe if I'd called her to cancel instead of only texting . . . ?

Baljit: What? You'd have told her not to jump?

Salvador: OUCH! Colder than ice, B!

Baljit: Like any of us could have seen this coming?

Reese: Poor JJ. She was never the same after Elaine's OD.

Salvador: 100%!! It totally freaked her out . . . Can't believe she's gone. What now?

Baljit: What do you mean?

Salvador: What happens to the tribe? And Dr. Danvers?

Liisa: How could we continue after this?

Reese: Not even sure I want to continue.

Baljit: Me, too. I'm a gambler, but two out of seven dead . . . Even I don't like those odds.

Simon can't help but think of his last conversation with JJ. All her suspicions about Elaine's death.

Simon: I spoke to JJ earlier, too.

Reese: You saw her?

Salvador: WTF, SIMON??

Simon worries that they'll think he tossed her off the balcony.

Simon: I didn't see her! I phoned her! After our session. I was concerned about her.

Liisa: What did she say?

Simon: She was acting weird. Asked me if I thought Elaine's death was suss.

Salvador: SUSS??

Liisa: What does that even mean?

Simon: Like could someone else have overdosed Elaine to make it look accidental.

Baljit: Come on!

Simon: Gets even weirder. JJ thought Dr. D suspected she was in-volved.

Salvador: JJ thought Dr. Danvers overdosed Elaine??

Simon: No! Other way around. She worried Dr. D suspected her of being involved.

Reese: That makes zero sense.

Simon: Agreed! I asked JJ if she knew something we didn't about the night Elaine OD'd. But she basically hung up on me.

Baljit: Could JJ have been involved? Might explain why she was acting so bizarre.

Reese: JJ? As if!

Baljit: Something made her jump. Maybe she fell off the wagon?

Liisa: It's a big stretch to go from falling off the wagon to falling off your balcony.

Simon: A roadie in my band used to get suicidal whenever he drank too much. Rest of us used to joke about it. Until the night he put a bullet through the back of his skull.

Salvador: WHOA! Can we ease up on the carnage and conspiracy theories?

Baljit: Should we meet to discuss?

All the others reply with yeses or thumbs-up emojis.

Simon stares at the screen, half expecting Baljit to add: *And then there were five.*

CHAPTER 31

Aaron stifles a yawn as he opens the front door to Holly. "Hi!" he says. "Why didn't you just use your key? You know you're welcome any time of—" But the look on her face stops him mid-sentence.

"JJ is dead," she says flatly as she steps inside.

"Dead? I . . . How?"

"Jumped, apparently."

He closes the door behind her. "How do you know?"

"I saw her. Her leg, at least."

"You were *there*?"

"I was too late."

Aaron steps forward to wrap Holly in a hug, but she's stiff in his arms. "I'm sorry, Holl."

She slips free of his embrace and heads into the kitchen.

"Glass of wine?" he asks.

"Tea, if you don't mind."

As Aaron fills up the kettle, he steals another glance at his wife. He can't tell if she's in shock or not, but her reaction is not what he would have expected after the death of a second client so soon after the first. Her expression is inscrutable, but with her arms folded and her chin held high, her body language borders on defiant.

As he passes her the mug, he asks, "What are you not telling me, Holly?"

"Nothing," she murmurs.

"What are you thinking then?"

She studies her tea for a long moment. "It's all too convenient."

"Convenient?" He grimaces. "For whom?"

"For me."

He exhales a sigh. "You're going to have to explain that one."

"Two clients. Both with potentially explosive dirt on me. Both die before they can go public."

It is a huge coincidence, but she doesn't need to hear that from him. Instead, Aaron shakes his head and asks, "Did you kill them?"

"No." She pauses. "Not directly, at least."

"How else do you explain the 'convenience' of it then? Do you think there's some ultra-violent guardian angel looking out for you?"

"I don't know how the hell to explain it, Aaron."

"Then stop trying, Holl."

"I have to."

"Why?"

"Because two of my clients are dead!" She lowers her cup. "Both of whom would still be alive if they had never met me."

Aaron silently agrees. But he also understands that once Holly's shock and outrage recede, they will be replaced by guilt and self-recrimination. She came to him first for a reason. And he intends to be there for her, protecting her however necessary.

"A hundred years ago," he says, "when I was a junior psychiatric resident, I did an elective at this clinic in Sausalito called the McMaster Institute. Have you heard of it?"

"I don't need an equivalency tale right now, Aaron."

"Hear me out. Please."

She shrugs.

"The McMaster was a well-regarded private psychiatric institute," he says. "Most of the residents were highly intelligent and educated. A couple were even former college profs. But they all suffered from debilitating illnesses ranging from schizophrenia to severe PTSD. All of them had been institutionalized at the McMaster for decades, after failing to cope in the outside world. By the time I got there, there were only nine residents left."

"Aaron . . ."

"While I was there, the psychiatrist who had been running the place forever dropped dead. And no one was willing to take the job. Also, remember that at the time there was intense public pressure to de-institutionalize such patients. In the end, the board decided to close the place and relocate the residents back into the community." He pauses, but she only stares at him. "Within one week of the announcement, four of the nine residents attempted suicide. And three succeeded."

Holly reaches out and strokes his arm. "I appreciate what you're doing. And I love you for trying. I do. But comparing a group of displaced, institutionalized residents to my high-functioning clients . . . that's no comparison at all."

"High-functioning or not, your clients were addicts. Their risk was always going to be much higher than others."

Holly shakes her head. "Not this high. No way."

Aaron glances down at her hand where it rests on his elbow. "You're going to have to accept that you might never know why they died. That you probably won't."

"Maybe." She releases her grip. "But I have to at least try to find out."

"How do you intend to go about it?"

"To start with, by figuring out how their deaths are connected."

"If they are—and that's a *huge* if—how will you do that?"

"I have no idea. But Elaine overdosed right after she launched a mission, misguided as it was, to expose me for sexual misconduct. And then JJ allegedly killed herself within days of admitting that she might have been the last person ever to speak to Elaine. And that she should have 'told'—though I think JJ really meant 'warned'—Elaine about something." Holly locks eyes with Aaron. "What are the chances they're not connected?"

"You think JJ felt responsible for Elaine's death and the guilt of it drove her to kill herself?"

"That's one possibility."

He squints at her. "What else?"

"There are five other clients in our group. All of them desperate to continue their psychedelic therapy. To not have it disrupted by scandal or anything else."

Aaron clicks his tongue. "That sounds like a reach."

"I have to fill in some of these gaping blanks. I'll go out of my mind if I don't." Holly swallows the frog in her throat. "Poor JJ. Despite all her wealth, she suffered. The alcohol . . . those lost pregnancies . . . And she cared about the tribe. She really did. Maybe too much." She also can't help thinking of Reese, wondering how the young lawyer is coping with the sudden loss of her best friend and primary ally in the group.

Aaron takes her hand and caresses her knuckles. "It's late, Holly. You're traumatized. Stay here tonight. Tomorrow, everything will be clearer."

She squeezes his hand. "I'm not going anywhere. I want to be with you tonight."

Her loving stare accentuates the gold flecks of her irises, and he smiles. "Good."

She lets go of his hand. "But tomorrow, I'm going to go speak to the police."

He fights off a sigh. *Oh, my love, will you ever learn to leave well enough alone?*

CHAPTER 32

Friday, April 19

Holly wakes up early and slips out of bed, grateful that Aaron is such a heavy sleeper. Her mind is made up, and she doesn't want to give him an opportunity to change it. She grabs her clothes and steals downstairs, hoping that Graham isn't lying in wait for her again.

All is quiet on the main floor, and she's relieved to make it out to her car without incident.

Though Holly has begun to question her own judgment of late, she recognizes that she desperately needs distraction. Something to shield herself from any more guilt or self-blame—and sadness—over two lives cut brutally short. Such a waste.

Holly is also desperate to regain some control. For too long now, she has merely reacted to each mounting catastrophe without a plan or strategy. She needs to follow the advice she would give any of her clients in a similar predicament: *Be proactive. Advocate for yourself.*

As soon as she gets into her car, Holly calls the Newport Beach Police. Once she explains who she is and how she's connected to the victim, she gets an appointment straightaway for an interview with the detective attached to JJ's case.

Within minutes of checking in at the Newport Beach police station's main desk, Holly is greeted by a thirtyish Black man in a well-cut gray suit who introduces himself as Detective Rivers and leads her into a small interview room. Having lived in Southern California for her whole life, Holly is used to meeting aspiring models and actors who work in the service industry. She almost expects to be served by gorgeous baristas and servers. But not cops. With piercing almond-brown eyes, chiseled cheeks, and flawless complexion, Detective Rivers is distractingly good-looking. She also can't help noticing that he doesn't wear a wedding band.

He leans an elbow on the desk that separates them as he scribbles in a notebook. "How long were you Ms. Jang's psychiatrist, Dr. Danvers?"

"A little over three months," Holly says. "But that's not how I would've described our professional relationship."

"You're not a psychiatrist?"

"I am, yes." Holly hesitates, still not entirely comfortable where to draw the lines of patient-therapist confidentiality when it comes to the dead. "But with JJ—Ms. Jang—I was treating her specifically for addiction."

"Addiction to?"

She hesitates. "Alcohol."

As the detective jots down another note, Holly notices that his expensive-looking pen is the same color as his suit.

"But JJ had been sober for the past two months," she adds.

His pen stills. "Sober? Are you sure?"

"Yes. Why?"

"We won't have the toxicology report back for a few days, but we found two empty bottles on her kitchen counter. One vodka, the other wine."

The words hit her like a slap. "JJ was drinking again?"

"We can't know for sure without blood tests," he says, though his eyes show little doubt.

Holly feels ashamed—as if she had failed JJ, as if she were the one who had downed the bottles—but refuses to let it deter her. "Are you certain she jumped, Detective?"

"No. I'm not certain of anything yet. Why do you ask, Dr. Danvers?"

"I just . . . Did she happen to leave a suicide note?"

"No. But more often than not, victims don't. Especially when alcohol is involved." Rivers lifts his pen off the page. "I don't need to tell you, Dr. Danvers, that suicide tends to be a more impulsive decision among the intoxicated."

She knows he's right, but it doesn't diminish her doubt. "Have you ruled out foul play?"

"We haven't ruled anything out." He angles his head slightly. "But it sounds to me like you have suspicions of your own."

Holly considers her words carefully. "JJ is the second death in my practice in the past few weeks."

"Second?" His eyelids flicker, but his expression is unchanged. "Who was the first?"

"Elaine Golding."

He jots down the name. "The activist who overdosed in Laguna?"

Holly nods. "I'm not convinced her overdose was accidental."

"Why not?"

"To begin with, Elaine always used oral opioids. Percocet and Vicodin, mainly. Never fentanyl. Which is what killed her."

"Isn't it common for users to cross over to other opioids?"

"Yes, but Elaine never had before. Besides, even if she did decide to try fentanyl, she could have smoked it instead of injecting."

"Can't someone overdose smoking fentanyl just as easily as injecting?"

"Sure. But Elaine had a severe needle phobia. I'd given her IV medications before, and she was terrified. It's hard for me to imagine her being able to inject herself."

"Hmm," Rivers mutters as he writes more notes. "You think the two deaths in your practice are connected then?"

She shrugs. "I have no idea what to think. But it would be quite the coincidence if they aren't."

His gaze is indecipherable. "Did Ms. Golding know Ms. Jang?"

Holly hesitates. "They were in group therapy together."

His eyes widen momentarily. "How many others in this group?"

"Five."

"Can you tell me their names?"

She holds up a palm. "No. That would be a betrayal of the other clients' confidentiality. I only told you about JJ and Elaine because . . . they're gone."

"All right. Can you tell me more about the purpose of the group? Were you treating all the members for addiction?"

"Yes. But for different types. For Elaine it was opioids, JJ alcohol. Others in the group have varying types of addictions."

The detective studies her for a few unnerving seconds. "You're the therapist who treated Simon Lowry, aren't you? I read something about that. He's one of my dad's favorites."

She doesn't see any point in concealing what is already public knowledge, so she nods.

"Was he in the same group as Ms. Jang?" he asks.

"I can't comment on that."

"He was getting psychedelics as part of his treatment, wasn't he? He said as much in that interview. Ketamine, right?"

"Yes."

"Can I assume Ms. Jang was also being treated with ketamine?"

"Yes," she says, knowing it will probably show up on JJ's toxicology testing.

The detective scratches more notes. "Is there any known association between ketamine and suicide, Dr. Danvers?"

"Yes, but in the reverse sense," she says. "Ketamine is one of the only medications proven to lower someone's risk of suicide. Even after a single dose."

"OK. Aside from the two victims being in the same group, what else makes you think their deaths might be related?"

Holly tells him how JJ admitted to speaking to Elaine on the night of her overdose and how she felt responsible for not sharing some kind of warning with her.

"Warning? Ms. Jang used that specific word?"

"No. I inferred it. JJ said she should have *told* Elaine something. But to me, it sounded as if she felt guilty for not warning Elaine about something."

"What?"

"I have no idea."

"All right." But his expression is doubtful.

Holly sighs. "Look. JJ had no history of previous suicide attempts. Or even depression. In my judgment, her jumping off the balcony . . . it just doesn't fit."

Detective Rivers lowers his pen. "We'll have to wait for the medical examiner's report and the toxicology results. Meantime, I'll liaise with the detectives in Laguna Beach who investigated Ms. Golding's death. But I can tell you this much: there was no evidence of a struggle found at the scene."

Holly feels deflated, but she's not ready to concede. "Let's say, hypothetically, that JJ didn't choose to jump and someone pushed her . . ."

"Go on."

"Would you always expect to see signs of a struggle if, say, she trusted the other person?"

"Not necessarily. No." His smile is almost apologetic. "I'll look into everything you've told me today, Dr. Danvers. If anything turns up, we'll absolutely pursue it. But it's more likely than not these deaths are just a tragic coincidence." His smile fades. "Or, at least, not murder."

CHAPTER 33

Aaron pours himself a generous two fingers of Glenmorangie, his favorite single malt. He rarely drinks alone, but this evening it feels appropriate to do so. Maybe even necessary. A day that started out with so much promise has rapidly turned to crap. Holly left his bed while he was still sleeping. And then she called to cancel her plans to stay over again tonight, but not before telling him that she had spoken to a detective in Newport Beach.

Just as he lowers himself onto the couch, he hears the deadbolt turn and hopes that Holly might have changed her mind. He's disappointed to see his son saunter through the doorway.

"Hey, Dad," Graham grunts. "Got anything to eat?"

"Did I know you were coming over tonight?"

"I had a date downtown. It's on the way home."

By the fact that it's barely nine o'clock and his son is looking for food, Aaron surmises the date didn't go well, but he asks anyway, "How was it?"

Graham shrugs. "She was a bit of a cunt."

"You know how I feel about that word," Aaron snaps, thinking that it's no wonder his son is perpetually single.

"If the shoe fits, Dad . . ." Graham says as he heads to the fridge and helps himself to the last bottle of Aaron's favorite imported Belgian beer.

"What exactly did she do?"

Graham returns to the living room and plunks down on the chair across from him. "For starters, she talked nonstop the whole hour while downing two glasses of very expensive pinot noir."

"Didn't you tell me you always split the bill on first dates?"

"But my half of her fifty-dollar wine tab was a lot more than her half of my ten-dollar beer."

"What else made her so insufferable?"

He takes a sip of beer. "She had this attitude, you know."

Aaron stifles a sigh. "What kind of attitude?"

"Like she was better than me or something. As if I was the one hitting out of my league. And, honestly, she wasn't that hot. A six-and-a-half. At best."

Aaron has long recognized that Graham's issues largely stem from a chronic sense of inadequacy, a lifetime of being the lesser brother, the lesser son. "What did she do to make you feel that way?"

"Do?" Graham's face scrunches. "I dunno. She just gave off that vibe."

"But how? What did she say?"

"Lots of shit." He snaps his fingers. "OK, I mentioned something about Nate being in med school at Columbia. And then she got all worked up. As if it were some big fucking deal or something."

Aaron summons a smile. "Did you ever think she might be showing you how impressed she was because she thought it reflected well on you, too?"

"Nah. She knew exactly what she was doing." Graham takes a swig and smacks his lips. "Anyway, who cares? I was glad she didn't stay for dinner. That I got to see her true colors before I wasted any more time or money on her."

Aaron is too tired to argue. "That's one way of looking at it."

"It's not like it was back in your day, Dad. When it comes to online apps, first dates are as plentiful as sand at a beach. The biggest challenge is juggling all the options. You know?"

"I really don't, Graham."

"You should! Even guys as old as you are getting lucky with these dating apps. Might save you a lot of the will-she-won't-she grief that you keep reliving with what's-her-face."

Aaron takes a breath. "Why do you do that?"

"I'm only looking out for you, Dad," Graham says with a smirk.

"It's just like with your date. Rather than give people a chance, you always assume the worst. As if they're always out to hurt you."

Graham screws up his face. "This isn't about me! Look at Holly's track record with you. How many times has she left you since you've been together?"

His son has a point, but he doesn't understand that for Holly, it's more of a coping mechanism when she feels overwhelmed. One that is inextricably related to the traumatic and sudden loss of her father. "It's a bit more complicated" is all Aaron is willing to say.

"Speaking of complicated, Dad . . ."

Aaron cocks his head. "Yes?"

Graham waves away the suggestion. "Nah, never mind."

But Aaron can tell in a glance his son is up to something. Graham is wearing that same sheepish look that he always did when he'd crossed a line at school, and Aaron would know to expect an angry call from a teacher or the vice principal. "What is it?"

"You're going to be pissed."

"Just tell me, Graham."

He shuffles in his seat. "This Justine Jang woman . . . the one in the news who took a header off her balcony?"

Aaron lowers his glass to the coffee table. "What about her?"

"She was also a patient of Holly's, wasn't she?"

Aaron's toes curl inside his shoes. "How do you know that?"

"I told you that you were going to be pissed."

"How, Graham?"

"Like I've been telling you, my new company is on the cutting edge of surveillance products." He grins. "We have the absolute dopest gear. And we get tons of new gadgets to test at the office."

Aaron can feel his ears heating. "Surveillance gadgets? As in bugs?"

"Yeah. Voice-activated shit. Some of them not much bigger than the head of a pin."

Aaron rises from his seat. "Did you tap my phone?"

"No, not your phone!" Graham gets up and hurries over to the far wall. He stops at one of Aaron's favorite paintings, a charcoal sketch of a woman in a dress drawn only from the neck down. He reaches behind the frame, fiddles for a moment, and pulls out what looks like a tiny USB plug-in. "It's the only one I placed in the house. I swear."

"Goddammit, Graham! How dare you bug my house!"

"What? I was just testing out the effective audio range. It's not like I bugged your bedroom or something."

"Christ! Even you have to know better than this!"

"I was going to tell you, Dad." Graham folds his arms across his chest. "It's only been there for like three days. I just happened to pick up another one of Holly's damsel-in-distress convos with you." He scowls. "And what do you mean, 'even you'? What the fuck, Dad?"

"You have no right to—"

"Kind of hard to overlook, though, isn't it? Two dead patients in a couple weeks. Both under sketchy circumstances. Both of whom had dirt on Holly."

"You don't have the first clue," Aaron growls.

"Come on, Dad. Just like Holly said to you last night. It's pretty fucking convenient!"

Aaron only glares at his son, feeling closer than he has in years to hitting the boy.

CHAPTER 34

Though it was Salvador's idea to meet, Simon is happy to host the others in his home, where they all sit in a circle on the blue velvet chairs in the living room. Salvador and Liisa are on either side of him, Reese and Baljit across from him. It's as close to a family as Simon has these days. But JJ's absence is palpable. And there's an edginess to the gathering. It reminds him of how awkward and painful things got with the band after Jeremy's suicide. Nothing was ever the same, and the band soon dissolved. He wonders if that will be the fate of the tribe, too.

"I heard a rumor that JJ was drinking again," Baljit says.

"Who told you that?" Salvador asks.

"A friend," Baljit says. "Her little brother is a paramedic in Newport. He says they found empty bottles at her place."

"JJ was drunk most nights before she began treatment," Liisa points out. "And she never jumped then."

"But she was completely bent out of shape over Elaine's OD," Simon says.

Salvador nods vehemently. "And throw in the shame of having fallen off the wagon . . ."

Baljit glances from Salvador to Simon and shakes her head. "Is that what you figure, *doctors*? That's literally what pushed JJ over the edge?"

Reese's head snaps toward the other woman. "What's wrong with you? Is nothing off-limits?"

"She wasn't exactly my friend," Baljit says unapologetically. "Besides, sometimes humor diffuses the tension."

"Well, she was *my* friend. And you're not funny."

Simon has a mental image of the two women naked and bloodied, tied at the wrists and ankles, wrestling on an oily mat. He forces the fantasy out of his mind, aware that he's slipping again.

"Why don't you dial down the meanness, Baljit?" Salvador says, siding with Reese. "We're all in shock after losing JJ the way we did."

Simon nods. "I can't imagine what was going through her head after she jumped."

Salvador glares at Baljit. "And if you say 'the pavement,' I swear to God I'll absolutely lose it!"

Reese massages her temples between her thumb and her fingers. Her eyes look tired, and Simon wonders if she's been drinking. "I shouldn't have canceled our get-together after that last session. Or at least I should have taken the time to call her. I knew something was wrong. JJ was just so . . . off."

Liisa looks over to Reese but doesn't offer any words of consolation. The room falls into a somber silence.

"OK," Simon finally says. "What about JJ's theory that there was something sketchy about Elaine's death?"

"You don't think there's anything to that?" Salvador asks.

"Not really," Simon says. "But JJ made it sound like Dr. D did."

"Then how come Dr. Danvers didn't say boo to the rest of us?" Baljit asks.

"Why would she, if she thought only JJ was involved?" Reese snaps, and Salvador nods his approval.

Liisa clears her throat. "Besides, she would never betray client-therapist confidentiality like that."

"Yet another reason Dr. Danvers won't want to resume group therapy," Reese points out.

Simon's heart sinks. "Dr. D's treatment has been working for the rest of us. And I, for one, need to continue it."

"I couldn't agree any freakin' more!" Salvador cries, practically bouncing in his seat. "I need it, too."

"Me, too," Baljit sighs.

Reese looks around the room. "After JJ and Elaine . . . can we really just go back to business as usual?"

"It definitely wouldn't be business as usual," Salvador says.

"Couldn't we go to another ketamine clinic?" Reese asks. "Or get our own supply? Vitamin K, as they call it on the street."

"Other clinics don't do IV ketamine," Liisa says.

"And snorting Vitamin K is not the same," Simon says. "Trust me. The effect is nothing like the IV stuff Dr. D gives us."

"Besides, Dr. Danvers is simply *the* best therapist," Salvador says. "At this point, I must've tried them all."

Baljit turns to Reese. "Are you sure you can keep away from the bottle without her help?"

Reese shrugs. "I'm not sure of much of anything at this point."

"Does anyone in this group feel unsafe to continue therapy with Dr. Danvers?" Salvador asks the others. "Now is the time to speak up."

No one does.

"I don't buy what JJ told Simon," Baljit says. "There's a perfectly simple explanation for what happened to Elaine."

"And to JJ, too," Salvador adds.

"Then we're agreed?" Baljit asks, staring into each person's eyes, landing last on Simon's.. "We reach out to Dr. Danvers and convince her to continue our therapy?"

"Who reaches out to her?" Simon asks.

"I will," Baljit says.

Simon shakes his head. "Uh, no. You lack tact. And judgment. Then again, so do I. It's going to take some world-class persuasion to convince Dr. D." He looks over to Reese. "I say we send in the best negotiator in the room. Naturally, the lawyer."

CHAPTER 35

Saturday, April 20

Holly sits at her desk and stares at the blank computer screen. She had begun to see clients every second Saturday to keep up with the crushing demand on her practice, but this morning she has only come into the office to work on her manuscript. She promised her editor in New York that she would submit a chapter of her book before the weekend. But Holly is totally uninspired. Besides, how she could write anything about the untapped power of psychedelics with all that has happened within the tribe and her own life?

Holly senses her assistant's silent presence outside the open door. As dedicated and competent as Tanya is, she's no poker player. And Holly can tell in a glance that something is troubling her. "What's wrong, Tanya?"

"Um, Reese Foster, is . . . er . . . here to see you."

Holly shuts her laptop. "I didn't think I was seeing clients today. Especially anyone from that group."

Tanya seems embarrassed. "And I told Reese that when she called."

"But she came anyway?"

Tanya holds out her palms, helplessly.

"Don't worry, Tanya." Holly musters a smile. "Give me five minutes, and then show her in please."

Five minutes later, Reese is seated across from Holly in one of the padded interview chairs. "Thanks for seeing me, Dr. Danvers."

"Not to nitpick, Reese, but I didn't actually agree to see you."

"True." Reese laughs. "I kind of muscled my way in, didn't I?"

"It's not that I didn't want to speak to you or anyone else in the group," Holly says. "But after all that's happened, I thought it best if we took a collective break."

"Of course, yes. That makes sense. I would've done the same, probably, in your shoes." Reese shows an apologetic smile. "I wanted to tell you in person how sorry I am for JJ's loss."

Unsure how to respond, Holly simply nods.

"It's been hard on all of us," Reese says. "But as her therapist . . ."

"I must feel responsible?"

"No." Reese shakes her head. "Not at all. I just assumed it must be very difficult to lose a client that way."

"It is, yes. Thank you." *Even more so when it's your second one in two weeks.* "What about you? It must be very difficult to lose a friend. You and JJ were close, right?"

Reese leans forward in her chair. "Not at first. But yeah. She grew on me. JJ was silly and goofy, and I don't think she ever did an honest day's work in her life, but she had a pure heart. And she understood loneliness. Probably better than anyone I'd ever met. So we had two things in common." Reese smiles sadly, then remembers herself and straightens her posture. "There's something else I wanted to ask, Dr. Danvers."

Holly waits in silence.

"There's a rumor circulating among the group about JJ and Elaine."

"Which is?"

"That you thought JJ might have been . . . involved in Elaine's death."

Holly struggles to keep her expression neutral, wondering how this could have possibly gotten back to the group. She considers her answer carefully. "All my discussions with clients are protected by privilege. As a lawyer, you must appreciate that."

"Of course, I do. But they're both dead. And if you believe something . . . nefarious happened to Elaine or JJ, then shouldn't the rest of us know?"

"I can't comment on this rumor. Or anything that came up during my private sessions. Client confidentiality is sacrosanct." Holly pauses. "But I can tell you the police are investigating. I've already spoken to the lead detective. As far as I know, they haven't reached any conclusions."

Looking disappointed, Reese only nods.

"Where did you hear this rumor?" Holly asks.

"JJ. Not directly, though. Through Simon. JJ told him that you thought Elaine's overdose could have been staged. And for some reason, JJ believed you suspected she might have been involved."

Clearly, JJ had misinterpreted Holly's questions about that night. And she must have been extremely distressed to have shared her worries with someone like Simon. He strikes Holly as an unlikely choice for a confidant. *Did JJ's anxiety over what she thought I knew lead her back to the bottle?* And did the guilt and the alcohol conspire to convince her to jump? Or was she pushed?

"I didn't come here to spread rumors," Reese says.

"What does bring you here?"

"The tribe sent me. As their envoy, of sorts."

"Why do they need an envoy?"

"To let you know that, despite what's happened, we're all committed to continuing with our psychedelic therapy with you."

Holly almost does a double take. "Two out of seven dead! And the rest of you still want to continue the same treatment?"

"We don't believe it had anything to do with the psychedelics. Or you. Not directly, anyway. We think it's all a freakish coincidence."

Holly can't wrap her mind around that possibility. "Even if you don't, others will. And as I said from the outset, our treatment isn't mainstream. You knew it would be under the microscope. That *I* would be."

"Our names are protected by therapist-client confidentiality."

"But mine isn't! And Simon has already gone public about his therapy with me."

"But not the rest of us," Reese points out. "No one outside of the tribe has to know that JJ or Elaine were in our group. That won't get out."

"Won't it?" Holly waves a hand. "Look how quickly the rumor spread about JJ."

"Only within the group, Dr. Danvers. None of us will say a word to anyone about JJ or Elaine. Or you. We promise. You don't have to stop the ketamine."

"We absolutely do. At least, for now."

Reese frowns. "I thought you believed in psychedelics. Wholeheartedly. Didn't your grandfather help pioneer the field?"

"Of course, I still believe. And so does my grandfather."

"Oh? He's alive?"

"Very much so. Here in Orange County. And at ninety, he's still active and highly respected in the academic world of psychedelia."

"Impressive."

"He is," Holly says without masking her pride. "But after everything that's happened, Reese, we have to hit the pause button on the ketamine infusions."

Reese looks Holly dead in the eyes. "We're scared, Dr. Danvers. All of us."

"About the risk of relapsing?"

"Yes." Her candor is bracing. "For the first time in years, each of us has found something to control our addiction. Something that actually works. All of us believe that if we were to stop now, we'd be bound to fall off the wagon. Likely sooner than later. And that terrifies us."

"There are other options, Reese," Holly says gently. "Other ketamine clinics and psychedelic practitioners."

"None like yours. None which offer ketamine intravenously."

Holly can't remember seeing Reese so unguarded, and she feels a pang of sympathy for the normally steadfast lawyer. "I have no choice but to put our therapy on hold for now. But I will consider what you said, Reese. And maybe, after the investigation is complete, we can discuss restarting."

"Thank you." Reese sighs as she rises to her feet. "Please do consider it, Dr. Danvers. We're relying on you."

After Reese leaves, Holly goes over their conversation in her head as if it were a court transcript. What else do members of the group know? Who else might be involved? What wasn't said?

Then an idea hits her. One she almost dismisses out of hand, recognizing it to be beyond unethical. But Holly is desperate for answers, and the prospect is too tempting. The longer she considers it, the more she realizes there's only one person she can turn to for guidance.

Holly grabs her bag, and hurries down to her car.

She finds her grandfather inside his crowded office, slouched in front of his computer screen. She kisses him on the forehead. "Hi, Papa."

"Hello, Koala," he says, but his words lack their usual warmth or enthusiasm.

"Everything OK? You don't seem yourself."

He waves off her concern. "What brings you by?"

"I was hoping to get your advice."

His chin drops. "Not about the accident?"

"I wasn't—"

"Please, Holly." He holds up a shaky hand. "No more questions about your father. I don't want to relive that." His voice is as tremulous as his hand. "It's too much."

"No, no, Papa," she says, feeling guilt all over again for having caused him such angst. "It has nothing to do with Dad. Or the accident. Promise."

He musters a grateful smile. "What is it, then?"

She pulls up a chair and sits down beside him. "I lost another client . . ." Her voice cracks unexpectedly. "A second one from the same psychedelic group."

He looks dumbfounded. "Another one?"

The words pour out of her as she recounts the story of JJ's death. She describes the crippling sense of responsibility as well as her suspicions surrounding the deaths. "I can't shake the feeling that someone in the tribe is hiding something. Something serious. Maybe more than just one of them."

He squints at her. "You honestly believe those deaths weren't self-inflicted?"

"I have no idea. But I have to find out."

"Isn't that for the police?"

"I'm not sure they'll look hard enough. Or at least in the right places.

Because they don't even know who the rest of the tribe is. And I can't tell them."

"What do you intend to do?"

"I have this idea . . . but it's not exactly ethical."

He gives her a stern look. "Tell me."

"Not sure you'll want to hear this."

"If it makes you feel any better, chances are I'll forget ten minutes after you tell me."

She laughs and settles deeper in her chair. "The only reason I know anything about JJ's concerns regarding Elaine is because I interviewed her while she was under ketamine. And she was so forthcoming."

Walter's bushy eyebrows furrow. "What are you suggesting?"

"If I could just speak to other members in a similar way. Under ketamine . . ." Holly says sheepishly. "And, if necessary, I could always add midazolam to blur the memories."

"Oh, Holly." He reaches out and clutches her wrist. "You didn't need to drive all the way here. You already know the answer."

"Yes, but—"

"You and I, we've been committed to harnessing the therapeutic powers of psychedelics." He lets go of her wrist. "But to now use them as some kind of truth serum? Nothing in the world would justify that."

"What if it's the only way to get to the truth?"

"The CIA used to say the same about waterboarding," he says, shaking his head. "There is no justification."

CHAPTER 36

Simon has just poured himself a second vodka soda when his phone buzzes with the distinct ring from the front gate doorbell. As usual, he opens the video app on his phone to check who's at the door and ensure it's not some crazed fan. A young Black man in a blue suit stares back at him through his screen.

"Can I help you?" Simon asks over the speaker.

"Detective Rivers with the Newport Beach Police," he says, holding up his identification to the camera. "I'm looking for Simon Lowry."

Simon's mouth goes dry. *Which one of them filed a police complaint?* "Now is not the best time."

"I need a few minutes at most, Mr. Lowry. Please."

Simon hesitates before tapping the button to open the gate. He dumps his drink down the sink and heads to the front door. His rib cage is thumping by the time he opens it to let the detective in.

After they sit down together on the velvet chairs, Rivers says, "Thanks for seeing me."

"Not a problem." Simon leans back, trying to appear as carefree as possible, but his hip throbs and his throat feels thick.

"I'm looking into the death of Justine Jang," the detective says.

"Oh, you mean JJ," Simon says, hiding his relief. But it's short-lived.

A new worry forms in his head. Maybe Rivers has come to ask him about the night JJ bolted from his house?

"You did know Ms. Jang, correct?"

Simon shakes his head. "Not that well."

"Were you in the same therapy group with Dr. Danvers?"

Simon folds his arms across his chest. "I'm not supposed to discuss the group."

"Of course." Rivers flashes a disarming grin. "I'm sure you hear this all the time, but I just have to tell you. My dad's a huge fan. He's got all your albums. On vinyl, too. I grew up listening to your music. *The Time Will Come* is still one of my all-time favorite albums."

"Thank you," Simon says, not fully trusting his flattery.

"You've been open in past interviews about your therapy with Dr. Danvers."

"I have nothing to hide," Simon says, uncrossing his arms. "But I don't have the right to talk about anyone else in the group."

"I respect your wanting to protect their confidentiality." Rivers sighs. "But Ms. Jang is dead."

The detective has a point. And the fact that he has come to see Simon means it's likely he already knows JJ was in the tribe. "All right, yes, we were in the same group."

"Being treated for alcoholism, as I understand it?"

Simon merely shrugs.

"When was the last time you saw Ms. Jang?" Rivers asks.

"At our last group session."

"Do you remember which day that was?"

"Last Thursday."

Lines crease the detective's otherwise smooth forehead. "The day she died?"

"That morning. At group session."

"How did she seem to you?"

"She was . . . quiet. Kind of withdrawn, I guess."

"Did she seem upset?"

"I suppose you could say that, yeah."

Rivers nods. "And that was the last time you spoke to her?"

Simon is about to answer in the affirmative when it occurs to him that the police might already have her phone records. "It was the last time I saw her in person."

Rivers tilts his head, waiting.

"I called her afterwards." Before the detective can ask, Simon adds, "I just wanted to check up on her. See how she was doing."

"And how was she doing?"

Simon thinks about his answer. "She said she was OK."

"Did she sound drunk to you?"

"Not that I noticed, no."

"Did she happen to mention Ms. Golding's death?"

Simon squints at Rivers. "You know about Elaine?"

He nods again. "I understand that Ms. Jang was extremely distressed about Ms. Golding's death. Did Ms. Jang mention anything to you about that?"

"I . . ." Simon starts, but something makes him clam up. He doesn't trust the friendly detective. If he goes into details about what JJ told him regarding Elaine, it might push the detective to look deeper into his own history. And Simon can't afford that now, not with a fresh accuser crawling out of the woodwork.

CHAPTER 37

Monday, April 22

The weekend passes without Holly hearing any further news on JJ's death. Rather than feeling reassured by the collective silence, it puts her more on edge. She is actually relieved to get a call from Detective Rivers asking if he can stop by her office this morning to give her an update.

Within ten minutes of hanging up, the detective is seated across from her in the chair that is usually reserved for clients, staring at her with those brown eyes that could melt butter. "Thanks for agreeing to see me on such short notice, Dr. Danvers," he says.

"Happy to, Detective. You got here quicker than I expected."

"I was only a couple blocks away. At the Laguna police station."

"Were you there about Elaine?"

He smiles. "As a matter of fact, I was."

"Did they tell you much? Anything you can share?"

"There's not much to share." He shrugs. "Everything found at the scene was consistent with an accidental opioid overdose. The coroner has already ruled it as such. In fact, the Laguna investigation into Ms. Golding's death is officially closed."

"I see," Holly says, feeling strangely deflated. "And how about your investigation?"

"I believe I've followed up on everything we discussed at our initial meeting."

When he doesn't expand on it right away, she says, "And?"

"In terms of physical evidence, the crime scene technicians went through Ms. Jang's home a second time without finding anything to suggest a struggle inside the condo or on the balcony. We also reviewed the lobby camera footage without identifying any unexplained visitors coming in or out of the building. And the property manager was able to confirm that Ms. Jang didn't buzz anyone in through the intercom the entire day."

"Oh," Holly says, feeling even more disheartened. "What about the bottles?"

Rivers frowns. "The empties at the scene?"

"Yes. Aside from them, did you find other alcohol in her home?"

"No. Just those two. But we did get results back from the toxicology testing. And alcohol was the only drug found in her system."

"No ketamine? Or . . ." Holly stops herself before asking about MDMA or midazolam.

"No." He clicks his tongue. "But her blood alcohol level was 0.37."

"Wow! That's almost five times the legal limit." Holly, herself, would be comatose with a level that high, but alcoholics like JJ often build up a degree of tolerance to such high concentrations in their bloodstream.

"Also, the preliminary autopsy results are consistent with someone who jumped," he says.

"They can tell that from a person who smashed into the pavement from eleven stories above?"

"Not with certainty, no. But there are indicators. For example, the medical examiner didn't find any ligature marks, circumferential bruising, or defensive wounds that might suggest homicide."

"I see," Holly murmurs.

"I've also spoken to Ms. Jang's siblings and two of her ex-husbands. None of them were aware of those concerns she shared with you. Ms. Jang never mentioned any regrets to them over Ms. Golding's death. Or not having warned her about something."

"JJ was spooked. She probably only told a select few." Holly thinks of what Reese told her about Simon's conversation with JJ. "I believe she did share her concerns with a fellow client in her group."

Rivers eyes her with a knowing smile. "But as you're aware, Dr. Danvers, I'm not privileged to the names of the other group members."

Holly considers it for a moment. "What if I were to put the client in question in direct contact with you?"

"That would be really helpful," he says with an encouraging nod. "So far, the only person I've been able to track down is Simon Lowry."

Her lip twitches. "You already spoke to Simon?"

"Yes. And he acknowledged he was in the same group as Ms. Jang."

"Simon is the other client I was referring to," she says, unable to conceal her disappointment. "Did he corroborate what I told you? About JJ's misgivings over Elaine's death?"

"No, he did not."

Why would Simon deny it?

"Look, Dr. Danvers," he continues. "I take your concerns very seriously, but so far, I've found no evidence of a crime. And I hope that reassures you."

"I wish it did."

"I'm willing to keep digging, Dr. Danvers. But Newport has a small detectives' division, and we're backlogged with cases." He studies her with what appears to be genuine sympathy. "I just thought you should know that the coroner is likely to rule Ms. Jang's death to be a suicide."

Holly can't hide the defeat in her voice when she says, "Thanks for letting me know, Detective Rivers."

After he leaves, Holly sits and stares at her blank computer screen. She tries to convince herself that the detective is right. That she should be relieved there's no evidence of foul play in either client's death. That as tragic and senseless as two self-inflicted deaths in one group are, homicide would be worse.

But it doesn't do much good. Her gut screams that a huge piece of the puzzle is missing. Holly thinks of Liisa's description of Elaine as "determined" in her final hours and how her death doesn't fit with a needle-phobic patient who was about to overdose by injecting fentanyl. And Holly can't overlook how coincidental it is that Elaine and JJ both fell off the wagon within hours of their deaths.

No. Despite the coroners' convenient conclusions, Holly knows she will not—cannot—simply accept them.

"I'm sorry, Papa," she mutters aloud. "I don't see any other way."

CHAPTER 38

Holly didn't plan the appointments in any particular order, but she's relieved that Simon is the first client to arrive for ketamine therapy since JJ's death. If anyone in the group can handle heavier doses of psychedelics, it has to be him.

Still, Holly's heart flutters as she slides an IV into his veiny, tattooed forearm. And her guts are knotted with guilt and worry. She feels as if she's on the verge of betraying her grandfather's legacy, but for the life of her, she can't think of a way around it.

"Ah, it's good to be back in the old recliner!" Simon bellows, and pulls the blindfold over his eyes before Holly suggests it.

Holly doesn't even ask Simon if he minds her playing the music over the speakers instead of the usual headphones. And as she launches his perennial choice of songs from Pink Floyd's *The Wall*, Simon settles back in the recliner and sighs contentedly. "I'd avoid Roger Waters like the plague if I saw him at a party, but there's no other album I'd rather trip to."

"Are you ready, Simon?" Holly asks, realizing it's evident he is.

"All systems check, Captain." He guffaws. "Ready for liftoff, Ground Control."

"Set and setting," Holly reminds him as she slowly injects the ketamine into his arm, adding 25 percent more than his previous dose. "Go to that happy memory, Simon. Somewhere safe and warm."

In less than a minute, a dreamy smile crosses Simon's lips as he begins to hum along to the music.

"How are you feeling, Simon?" Holly asks.

"Awesome," he says, sweeping his free hand toward the ceiling. "Stars and planets and moons and asteroids . . . I see them all. A whole galaxy. Like I'm in a goddamn planetarium."

"Good," she says soothingly. "Go with it."

He breaks into song, singing along to the soundtrack.

"Simon?"

"Yeah?"

"How do you feel about everything that's happened to the group?"

"Not exactly ideal, is it?"

"No, it's not."

His smile fades. "I can't believe there's another one."

"JJ?"

"I can't remember her name. Kyla? Maybe."

"Kyla?"

"She came forward for the money. Just like her friend, Brianna. Fleeced me dry. Greedy bitches."

"Simon, who is Kyla?"

"They begged to come on tour with me," he mutters. "They crawled into my bed."

Simon has alluded to similar accusations of sexual misconduct in the past without going into specifics. Then again, Holly has never interviewed him under the influence of ketamine before, only afterwards, during their debrief.

"I told them . . ." he mumbles. "I got their consent. Always do. The restraints, the gags, the chains, the hoods . . . they were into it. They said it was super-kinky."

"And now they're accusing you?"

"The second one is, yeah," he grumbles. "Brianna already won the lottery at my expense!"

"You reached a settlement with her?"

"I didn't mean to hurt her. I'm always careful. I have no idea where the bruises came from. I only wanted to restrain them. To enslave them. Give them the full thrill of being dominated."

"Bruises?"

"Dr. D, you've helped me soooo much. Those urges are almost gone. They don't drive me anymore." He chuckles. "I don't even fantasize about you chained to my bed, like I used to."

Holly fights off repulsion at the thought. She remembers JJ's comment about not telling Elaine. Had she meant to warn her about *Simon*? "What about Elaine? Or JJ? Did something . . . sexual . . . happen with one of them, Simon?"

He grips the armrest and the veins in his forearm pop. "Did she tell you?"

"Who?"

"JJ."

"No."

"It was just dinner! Friendly like. We got into this deep conversation about our addictions. She told me a bunch of stuff about how she fell into the bottle. After all those lost pregnancies. And I thought it was only fair for me to share, too. I told her about my . . . you know . . . kinks. I thought she was into them, too. But as soon as I mentioned how sexy it would be to chain her up, she completely freaked out. And bolted. Like I'd pulled a chainsaw on her!"

Holly's mind races as she absorbs the details. "Was JJ threatening to expose you?"

"Expose?" He grunts. "No, no. She ghosted me. Would barely say two words to me after."

"But you saw JJ again, Simon?" Holly has to stop herself from telling him that Reese told her as much. "The night she died."

He shakes his head. "I spoke to her on the phone. In the afternoon."

"And what did JJ tell you?"

"That something happened between her and Elaine. And JJ thought you suspected she was involved in Elaine's death."

Holly forces herself to speak in a conversational tone. "Did JJ tell you what happened between her and Elaine?"

"Nope. JJ couldn't get off the phone fast enough. Like she regretted bringing it up." Simon reaches up and touches his mask. "What's going on, Dr. D?"

"Nothing, Simon. You're doing fine."

"Why the million questions?"

Holly can tell from the clarity in his voice that the ketamine is wearing off, and that he's gaining insight. She glances at the two syringes in her hand. For a moment, she considers administering more ketamine to put him back under, but she banishes the thought.

"Do you know something about Elaine and JJ?" His voice borders on frantic. "Something I don't?"

"No, no. It's only talk, Simon."

He wriggles on the recliner. "What the fuck is going on here?"

Holly feels trapped. Without a choice. Hand trembling, she attaches the syringe of midazolam to the IV and pushes in a full dose.

Within seconds, Simon is snoring.

Staring at his sleeping form, Holly feels sick to her stomach.

Ten minutes later, he wakes with a start, pulling the blindfold off his eyes and sitting up. "Whoa! That was a fucking weird trip!"

"What do you remember, Simon?" Holly asks, trying to steady her breathing.

"Lots of stars. Not much else. It's so foggy." He grimaces. "Did I say anything?"

She forces a smile. "Nothing very coherent."

Holly removes his IV and escorts him out to the waiting room, staying close by his side in case he loses his balance on the way.

After asking Tanya to call him a taxi, Holly hurries back to her office, closes the door, and drops into her seat. She has to fight back tears. She has never knowingly lied to a client before. At least not for personal gain.

Before Holly is even close to settling her nerves, Tanya knocks at the door and ushers Baljit into the room.

"How's it going, Dr. Danvers?" Baljit plops herself onto the recliner and rolls up her sleeve, wordlessly demanding her IV therapy.

"OK, Baljit. How are you?"

She looks skyward. "Been better."

"Are you sure you want to proceed with this today?" Holly asks, hoping the answer will be no.

"Want has nothing to do with it. I need."

Holly has to steady her hand to insert the IV into Baljit's forearm. After it's secured, Holly turns on Baljit's playlist of nineties female folk rock, straight out of Lilith Fair, and then robotically recites the same spiel she gave Simon about set and setting. Within minutes of the ketamine infusing into her vein, Baljit's shoulders relax, and her right arm slips off the armrest.

Holly keeps her mouth shut, determined not to interrogate Baljit like she did Simon.

"God, I needed this," Baljit murmurs. "Especially today."

"Why today?"

"Because I didn't think I'd ever be able to forgive him."

"Who do you have to forgive?"

"My evil fucking dad," she says with a laugh.

"What did he do to you?"

"What didn't he do?" Baljit mutters. "Look, he can undermine me at the office all he wants. That's fine. But to turn my daughter against me? That's too shitty even for him."

"How did he do that?"

"He told her I wasn't a proper mom. That I put my own wants and needs first. That I'm not there for her like her *Biji*. Her grandmother." Baljit groans. "Can you imagine anyone saying that to a seven-year-old? The one person in this world I love unconditionally. Sometimes, the only one I love at all."

"That must have been difficult to hear."

"No shit. But I forgive the bastard." She laughs again. "You know why?"

"Why?"

"Because right now the universe wants me to forgive everyone. I can feel it."

As tempted as Holly is to ask Baljit what she knows about Elaine and JJ, she can't do it. Not after Simon. Instead, they lapse into silence, and Baljit's head rolls from side to side along to the music.

"Liisa was so wrong about you," Baljit says groggily.

"Liisa? Why do you mention her?"

"She tried to convince me what Elaine said about you was true. As if!" Baljit huffs. "You're all right, Dr. Danvers."

Holly's breath catches. "Convince you, Baljit? I'm not following."

"After . . . you know . . . the whole thing with Elaine and the touching."

"What exactly did Liisa say?"

"She told me that women hardly ever make up claims like that."

The hairs on Holly's neck bristle. "Liisa told you that?"

"She said that abusers know how to turn accusations upside down. Make none of it sound credible. Typical victim-blaming stuff."

Gaping at her blindfolded client, Holly struggles to keep her voice in check. "Liisa told you all that?"

"Yup. She even tried to convince me that maybe you'd also touched me while I was under. As if I'd let anyone get away with that shit!" She shakes her head. "Fuck Liisa! Acts like a know-it-all, but she's as much of an addict as any of us. And Jesus, does she have a hate-on for you."

CHAPTER 39

The hike along the Water Tank Loop trail was Aaron's idea, but he's already feeling winded as he pushes himself to keep up with Holly, who scrambles up the steep incline ahead of him. She finally slows to a stop at a viewpoint that overlooks the shoreline and the town of Laguna below.

Still panting, Aaron rests an arm across Holly's shoulders. She doesn't lean into or away from the embrace, and he enjoys the contact as they stare down at the endless Pacific. He inhales the warm breeze, picking up floral notes from the spring wildflowers dotting the landscape.

"Can we talk about it?" Aaron asks.

"What's there to say?"

"A lot."

"Papa was right," Holly says. "Nothing in the world could justify me using a therapeutic agent to roofie my own clients. But I did it anyway."

"You didn't roofie anyone! You gave them the ketamine they were begging for," Aaron says, finding himself once again in the paradoxical position of trying to defend her practices, when he doesn't actually believe in them.

"These clients of mine, Aaron. Behind all their trappings of success, they're so broken. They depend on me." She sighs. "I'm supposed to counsel them, goddammit! Not interrogate them."

"It was only Simon, right?"

"One is more than enough! Especially considering I even gave him midazolam to cover my own ass."

"Wasn't he having a dysphoric reaction?"

"Maybe." She shrugs. "But that's not why I gave it to him."

"Sounds like he's doing fine."

Holly turns to him, her expression pained. "Ironically, I learned the most when I wasn't even trying to pry," she mutters.

He lifts his arm off her shoulders. "Care to elaborate?"

"My very next client, Baljit, blurted something about another member of the group while under ketamine. I'm still struggling to absorb it."

Aaron stares at Holly, waiting.

"Remember the psychologist in my group?" she says.

"Liisa Koskinen?"

"Oh, yeah. She trained under you, didn't she?"

He shrugs. "Not exactly. Liisa was doing a month-long rotation at my hospital during her doctoral internship. I was one of a number of psychiatrists who taught her."

"Regardless," Holly says, clearly uninterested in the distinction. "I can't believe how badly I misread her."

"In what sense?"

"Liisa was by far the most reluctant member of the group. The slowest to reach sobriety. And the most skeptical, too. Initially, I regretted including her. I saw her as a hindrance to me and the others. But after a few months, with dual therapy, Liisa had a breakthrough. I could feel her belief blossoming. I saw her as more than just a client."

"A friend, too?"

"No, more like an advocate. Someone with the expertise and the clout to back me up in group discussions. And to be honest, it was validating to see a colleague respond so well to my therapy."

"I'm confused," Aaron says. "What does this have to do with what Baljit told you?"

"I was wrong about Liisa. So wrong." Holly sighs. "She's been trying to undermine me the whole time."

"*Undermine?* How?"

"Liisa told Baljit that Elaine's accusations about me were probably true. She even tried to convince Baljit that I might have molested her, too."

"What the hell?" Aaron's voice rises. "Why would Liisa put herself into counseling with you—especially group therapy!—only to sabotage it?"

"I don't have a fucking clue, Aaron."

"How do you know what Baljit told you is true?"

"I didn't ask her. She just offered it."

"While high on ketamine?"

"While medicated, yes."

Aaron exhales. "Did you confront Liisa?"

"No. Not yet."

"How reliable are memories shared under the influence of psyche-delics?"

"It depends how deep the person is. How altered."

"But isn't it possible that Baljit misremembered?"

Holly stops to consider it. "Possible, I suppose. But unlikely. It was a spontaneous utterance. She believed what she was saying. I'm sure of that."

"Are you going to tell that detective?"

"You know I can't betray patient confidentiality like that. And as of now, it's all just conjecture."

Aaron knows his wife won't be able to leave it alone. "What do you plan to do, Holl?"

"I haven't decided. But I have an appointment with Liisa tomorrow."

Aaron shakes his head. "This tribe of yours . . ."

"It's not my tribe. It's theirs." Holly locks eyes with him. "But if Liisa really was so determined to sabotage the group, to convince members that they'd been molested under the influence . . ."

"Yes?"

"Isn't it possible she could have gone further?"

"Holly . . ."

"Think about it, Aaron. What if Elaine began to resist Liisa's sugges-tions, like Baljit did? Maybe Liisa was worried Elaine might expose her? Maybe Liisa thought she had to silence her?"

"Wasn't Elaine laser focused on exposing you before she died? Where's the resistance in that? And besides, how do you explain JJ?"

Holly snaps her fingers. "OK, let's say Elaine did OD on her own. But then Liisa tried to pull the same routine on JJ. To convince her that she'd been a victim, too. And then after Elaine died, maybe JJ felt guilty for not having warned her about Liisa. Maybe that was what was stressing her out?"

"And then what? Liisa silenced JJ by pushing her off her own balcony?" Aaron digests it for a moment. "It seems so . . . outlandish."

Holly eyes him intently. "How else do you explain what's been happening?"

Aaron reaches out and caresses her cheek. "Do I need to give you my not-everything-makes-sense-in-the-cosmos speech again?"

Holly spins away from his palm and sets off up the trail. Aaron hurries after her, relieved that the incline has lessened. By the time he catches up to her, Holly wears a distant look, and she avoids his eyes. She motions to the taller hills ahead of them and says, "Back there somewhere is Route 73."

"And what's the relevance of that?"

"It's where my dad died."

In the twelve years he has known her, Aaron has never once heard his wife willingly mention the car accident that killed her father, despite all the times he tried to get her to open up about it. He has no idea why she's raising it now, but he senses it's best to let her volunteer more.

"I found the site of the crash, Aaron," she murmurs without looking at him. "I went to see it. For the first time since the accident."

He wants to touch her, but he resists the urge. "And how did it feel to be back there?"

"Nauseating."

"Anything else?"

She kicks away a small rock. "Incomplete, maybe."

"Why incomplete?"

"For the last twenty years, since Peru, I stuck my head in the sand. I avoided talking or even thinking about the accident. And then, after Elaine . . . and my intense DMT trip . . . I decided I had to know. But what did I discover? Absolutely nothing. There was no explicable reason for the accident. Just more of that senselessness and randomness you love to fall back on."

"It's a huge step that you even tried, Holl. You confronted your fears, your denial."

"And what good did it do me?"

"You can't know that yet. Not right away."

"I'm not convinced, Aaron." Her voice thickens. "And you want to hear the worst part?"

"I do."

"I hurt Papa. Badly."

Aaron shakes his head. "What does this have to do with Walter?"

"It was my choice to confront those memories. Not his." She stops to swallow. "And it wasn't until I started pressing him for details that I came to realize he's been struggling to bury the memory of that day as much as I have."

"You didn't mean to, Holly."

Her shoulders rise and fall. "Poor Papa. My rock." She sniffles. "The strength it must have taken him to shield me from his devastation at losing his only son. He could've plummeted into despair like my mom did. But instead, he showered me with all the love and support I needed. What my mom wouldn't give me. What she couldn't give me."

"Holl . . ."

"Every time I go looking for answers, Aaron, I make things worse. But I just can't help myself."

He swallows her in a hug, feeling her chest pound against his, as her chin presses into his neck.

Walter might be your rock, but I'll always be your protector.

CHAPTER 40

Tuesday, April 23

*P*atients lie. All the fucking time, one of Holly's early mentors used to love to tell her. It's a lesson that has been reinforced over the years.

But Holly has never viewed her role as one of fact-checker. If a client chooses to lie, they have their reason. God knows they lie enough to themselves. Consequently, Holly has never before looked for objective sources to corroborate what a client told her. Until today. Now Holly is desperate to learn as much as she can about Liisa. And as she studies the Google page in front of her, she can only think: *How could I have been so naïve?*

Liisa's practice in Huntington Beach is closed. As best as Holly can tell, it has been shuttered for over a year. There are oblique mentions of disciplinary actions against Liisa, along with some scathing reviews from clients who felt abandoned by her in mid-therapy.

Tanya knocks at her open door. "She's on the phone again."

Holly closes her browser. "Who is?"

"Katy Armstrong."

In light of all that has transpired in the past week, the reporter had slipped her mind. Holly could only imagine how quickly she would jump all over the deaths associated with her ketamine practice and, for a fleeting moment, wonders if she should just tell Katy. To see if the dogged reporter could sniff out how it was all interconnected. But she dismisses the thought almost as quickly as it forms. "Not now, Tanya."

Her assistant nods. "That's what I thought. Also, Liisa is here for her appointment."

"OK." Holly's neck tightens. "Please bring her in."

A minute or two later, Tanya leads Liisa into the room. Rising from her desk, Holly wills herself calm as she greets the psychologist.

Liisa looks confused as she settles into the interview chair across from Holly. "I don't understand. No ketamine today?"

"Later." Holly forces a smile. "I thought we'd talk first."

Liisa accepts it with a shrug. "All right."

"I've been thinking a lot about your group lately," Holly says. "Did I ever tell you how I chose its membership?"

"Not explicitly, but it always seemed obvious."

"Oh? How so?"

"All of us high-functioning professionals, artists, or influencers who excelled in our spheres despite having what could be considered crippling addictions."

"Exactly. But apart from that, you couldn't be much less alike."

"I'm not sure that's true."

Holly interlocks her fingers and leans forward in her seat, keeping her body language as neutral as her tone. "Tell me more."

"Even putting aside education, wealth, and entitlement, there are parallels," Liisa says. "Simon and Salvador are both artists with predictably histrionic and narcissistic traits. Baljit and Reese are two driven, ultra-competitive corporate types. The textbook definition of alpha females. And of course, Reese and JJ are—was in JJ's case—both childless alcoholics who became fast friends."

"True enough. What about you, Liisa? Who are you most like?"

She thinks about it for a second or two. "You, I suppose."

"Maybe so." Holly swallows her disgust. "Do you recognize the other common thread among the members?"

"No. What's that?"

"There are actually two of them. First, like most people with addiction, all of you have suffered major traumas in your pasts. And the second is the secrets you keep."

Liisa crosses her legs. "Everyone harbors secrets."

"Maybe. But it's a matter of scale. By necessity, high-functioning addicts have to hide massive secrets to survive in their worlds."

Liisa tilts her head from side to side.

"Take you, for example, Liisa," Holly says. "A therapist who has to deal with addiction and trauma every day while hiding a benzodiazepine dependence of her own. That can't be easy."

Liisa laughs uncomfortably. "I'm here, aren't I?"

"Weren't there times when you felt as if you couldn't offer your clients the hard truths they needed to hear because of your own . . . situation?"

Liisa's gaze drops to her lap. "I've been able to compartmentalize my professional and personal lives."

"You've been working throughout the worst of your addiction, then? You've never had to take a break, right?"

"There have been times when I've had to cut back," Liisa says without making eye contact.

"How many days a week do you see clients now?"

"It varies from month to month."

"This month?"

Liisa's mouth tightens, and she sits up straighter. "What's this about?"

"You're not practicing at all, are you, Liisa?"

"I'm on a sabbatical."

Holly peers at her over the rim of her glasses. "A sabbatical from a clinical practice?"

"I needed a break," Liisa mutters. "I don't see what any of this has to do with our ketamine therapy."

"One of the main points of group therapy, Liisa, is to share your vulnerabilities, not to hide them."

"I've shared plenty. More than what I wanted or intended to."

"Did you choose to close your practice?" Holly presses. "Or did the Board of Psychology force you to?"

Liisa's nostrils flare slightly. "How is that any of your business?"

Holly only stares at her.

"All right," Liisa says. "Yes, there was a disciplinary action. One of my clients reported me after I fell asleep during a session. It had been a long day, and I hadn't slept the night before. But no, the Xanax did not help the situation."

"Is that right?"

"There were a couple of other complaints, too. Both trivial in my opinion. And not reliable complainants. But after an aggressive and, frankly, biased investigation, my license was suspended. And I was forced to seek treatment."

Holly is certain Liisa must be downplaying the incidents if they led to a suspension. "And that's how you ended up here? With me?"

"Not directly. As I told you before, none of the other programs I tried worked."

"You came to see me because you had no choice." It all begins to make sense to Holly. "You were extremely resentful about it, though, weren't you?"

"No, I was doubtful," she said. "That is, until your therapy began to help me. And then, as I've told you, my doubt turned into belief."

Holly chooses her words carefully. "But while you were still 'doubtful'— when you hadn't yet found sobriety—did you speak to the others in the tribe about me?"

"In what sense?" Liisa shifts in her seat. "We all discussed you and our therapy with one another."

"Did you encourage Elaine to pursue her allegations against me?"

Liisa's upper body stiffens. "Elaine came to me. She told me about her concerns with you and the way you'd touched her . . . hugged her."

"And what did you tell Elaine?"

"I told her it seemed far-fetched." She hesitates. "But stranger things have happened."

"Is that all?"

"I also told her the truth. That it's rare for a victim to misinterpret abusive intentions."

"You did encourage her to pursue it, then?"

"I encouraged her not to bury her feelings. To speak to you. To clarify what really happened."

"What about the other women in the group?"

The color leaves Liisa's cheeks. "What about them?"

"Did you suggest to any of them that I might've also been abusing them under ketamine?"

Liisa hops to her feet. "What is this? I feel like I'm back in front of the Board. Another inquisition!"

Holly rises from her own chair. They stand a few feet apart, the air electrified between them. "What have you done, Liisa?" she asks in a low voice.

Liisa shakes her head and begins to pace. She waves her hand around the office, contempt contorting her features. "Look at you!" she spits. "With your designer office. Your multimillion-dollar practice. Your celebrity clients. Is your board hounding you over your reliance on psychedelics? No! You've become rich and famous off them! While the Board of Psychology has turned me into a pariah!"

Holly gapes at her. "Does your resentment and bitterness run so deep that you'd throw away everyone's shot at sobriety? Including your own?" *Would you kill for it, too?*

Without saying another word, Liisa snatches her bag off the chair and storms out of the office.

CHAPTER 41

Simon's hip aches as he paces his deck, trying to force the memories to the surface. But only snippets of his session with Dr. Danvers float back to him. Something about Brianna and Kyla. He wonders why the memories are so fragmented. It didn't happen with any of his previous ketamine sessions. Even when Dr. Danvers added MDMA to the mix.

"Hey, Simon!" some stranger on the beach calls out to him. The man is ripped, but with long, graying hair, he looks to be at least fifty. He pumps his arm in the air and makes the heavy-metal horn sign, extending his index and little fingers while tucking the others into his palm. "You rock, man!"

"Thanks, dude!" *Grow up, asshole.*

Simon has rarely felt this on edge. Ever since his lawyer called to tell him about Kyla's complaint, his anxiety has peaked. He's aware that he's verging on paranoid, but that doesn't help to calm him any.

What the fuck did I tell Dr. D about those girls?

Simon decides he needs to talk it through with someone else in the tribe. Maybe one of them has heard something? Stepping back inside his house, he grabs his phone and calls Reese. It rings through to voicemail. He texts her: *Call me. Please. Important.*

After fifteen minutes without a response, he decides to try someone else. But Salvador would be as good as useless, and Simon is afraid Baljit would bite his head off. Or worse, side with Kyla and Brianna. That leaves Liisa. Who happens to be a therapist, as well. If anyone has insider's information, it will be her.

She answers on the fourth ring. "Simon?"

"Hiya, Liisa. How goes the battle?" he asks, realizing he's trying too hard to sound casual.

"Did something happen?" Her voice is strained.

"Noooo." He chuckles. "Just checking in. You know? After we all piled back onto the K-train. One at a time, of course. And since we don't have a group session for a couple days, I thought you and I could debrief early. How did your session go?"

"Oh." There's a long pause. "Fine. And yours?"

"Same here," he says, then calculates how much to reveal. "Except the whole thing is really cloudy. The other trips I remember so well. In fact, super-intensely. But this one . . . it's all kind of murky, you know?"

"If you say so."

"You're a doctor, right? Do you have any ideas why my trip might have been like that?"

"I'm a psychologist, not a medical doctor," Liisa says. "Maybe Dr. Danvers used a higher dose of ketamine this time?"

"Maybe, yeah. It's just so weird to have this select chunk of memory missing. I don't suppose Dr. D mentioned anything to you about me or my session, did she?"

"A therapist would never talk about one client with another. That would be an unforgivable breach of conduct."

He sighs inwardly. "Guess not, huh?"

"Why don't you just ask her what happened?"

Because Dr. D might be too repulsed to ever speak to me again. Or worse, she might have already reported me. But all he says is "Yeah, that's probably my best move."

As he is about to disconnect, Liisa says, "Simon, while I have you on the phone . . ."

"Yes?"

"That evening you saw JJ for the last time, I—"

"I didn't see her! It was a phone call. In the middle of the day."

"Of course. My mistake. But after JJ told you about Dr. Danvers's suspicion that she was involved in Elaine's death . . ."

"What about it?"

"Did JJ mention if Dr. Danvers suspected anyone else?"

"Like who?"

"Baljit? Reese? Salvador? Even me?"

"No," Simon says as he stretches his aching hip. "It was just a brief call."

"All right, thanks."

"Cool," Simon says, wondering why Liisa would care. "Guess I'll see you at the next group session in a couple days."

"About that." Liisa pauses again. "I probably won't make it to the next few. I have a bunch of conflicts."

CHAPTER 42

After her confrontation with Liisa, Holly lumbered through the rest of the afternoon's appointments on autopilot, struggling to focus on her other clients.

As she is packing up her bag to leave the office for the day, her mobile phone rings with a number and an area code that she doesn't recognize. When she answers, a woman says, "Hello. Is this Dr. Holly Danvers?"

"Yes. Speaking."

"This is Dr. Shayna Pearlman from the California Board of Psychology," she says in a friendly tone. "Sorry to return your call so late in the day. I was trapped in meetings."

Holly drops back into her chair. "Thanks for getting back to me, Dr. Pearlman."

"Happy to. You were looking to speak to me concerning a disciplinary matter, Dr. Danvers?"

"Not you specifically. But yes. I was hoping to speak to someone in your office."

"I'm probably as good a place as any to start. I'm the chair of the Enforcement Committee."

"Perfect," Holly says. "I wanted to inquire about one of your members, Dr. Liisa Koskinen."

There's a momentary pause. "What about Dr. Koskinen?"

"I'm a psychiatrist with a practice in Laguna Beach. I'm professionally . . . acquainted with Dr. Koskinen," Holly says, being deliberately vague. "And I've recently learned about licensing issues involving her and the Board."

"Dr. Koskinen is not practicing in Laguna, is she?" Dr. Pearlman asks, sounding concerned.

"No, no. Nothing like that. It's more of a . . . historical issue."

"Ah, all right. Just a moment please, while I pull up her file."

Holly hears the clicking of a keyboard. She understands Dr. Pearlman must assume that she and Liisa shared, or at least counseled, the same client. Rather than correct the misconception, Holly says, "I was hoping to get some more clarity on Dr. Koskinen's interactions with the Board."

"Certainly," Dr. Pearlman says. "It's a matter of public record that Dr. Koskinen's license is currently suspended."

"Can you share the details of the complaint that led to her suspension?"

"In the state of California, all the Board's disciplinary actions are part of the public record," Dr. Pearlman says, although Holly picks up a trace of reticence in her voice. "But do you mind if I ask why you're inquiring?"

"Of course." Holly clears her throat. "It has a direct bearing on the course of at least one of my clients."

"All right," Dr Pearlman says, seemingly satisfied. "Two years ago, the Board received complaints about Dr. Koskinen's conduct."

"Complaints? Plural?"

"Yes. And after a thorough investigation, the deputy attorney general formalized charges. Then last year, we reached a stipulated agreement with Dr. Koskinen whereby she accepted a suspension of her license for a minimum of eighteen months."

"Can you tell me more about the complaints themselves?"

"The misconduct was related to issues of substance dependence."

"I understand that, but it would be really helpful if I could understand the specifics of those complaints, Dr. Pearlman."

"Plain English. Sure. Why not? After all, the complaints are no longer confidential." Dr. Pearlman is quiet for a moment. "The first two
were submitted by clients who noticed that Dr. Koskinen appeared intoxicated during their sessions. Not from alcohol, mind you, benzodiaz-
epines. Xanax. Apparently, she fell fast asleep during one session. And in
another case, she stumbled and fell in front of a client, cutting her head.
The client had to apply pressure to Dr. Koskinen's bleeding wound."

"Oh." Holly is shocked to hear how much Liisa's addiction had im-
paired her at work. In Holly's experience, most high-functioning addicts
hide their substance abuse better. "Under what conditions can Dr. Koskinen regain her license?"

"To be reinstated at the end of her suspension, Dr. Koskinen would
be required to provide proof of completion of a substance dependence
rehabilitation program, as well as verified, regular attendance with an addiction counselor. And, of course, she'd need to submit to random drug
screening."

"That all makes sense."

The line goes quiet again. "I probably should tell you, Dr. Danvers,
those were only the two complaints that fell under the stipulated agreement."

Holly's neck tenses. "There were others?"

"One other. In my opinion, it was more serious in nature. But the
complainant decided to withdraw it after the charges were already
drawn up."

"Can you talk about it?"

"It's a little unorthodox to discuss, but since charges were drawn up
by the attorney general's office, it is also in the public realm. However,
I have to stress that since the complainant didn't cooperate fully, the allegations are not in any way substantiated."

"I understand," Holly says.

"This client claimed that Dr. Koskinen took her prescription medications from her."

"Took?" Holly gasps. "As in stole?"

"Not exactly. The client claimed that Dr. Koskinen badgered her into stopping—cold turkey, mind you—her daily Xanax that her psychiatrist had been prescribing. And allegedly, Dr. Koskinen convinced the client to bring in the bottles that contained a three-month supply. But later that day, when the client had a change of heart, Dr. Koskinen refused to return the pills to her, insisting she had already disposed of them. And the client further alleged that Dr. Koskinen tried to coerce her into silence."

"Coerce?"

"Apparently, Dr. Koskinen threatened to reveal personal and sensitive information to the client's prescribing doctor if she insisted on telling him what had happened to her medication."

"Liisa was blackmailing her own client?"

"I can't stress enough that these allegations were never substantiated, Dr. Danvers. And they had no bearing on the eventual disciplinary action against Dr. Koskinen."

"But you have no idea why the client retracted her claim?"

"No, I do not."

"Did you believe her, Dr. Pearlman?"

Her pause is confirmation enough for Holly. "It's not my role to speculate," Dr. Pearlman says. "We investigate. And we only proceed if the evidence supports the charges, *and* the complainant wants to go forward."

If Liisa was capable of stealing drugs from a client and then black-mailing her into silence, who knows how far she would go to protect herself? Would murder be too far?

Holly thanks Dr. Pearlman for her time. After she hangs up, she grabs her bag and heads for the door. She waves goodbye to Tanya without stopping to chat and then heads down to the underground garage.

Holly is so lost in her thoughts that she doesn't even notice the object in front of her driver's door until she kicks it with her foot. She kneels down and spots the empty glasses case lying by the front tire. Even before she reaches for the case, she recognizes it: one that she sometimes carries to hold either her corrective lenses or her sunglasses.

Holly's pulse quickens as she unlocks the door and tucks the case back into the side pocket where she always keeps it. She is certain she didn't remove it when she got to work, and there is no way it could have fallen out of the deep side pocket on its own.

Even more alarming, Holly knows that her car automatically locks as soon as she walks away with the key.

CHAPTER 43

The throb in his hip is almost comforting to Simon as he lies in bed and stares up at the light fixture that he has always hated. The brainchild of his eccentric designer, the thing cost tens of thousands of dollars and reminds Simon of a gaudy, mismatched collection of Christmas baubles. He wonders why he hasn't replaced it. Maybe because he doesn't deserve anything better.

Mom was right about me, Simon thinks for the umpteenth time. She never respected him, not once in her entire life. Even after he found worldwide fame with the breakout success of his debut album. Even after he bought his mother her dream home on the Malibu waterfront, one of the last lucid things she ever said to him as she lay dying of lung cancer in that house was: *Life would've been better without you.*

She never even stipulated *her* life. Simply life in general. And it was probably true.

The familiar ding of a new group text pulls Simon from his miserable thoughts. He pats the bed beside him until he finds the phone. Raising it to his face, he glances at a text.

Liisa: I'm out.

While Simon is still trying to figure out what Liisa means, another text pops up below the first.

Liisa: If you're smart, the rest of you will quit, too. She's toxic.

Baljit: Who's toxic?

Liisa: Holly Danvers. She's been manipulating us while she snows us with psychedelics. She's no therapist! We're only pawns in her scheme to get richer and more famous. She's willing to sacrifice all of us for her success.

Simon is confused. Liisa didn't express any such bitterness on their call earlier today. Why does she sound so different now? Did something happen between Liisa and Dr. Danvers since he spoke to her?

Salvador: WTF, LIISA? HAVE YOU BEEN DRINKING?

Liisa: Not my poison. I'm done. Our tribe is done. I'm going away.

Reese: What happened with Dr. Danvers, Liisa? And where are you planning to go?

Simon stares at the screen for several seconds, but Liisa doesn't respond. Another text pops up.

Baljit: When did you turn into such a drama queen, Liisa?

Still no reply.

Salvador: LIISA???

The others in the chat go quiet again, but there's still no response from her.

Reese: She must be offline.

A new group text pops up on the screen. It only includes the other four tribe members, not Liisa.

Salvador: WTF happened between Liisa and Dr. Danvers??

Baljit: Professional jealousy?

Reese: There's got to be more to it.

Simon: I called Liisa earlier. She didn't mention anything about quitting the tribe or blaming Dr. D.

Baljit: Jesus, Simon! Every time you speak to someone in private . . .

Simon: What?

Baljit: Elaine, JJ, and now Liisa . . . Do me a favor and don't ever speak to me outside of a session, OK?

I am toxic, Simon thinks, realizing his mother would have loved Baljit.

Salvador: Ease up there, Maleficent!!

Baljit: What? He's a big boy. And Liisa will be fine. You're probably right. She must've had a few drinks.

Reese: Liisa doesn't drink. Try to keep up.

Baljit: I forgot we had an expert online.

Salvador: JESUS!!

Reese: Did Liisa say what had upset her, Simon?

Simon: No. But she asked me about the day JJ died.

Reese: What about it?

Simon: Whether JJ had mentioned anyone else in the tribe aside from Elaine.

Salvador: WHY? Weird!

Baljit: Did she, Simon?

Simon: No.

Reese: Hold on. Let me see if I can reach Liisa on the phone.

The conversation pauses again while everyone waits.

Reese: Straight to voicemail.

Salvador: Liisa is right! The tribe is DONE!

Baljit: Easy there, Lindsay Lohan. Enough catastrophizing. Why don't we see where we're at in the morning?

Reese: Does anyone know where Liisa lives?

Salvador: Newport. A few blocks from JJ's place.

Baljit: And you know this how?

Salvador: Because I once drove her home when her car was in for service. And unlike you, Ballsack, I care.

Salvador: *Baljit. Damn autocorrect.

Salvador: 😌 😴

Simon laughs for the first time in days.

Reese: Maybe one of us should drop by to check up on Liisa in the morning?

CHAPTER 44

Wednesday, April 24

Holly got to her office early this morning, but she hasn't written a paragraph, let alone finished a few pages for her book as she had intended. Instead, she keeps dwelling on yesterday's events: the revelations about Liisa's professional misconduct, the break-in of her car, and the troubling conversation she had with Aaron last night.

After she discovered the break-in, Holly drove straight over to Aaron's place. But for the first time since Elaine's initial allegation triggered an avalanche of crises, he didn't offer his unconditional support. In fact, Aaron didn't hide his annoyance as he sat beside her at the kitchen counter, twirling his wineglass aggressively by the stem. "For Christ's sake, Holly! Now you think someone's breaking into your car as part of this never-ending patient drama?"

"I didn't drop the glasses case, Aaron."

"Was anything else missing?"

"No. They left my sunglasses. Which makes it even weirder. Like someone was looking for something specific."

He sighed heavily. "Even if someone did break in, why the hell do you immediately assume it has to be related to Liisa or any of your patients?"

"What? Am I supposed to assume it's just another random coincidence?"

"Come on, Holly. This whole thing is beginning to sound a little . . ."

"A little what?"

He eyed her steadily. "Like some conspiracy theory."

She could see his point. Elaine's overdose. JJ's apparent suicide. Liisa's attempt to sabotage the group. And now someone rooting through her car without stealing anything. It would be hard to tie it all together. Unless Liisa was pulling all the strings. "Do you think I'm acting paranoid?"

"I'm not saying that," he grumbled. "But these days, you keep flailing to find one tidy explanation for everything. Life doesn't always work that way."

"Time will tell, I guess."

"Now what?" he grunted. "You go running back to the police?"

"It's been a long day." Holly stood and stepped away from her untouched wineglass on the counter. "Right now, I'm going home."

Holly had intended to stay the night. She was even considering moving back in. But those flashes of the old Aaron—the intolerance, the superiority, the disdain for her work—reminded her of the reasons she left in the first place.

Tanya knocks at the door, snapping her out of the memory. "Simon Lowry is here to see you."

"Simon? He's not on my day sheet, is he?"

"He just showed up," she says, glancing at her watch with concern. "It seems to be becoming a pattern with this group."

"No problem, Tanya," Holly says, still guilt-ridden over her previous session with him. "Please show him in."

Moments later, Simon is seated across from her, fidgeting with his hands and refusing to make eye contact.

"You don't seem yourself this morning, Simon," Holly says. "How can I help?"

"There's just so much shit going on these days," he mutters, still not looking up at her.

"With the tribe?"

He nods. "But it's not just that. I'm also dealing with this . . . um . . . legal situation . . ."

"Kyla?"

His head jerks up, and his eyes lock onto hers. "I told you about her?"

Holly nods. "And her friend, yes."

"It's a shakedown, nothing more!" His expression is almost pleading. "They're jumping on this vulnerable political climate to extort me."

Holly musters a sympathetic nod.

Simon's face crumples, and he suddenly looks very old to her. "I can't remember our last session," he says. "Practically nothing about it. What else did I tell you? I've got to know!"

"Nothing too different from what we've discussed before," Holly says, deliberately easing the blow. "You did touch on your legal challenges with the two young women."

"Shit," he murmurs.

Holly doesn't have the heart to tell him that he also described including her in his bondage fantasies. Instead, she says, "You mentioned JJ, too."

Simon's head twitches. "JJ? What did I say?"

"Just that you two had had a run-in last month after you shared some of your . . . proclivities with her."

He sinks lower into his chair. "That was nothing. I thought we were having a . . . connection. I was only trying to be up-front with JJ."

"It's all right, Simon."

He doesn't say anything for a few seconds. "Why are my memories from that last session so jumbled? That's never happened before with ketamine. Even that time you added in MDMA."

"That's my fault, Simon."

"Your fault? How?"

"You became very distressed. I gave you a sedative, midazolam, at the end of the session to help calm you. But it often causes short-term amnesia."

Simon looks back up at her. For a moment, Holly senses hostility, even hatred, behind his tight stare. But then his face relaxes into a more familiar, affable smile. "You yanked me out of a bad trip. I guess I should probably thank you."

"No, you shouldn't. I had no right to pry while you were on ketamine. It stressed you out. And I'm sorry."

He folds his arms across his chest. "Eh, live and learn."

His body language suggests that he's far less accepting of her explanation than what he is letting on, but Holly feels too sheepish to prod or dig any deeper. "Thank you for understanding."

Simon sighs. "Look, Dr. D, I know you must be disgusted by my . . . how do the French put it? . . . peccadillos."

Holly smiles. "I think that word might be Spanish."

"The point is I've been plagued by these fantasies since I was a kid. The urge to tie women up. To dominate them."

Holly pushes away her discomfort at the thought of him fantasizing about her that same way. "Fantasies aren't always voluntary."

"Right! Exactly. Listen, I'm no shrink, but it has to all go back to my relationship with my mother. That woman raised me single-handedly. But she also resented the fuck out of me. I could never win her approval, let alone her love."

Holly nods. "A repetitive childhood trauma like that could contribute to your sexual predilections. And to addiction. No question."

"Another therapist once told me that my bondage fantasies are related to my very deep insecurity. How I was starved for love and approval as a child. The way he explained it was that basically I physically restrain—trap—the women I'm with for fear they'll otherwise slip away. Metaphorically speaking, to prevent their love from escaping."

The rationale sounds rehearsed to Holly. And in her mind, it's too literal an explanation, not to mention very convenient, for his dark fetishes. But all she says is "There could be a connection, yes."

"But you have to understand," Simon pleads. "It has nothing to do with pain. I'm not a sadist. I've never wanted to hurt anyone."

Holly leans forward. "I believe you, Simon."

"All this work we've done. All this progress I've made under your therapy. Taming those urges that have handcuffed me all this time," he says, seemingly oblivious to the irony of his metaphor. "It's been such a waste."

"Why a waste?"

"I heard from my lawyer this morning. Kyla has upped her demands. On top of millions, she wants a written apology, too. Or she won't sign an NDA." He holds out his palms. "What's the fucking point of an NDA if I sign some kind of confession?"

"Your lawyers will work it out, I'm sure."

"I don't trust them anymore," he grumbles. "I tried to get a second opinion from Reese, but I couldn't reach her yesterday."

"I can't help you, Simon. This is way out of my realm."

He sighs heavily. "It's more than just the accusations. I think Liisa is right. I mean who the fuck are we kidding? The tribe is finished."

A chill runs between Holly's shoulder blades. "Liisa said that?"

He nods. "She texted us all. In a group chat. She said she was dropping out. And she told us to do the same."

"Can I see those texts?"

He hesitates. "Don't think that's the best idea."

She extends a hand toward him. "Simon, please," she says in a firm tone. "I *need* to see this conversation."

After a moment, Simon digs his phone from his pocket, taps on the screen a few times, and then, with obvious reluctance, hands it over to Holly.

Holly scans the text chain on the screen. Her chest burns as she reads words such as "toxic," "scheme," and "sacrifice," which Liisa used to describe Holly's intentions.

She scrolls down below the point in the chat where Liisa announced she was leaving, but there are no more texts from her.

At the bottom of the text chain, Holly spots a message from Salvador that was sent at 7:22 this morning. *I stopped by Liisa's townhouse on my way to the studio. Totally dark. And her car wasn't out front.*

Baljit replied: *Wonder if she's flown the coop.*

"I think she's gone," Holly mutters, more to herself than Simon.

Simon eases his phone out of her hand. "Liisa told me she was going to miss some upcoming sessions. Conflicts or something?" He frowns. "Maybe she'd already planned a trip?"

"You spoke to Liisa?" Holly motions to his phone. "After those group texts?"

"No. Before. Earlier in the day. But man, was she singing a different tune. She didn't seem angry. She certainly never mentioned anything
about you being . . ."

"Toxic?"

"Yeah."

She's definitely gone.

CHAPTER 45

Holly finds herself back inside the same cramped interview room at the Newport Beach police station, sitting across from Detective Rivers, whose light-blue shirt sets off his ochre skin tone.

He jots notes with the same pen as before while Holly describes the incident involving her car. "What type of car do you drive, Dr. Danvers?"

"A BMW X3."

He nods. "And you had the electronic key in your possession the whole time?"

"Not on me," she says. "But it would've been in my purse, yes."

"What about the backup key?"

"It's at home somewhere, I think."

He looks up from his notebook. "If the doors were locked, then either someone would've had to use one of your keys or a fairly sophisticated relay system to open it."

"A relay system?"

"Basically, a hacking device that amplifies or relays the signal from the electronic key to another device near the car, allowing it to open the door remotely."

"That doesn't sound like some bored teen looking for loose change."

"No, it doesn't." Rivers taps his pen on the pad. He offers her a sympathetic smile. "But there's not much I can do. This apparent break-in happened at your office in Laguna, and I have no jurisdiction there."

"Even if it were connected to JJ's death?"

He eyes her skeptically. "Connected?"

Holly wavers. She still feels conflicted about sharing the name of a living client with the detective, but if Liisa has fled, then the detective needs to know. "As a psychiatrist, I have a duty to report if I have concerns that a client's life might be in danger."

"Yes, you do," he says. "Which client?"

"Dr. Liisa Koskinen."

He jots the name down, confirming the spelling. "But what does this have to do with your car?"

"Maybe nothing."

"OK, what makes you believe Dr. Koskinen's life is in danger?"

"Believe might be too strong a word," Holly says, wondering when it comes to Liisa if the threat is more suicidal or homicidal in nature. "I couldn't find her this morning. And no one seems to know where she went. I'm concerned."

"Is Dr. Koskinen a Newport resident?"

"She is. I went by her place on my way here. There was no answer. And her car was gone."

"Can we backtrack a little? Why would Dr. Koskinen's life be in danger?"

"Liisa is in . . . turmoil. Both professionally and personally." Holly's stomach twists, hearing herself divulge private information on a client. "She is—or at least was—a member of the same therapy group as JJ and Elaine."

The detective's eyebrow shoots up. "Another one?"

Holly nods.

"Does Dr. Koskinen also suffer from addiction?"

"Yes. Xanax." Holly hesitates. "But I only recently learned she'd also been hiding other secrets."

"Can you be more specific, Dr. Danvers?"

Holly tells him about the misconduct complaints with the California Board of Psychology, stressing that all of the information is already in the public realm. "Also, I just found out that Liisa was trying to convince other women in the group that I'd been molesting them, too."

He angles his head. "Too?"

Holly swallows. "I should've told you sooner, Detective. But Elaine—who was sexually abused as a child—misinterpreted an incident with me while under ketamine." And she goes on to summarize her allegations.

He eyes her steadily. "And you think Dr. Koskinen planted the suggestion with Ms. Golding that you were abusing her?"

"Not necessarily. But Liisa certainly capitalized on it. Turns out she has resented me all along. And at that point, when Elaine first accused me, Liisa was the only member who hadn't reached sobriety. She was more bitter about it than I realized. I think she wanted to sabotage me and, by extension, the whole group."

Rivers is quiet for a few moments. "Sounds like a complicated group," he finally says.

Holly can only sigh.

He lowers his pen. "Dr. Koskinen's behavior does sound erratic. But do you think she would go as far as to stage the deaths of two others?"

"I have no idea, Detective Rivers. Truly. But I've always struggled to believe that both my clients took their own lives. It never added up with their clinical presentations. And now I find out that Liisa—as vindictive and damaged as she is—was trying to manipulate Elaine and others behind the scenes. And I think JJ knew about it, too."

He frowns. "Would that be motive enough to kill them?"

"I know how this sounds, Detective. I can't explain it. Maybe something backfired between Liisa and Elaine? Or maybe Elaine really did overdose and JJ threatened to expose Liisa for pushing her into it? And then Liisa got rid of JJ." She sighs. "Who knows? But clearly, Liisa has a history of suspect behavior. If she's capable of stealing pills from a client and trying to blackmail her into silence, then it's hard to imagine a line she wouldn't cross."

Inwardly, Holly cringes. She's one to talk, having already proven herself capable of vaping DMT in her own office and of interrogating her clients while they're medicated. *What lines am I not willing to cross?*

The detective's face is as impassive as ever, but his tone takes on a slight edge when he asks, "Is there anything else you've neglected to share with me?"

"I don't think so, no."

He nods. "Obviously, I don't need to tell you how erratic and impulsive addicts can be. But to go to this extent? Hard to imagine anyone constructing such an elaborate conspiracy simply to cover their tracks."

There it is again. *Conspiracy.* The word grates after the way Aaron already turned it against her. "Even if Liisa had nothing to do with either death, it still concerns me that she would disappear in her current state of mind. In my professional opinion, she is not stable or safe."

"I suppose that's true," Rivers says as he rises from his chair. "I'll see if I can track her down."

CHAPTER 46

Aaron sits on the couch and stares into the bottom of his empty tumbler of scotch, wondering whether or not to pour himself a second glass. He hasn't heard from Holly since she walked out on him yesterday evening, carrying the overnight bag that she had arrived with less than thirty minutes before.

He realizes his bluntness and lack of sympathy drove her away, but he couldn't help himself. Why does she always insist on trying to connect everything? The situation is bad enough as is.

Then again, what else could he expect from her?

Holly's intransigence has been the bane of their relationship. It led to their first fight, which happened before they were even romantically involved, while Holly was still a junior resident in psychiatry. She had admitted a violent patient from the ER, a biker who was suffering from crystal meth–related psychosis. Despite Aaron's strong warning against it, Holly had insisted on releasing the patient from his four-point restraints, claiming the man had calmed enough, and that it would be cruel to keep him bound any longer. As soon as the patient was freed, he tried to smash down a door with a chair. It took three security guards—one of whom ended up with a broken nose—to subdue him. Despite Holly's remorse over the incident, the experience had taught her little. Her obstinance led to further mistakes during her residency and early in her practice. If anything, she is even more stubborn now. And she has never been able to leave well enough alone.

Just as Aaron gets up to refill his glass, the door opens, and Graham trudges into the living room wearing a deep scowl.

Aaron steps over to the counter and pours himself another glass of scotch before asking, "What happened, Graham?"

"Those fuckers canned me."

Aaron takes a slow breath. "Why?"

Graham helps himself to a beer from the kitchen fridge. "Some bullshit about my attendance. But I have zero doubt Hassan got me fired. That little prick has been up my ass since day one."

"What about your attendance?"

"I'm not working an assembly line, Dad. I took a couple afternoons off. What do they care? I got my work done on time."

"Why are you taking time off in the middle of the day from a new job?"

"I had shit to do, OK?" Graham grumbles. "Little did I know that Hassan was just waiting to rat me out."

Aaron rubs his temples. "It was going to be different this time, remember?"

"Yeah, yeah, I get it, Dad. I'm a habitual fuckup. There's no hope for me." But his tone sounds bored, not repentant.

"What do you think, Graham?"

He takes a long swig from the bottle. "About what?"

"Are you aware how deliberate your self-sabotage is?"

"And are you aware that things don't come as easily to me as they do to the Golden Boy, Nate?"

"Constantly."

"Yeah, well, then cut me some slack."

"Which is what I've been doing your whole life," Aaron says. "Always giving you the benefit of the doubt. Always bailing you out. But who's it helping? It's not a safety net, is it? It's more like a web that's keeping you trapped."

Graham's eyes narrow with a flicker of concern. "What does that mean?"

"It's time I cut you off, Graham. After this month, I won't pay your rent anymore. And I'm canceling your credit card."

"What kind of bullshit—"

"I can't keep reinforcing your self-destructive behavior."

"You're abandoning me?" Graham glares at him. "Your own son?"

"I'm doing this *for* you."

"Bullshit!" he cries. "You want to talk about reinforcing behavior? You let that wife of yours walk over you like a doormat."

"This is about you, Graham. No one else."

But Graham ignores him. "You let her humiliate you. Constantly. You dote on her when she needs something and then ignore the tire tracks she leaves across your back on her way out the door." He lays a hand across his own chest. "And all the while, she just keeps poisoning you against me."

The words sting more than Aaron is willing to let on. Holly does have a habit of loving and leaving, but all he says is "You'd be surprised how little thought Holly gives you, Graham. There's so much you don't understand."

"Oh, I understand plenty. Her patients are dropping like flies. And what do you do? You help her dispose of the bodies."

Aaron shakes a finger at the door. "It's time for you to leave."

Graham pivots and stomps to the door. He looks back over his shoulder, his lip curled into a sneer. "Did it ever occur to you that she might be the one killing them?"

CHAPTER 47

Thursday, April 25

Holly is clear with Walter as soon as she steps into his home. "I didn't come to talk this morning," she says as she wraps his bony frame in a gentle hug.

"You prefer semaphore now?" he asks as soon as they separate, moving his arms as if using imaginary flags to communicate.

She grins. "I mean I'm not here for heavy discussions about death. Or divorce. Or professional disgrace." What she doesn't say is that his proximity alone is enough to make her feel more grounded. Safer.

But Walter's spark is back, and he isn't willing to leave it at that. "Don't be boring, Koala. I can talk about the weather with the few nearly dead friends I have left. Tell me what's going on with this volatile tribe of yours. And the police investigation."

Holly provides a sanitized update. She leaves out any mention of having questioned her clients while under the influence of ketamine, wondering if she's doing so more to protect his feelings or to shield herself from his disappointment.

After she finishes, Walter stares in disbelief. "This psychologist was blackmailing her own patients?"

"Apparently."

"You could probably stand to tighten your client-vetting process a notch or two."

Holly can only laugh. "No kidding. It never occurred to me to look into Liisa's background."

"What do the police think?"

"I haven't heard from the detective since I left his office yesterday. To be honest, I get the feeling he's sick of me and my off-the-wall theories."

"Are they? Off-the-wall?"

She sighs. "Aaron seems to think so."

"Does his opinion matter that much?"

"It does to me, Papa. Yes."

"You've always known your own mind. Since you were this tall." He levels a hand with the height of the table. "What do *you* think, Koala?"

"Look, it could all be unrelated."

He eyes her without comment.

"An opioid user relapses and overdoses," she continues. "That happens all the time. An alcoholic falls off the wagon, gets incredibly drunk, and rashly decides to jump off her balcony. She certainly wouldn't be the first. And an unethical psychologist takes her bitterness and jealousy over her professional downfall out on another colleague by trying to prejudice a few patients. That one actually makes some twisted sense."

Walter views her for a long moment. "All in the same group. Do you believe in coincidences that large?"

Holly shakes her head.

"Neither do I, Holly. So what are you going to do?"

"What can I do?"

"Look for a better explanation."

She nods.

Walter sips his tea. "Can I ask you something?"

She can tell by the quietness of his voice that he is feeling vulnerable. "Of course, Papa. Anything."

"This group . . . all the tragedy and adverse outcomes . . . do you believe the psychedelics are to blame?"

Holly has wondered the same recently. But she knows it would contradict all the data that has been accumulated for decades on the effects of psychedelics. "This group consisted of seven highly accomplished people. But all of them are—were—addicts, deeply scarred by personal traumas. And each of them had been hiding secrets for years. Essentially, their whole lives have been facades. Ready to topple at any moment." She pauses. "No. I don't blame the psychedelics. Not directly, anyway."

He tilts his head. "What does that mean? 'Not directly.'"

"I think the buried traumas and memories that have surfaced during therapy have affected their states of mind. But blaming psychedelics would be like blaming the ocean for the rocks that appear at low tide."

He grunts. "Then again, those rocks would stay buried forever if not for the tide."

She shakes her head. "Honestly, I think it's the group itself. Not the medication. Getting the seven of them together has somehow created a very . . . combustible environment."

Walter accepts her theory with a shrug.

They sit in silence for a few moments, until Holly's phone rings. She glances at the screen and sees that the call comes from her office line. She raises the phone to her ear. "Hi, Tanya."

"Sorry to bother you, Holly," her assistant says. "But I have Liisa Koskinen's daughter, Kimberly, on the other line. She insists on speaking to you."

Holly's heart skips a beat. "Of course, patch her through, please."

"Dr. Danvers?" Kimberly asks in a voice that is similar to but higher pitched than her mother's.

"Speaking. Hello, Kimberly."

"Do you know where my mom is?"

"I . . . I haven't seen her in a few days. Why do you—"

"She was supposed to come here yesterday, but she canceled last minute."

"Where is 'here,' Kimberly?"

"San Diego. I'm a senior at UC San Diego. Mom always drives down on the day of my infusion."

"Infusion? I'm not following you."

"For my Crohn's disease. I get an intravenous infusion every six weeks. But sometimes I react to it. Not to be gross, but like puking and gut rot. Mom usually stays the night with me."

"I see," Holly says, wondering why Liisa never mentioned anything about her daughter's illness. "Did your mother tell you about me, Kimberly?"

"She said you were helping her. That she'd gotten off the Xanax thanks to your therapy."

"She did?" Holly can't hide her surprise. None of it squares with her impression of Liisa as a woman driven by grievance and bitterness. "Did your mom call to tell you she wasn't coming?"

"She texted." Kimberly sighs. "I'm really worried, Dr. Danvers."

Holly grips her phone tighter. "Why?"

"It was a weird couple texts. And now she's not answering my calls. Which isn't like her."

"Did your mom say why she couldn't make it?"

"No. Only that she had something urgent to do."

"Urgent?"

"Yeah. And then she texted to say she wouldn't be reachable for a while."

"Did she say why?"

"No. Her last text simply said . . . 'I'm sorry, Kimmie. I love you.'" Her voice catches. "She hasn't replied to any of my texts since."

Holly feels cold invisible fingers wrap around her neck. "That was yesterday?"

"Yeah, in the early evening." Kimberly's pitch rises. "In the text, she called me Kimmie, Dr. Danvers!"

"She doesn't usually?"

"All the time. Except when she has something serious to tell me. Then she always calls me Kimberly. And Dr. Danvers?"

"Yes?"

"Mom has never once texted to say that she loves me." Holly can hear Kimberly swallow. "It just . . . didn't sound like her."

CHAPTER 48

As Holly steps into her office after lunch, she's surprised to see Detective Rivers, dressed in a sleek gray suit and royal-blue tie, standing at the desk and chatting with Tanya. She can tell by the flush in her assistant's cheeks, which only deepens at the sight of Holly, that Tanya is likely crushing on the attractive detective.

He turns to face Holly. "Dr. Danvers, hello. Do you have a moment?"

"Absolutely. In fact, I was about to reach out to you." She points down the hallway. "Why don't we speak in my office?"

"Yes, please," he says in a friendly tone, but his smile seems pinched.

After they're seated across from each other in the interview chairs, Holly asks, "Have you found Liisa yet?"

"Not yet. No. But I did speak to her daughter."

"Me, too. In fact, I encouraged Kimberly to get in touch with you."

"Thank you for that." His expression is unreadable.

"Kimberly told you about her mother and those texts? How she doesn't believe her mom even wrote them."

"She did."

Holly is growing impatient with his poker face. "What do you make of it?"

He flattens a tiny crease in his pant leg. "It's unusual. For sure. But it's a stretch to jump to the conclusion that someone else wrote those texts."

"How else do you explain it?"

"Maybe Dr. Koskinen meant it as a goodbye to her daughter?"

Holly shakes her head. "But Kimberly said it didn't even sound like her. And everything I know about Liisa tells me she's driven by a strong survival instinct."

He only shrugs.

"But you're not discounting the possibility someone else could be using her phone?" she asks.

"I'm not discounting anything."

"Listen, Detective, if someone has her phone . . . they might also have Liisa."

"Or maybe Dr. Koskinen doesn't want to be found?"

Holly squeezes the armrest in frustration. "Even if she took off on her own, her behavior is worrisome, isn't it?"

"Unusual, yes."

"What then?" Holly snaps. "You're just going to wait and see if she surfaces or not?"

Rivers pulls his phone out of his jacket pocket and consults the screen. "Dr. Koskinen is in Monterey," he says. "At least that's where she was when she sent her daughter those texts last night."

"Monterey? That's where Liisa grew up," Holly says. "But she told me her family had all left."

"Maybe she still has friends there from childhood? We tracked her phone there. But the signal has been intermittent."

"How do you explain that?"

"She has kept it off most of the time. Or at least not connected to a WiFi or cell signal."

Holly's gut churns. "That's odd, isn't it?"

"Maybe, but not necessarily criminal." He looks down at his phone. "I was also able to access her credit card records. She filled her car up yesterday outside Carmel. And then she paid for an Uber Eats delivery last night at a condo in Monterey."

"Then you do know where she is!"

He shakes his head. "Where she *was*. I spoke to the owner of the condo. It was rented through Airbnb, but Dr. Koskinen had already checked out by the time I reached the landlord this morning."

"Did he see her leave?" Holly demands.

"No. He never met her. It was all done online via a remote key code entry for the door."

"And there's been no trace of her since?"

"Not electronically, no."

"This isn't good, Detective. Either Liisa has been abducted, and someone is impersonating her, or she is on the run. Which makes her behavior look particularly suspect with respect to Elaine and JJ."

He tilts his head side to side.

"Are you going to put out one of those BOLO alerts?" she demands.

"We don't have enough for that," he says. "But we have opened a missing person's file."

"And what good will that do?"

"For starters, it's already allowed me to access her electronic trail. It will also feed her information out to other police departments across the state. And to the public, through our department's social media channels."

Holly scoffs. "You think she'll be found via Facebook?"

Rivers stares at her for a few seconds. "If Dr. Koskinen did disappear after leaving your office . . . then you might have been the last known person to have seen her." He pauses. "Weren't you also the last person to have seen Ms. Golding?"

"Elaine had been dead for hours when I got there." She narrows her gaze. "What are you suggesting?"

"Only that the timing is coincidental," he says. "Two unusual deaths in your practice. And then the person you think might somehow be responsible vanishes almost as soon as you report her."

She gapes at him. "You think I'm involved in this, Detective?"

"You are involved, Dr. Danvers. One way or another. This all started with Ms. Golding's allegations against you."

"I . . . I was the one who came to you," she sputters. "Concerned something wasn't right."

"I know. And as I keep reminding you, it's too early to conclude any-thing." He shows her another tight smile and then raises his phone again. "I also got a copy of Dr. Koskinen's cell phone records."

"And?"

"She hasn't made many calls in the last few weeks. And most of the ones she did place were to her daughter and unlisted numbers. But then, two days ago, she did make a call that might interest you."

"Why's that?"

He glances down at his phone and recites a phone number.

Holly's veins turn to ice. The invisible grip around her neck feels like a chokehold.

The detective looks back up at her. "Do you have any idea why Dr. Koskinen would've been calling your husband's office?"

CHAPTER 49

Simon doesn't even read the contract as he swipes his finger across the screen to sign it electronically. His lawyer assured him that the nondisclosure agreement with Kyla is as airtight as the previous one, though it's going to cost Simon an extra five hundred thousand to forgo the written apology that she had been demanding. That doesn't matter to him. He has more money than he will ever want or need. And besides, he has no family or loved ones to spend it on or leave it to. What the hell? Why not support these parasites in a lifestyle that would've otherwise been completely foreign to them?

While Simon feels relieved that Kyla now poses less of a threat to him, he can't say the same for Dr. Danvers. That last ketamine session still eats at him. He can't shake the feeling that Dr. Danvers didn't share everything he had disclosed to her. And he doesn't understand why she felt the need to erase his memory of it.

Moments after he emails the signed contract back to his lawyer, a group text pops up on his screen.

Salvador: CAN YOU FUCKING BELIEVE THIS?!?

Attached to the text is a link to a tweet from the Newport Beach Police Department. "#Missing. Newport resident, Dr. Liisa Koskinen.

Age forty-eight. Last reported in Monterey yesterday." It went on to list the department's contact details and included a photo of Liisa. She is as unsmiling as ever in the shot, but her hair is longer. Simon can't tell if it was taken in the last year or over a decade ago.

Simon: Why Monterey?

Baljit: That's the part that concerns you?!

Salvador: IS LIISA DEAD, TOO????

Reese: Why would you jump to that conclusion?

Baljit: Because clearly we've become the cast of some cheap Agatha Christie knockoff!

Baljit: And then there were four! ☠

Reese: How is that helping??

Simon: Maybe Liisa is a suspect in Elaine's or JJ's death?

Reese: Why would you suggest that?

Simon: A detective came to see me after JJ's death. Then, when I saw Dr. D last time, she got all bent out of shape about the texts Liisa sent us before she went dark.

Salvador: Liisa did say she was going away!!

Baljit: But she never mentioned anything about faking her own death or whatever the fuck this #missing tweet is about.

Reese: Maybe Simon's right? Maybe the police are looking for Liisa in connection with what happened to JJ or Elaine?

Baljit: There's only one common denominator here: Dr. Danvers. Her patients. Her therapy.

Salvador: Dr. Danvers?? You think she's behind this?!

Baljit: With this group of fuckups? All the weird bullshit? Nothing's out of the question.

Simon can't help but think of his last ketamine session again.

Simon: Did Dr. D give any of you that midazolam along with the ketamine?

Baljit: The stuff she gave Elaine? For panic attacks?

Simon: I've never had a panic attack in my life. But Dr. D pumped me full of that crap during my last session. Wiped my memory clean.

Reese: Why?

Simon: She said I was having a bad trip. She told me it was her fault, too. For pressing me too hard. But I don't remember shit from our actual session.

Reese: Nothing?

Simon: I feel like she was grilling me about the tribe.

Reese: What kind of questions?

Simon: Don't remember.

Baljit: Of course not. Why would you become helpful at this point, Simon?

Salvador: Put the broom away, Baljit!

Salvador: Liisa will turn up. And I 110% guarantee she is no killer! Same goes for Dr. Danvers!

Reese: Let's hope you're right, Salvador.

The text chain goes quiet. But the change in the group dynamic is palpable. No one seems certain of anything, least of all Simon. None of them know whom to trust. And no one is talking about restarting ketamine therapy.

Even though Baljit's joke was tasteless and totally on point for her, Simon wonders if she might be right about Liisa. Maybe there are only four of them left now? And if so, will it end there?

CHAPTER 50

Holly hasn't eaten all day, but whatever appetite she brought with her to the restaurant vanishes the moment she spots Aaron sitting at their usual table on the far side of the deck. She can tell from his light-blue blazer, his favorite jacket, that Aaron must have assumed she meant tonight to be a date night. She didn't. Holly only chose this spot because it's a safe and public venue.

Aaron stands up and pulls back her chair as she approaches. She forces an over-the-shoulder smile as she allows him to slide the chair back under her.

"This is an unexpected treat," he says as he sits down beside her.

"It's a nice night," she says, but the starry sky and the lit boats and yachts dotting the water hardly even register with her. She wonders if she is going to be able to fake her way through enough small talk to get him off his guard.

"How do you feel about white?" Aaron says, offering her the wine list.

She holds up a palm. "I trust you." But nothing could be further from the truth.

"I feel empowered," he says with a chuckle, as he puts on his reading glasses and consults the list. "I know just the one."

With glasses on and a full head of salt-and-pepper hair, Aaron is still handsome in the professorial way that had originally drawn her to him. But all she feels now is queasiness in his company.

As if sensing her underlying emotion, Aaron lowers the list to the table and stares at her apologetically. "I am sorry, Holl. I really am."

"Oh? What for?"

"Hurting you."

It takes all her restraint to keep her tone in check. "When did you hurt me, Aaron?"

"Last time you came over. I was awful. After everything you'd been through with Liisa. Not to mention the others in the group. What you needed was a sympathetic ear, not a condescending lecture from a pompous ass like me. I was tired. And Graham has this crazy idea that . . . It doesn't matter." He shows her a contrite smile. "Any chance you'd be willing to give me a do-over?"

Aaron sounds so sincere that any other time Holly might have been moved to forgiveness. Not tonight. "Remind me, Aaron. When was the last time you worked with Liisa?"

"When she was my student. Must've been fifteen years ago. Maybe twenty."

"And you haven't seen her since?"

He shrugs. "Not that I can recall, no."

"Not even a phone call?"

"No, no phone calls." His smile fades, replaced by a look of suspicion. "What am I missing here?"

"It's probably nothing." Holly buries her face in her menu.

He gently pushes it down. "It doesn't sound like nothing."

"Liisa is missing," she says matter-of-factly.

He cocks his head. "As in missing her appointments?"

"She has been listed by Newport Police as a missing person." She meets his bewildered stare. "And because of that, the police got access to her phone records."

Aaron nods. "Were they able to track her through GPS or whatever?"

"Her last known location was in Monterey. Where she grew up. But her phone has gone dark. And they don't know where she is now."

"And you think this is somehow related to the deaths in the group?"

She ignores the question. "The police also got access to her calling history."

He leans forward, expectantly. "And?"

"Coincidentally—or not—one of the last phone calls she placed was to your office."

Aaron chuckles. "Of course. Why wouldn't she call me?"

She views him stone-faced. "Liisa called your office the day she disappeared."

His eyes go wide and his nostrils flare. "She absolutely did not!"

Holly folds her arms across her chest. "It was there in black-and-white. Liisa also placed several calls to unlisted numbers. I assume some of those were to your cell phone. A burner phone, maybe?"

"Nonsense!" He taps the table aggressively with his finger. "I haven't spoken to Liisa Koskinen in fifteen years."

"Then how do you explain it?"

"When did this supposed call happen?"

"The day before yesterday. In the early afternoon."

"Tuesday! My hospital teaching day!" he trumpets. "My assistant, Amy, isn't even in the office on Tuesdays. And how long did the call last?"

"Less than a minute," she concedes.

"Because it would have gone straight to voicemail. And I promise you, if Liisa did call, she sure as hell didn't leave a message. Amy would've told me."

"Why would Liisa even try to call you?"

"How should I know? I have no idea what any of this has to do with me."

Neither Aaron's voice nor his body language suggests he's hiding anything. His outrage comes across as genuine. But then again, she reminds herself, as a seasoned therapist, he would know how to feign sincerity better than most.

"A quick Google search would've told Liisa I was your husband," he continues. "It was in all the articles. Maybe, in desperation, she thought she could reach you through me?"

"Reach me for what, Aaron? Liisa and I had just spoken that morning."

"But you told me she stormed out. Distraught. Maybe after she calmed down—"

"What? She thought the best way to reach me was through my husband, whom she hadn't spoken to in fifteen-plus years?"

"I can't explain it, Holly. I didn't even know about this call until now." He squeezes the bridge of his nose. "But I suppose it explains why that detective was looking for me earlier."

"Detective Rivers?"

"I think so, yes."

"When was this?"

"Around five-ish. I got a message from Amy. I just assumed it had to be about Graham." Aaron laughs bitterly. "I was going to call him back in the morning."

Of course, Aaron would assume the detective was calling about Graham, but Holly doesn't say anything.

"I didn't want it to ruin tonight, Holl."

She doesn't know what to think. But she isn't ready to take him at his word, either. He has always had that effect on her—the ability to sow doubt when she thought her mind was already made up. She rises from the table. "I need a little time and space to think."

He doesn't get up. "Space," he mutters. "You always use that word when you're running away from me. From us."

Holly is unmoved. "Do you have any idea how sketchy this all sounds? My client—who might be abducted, on the run, or even dead—calls my husband's office only hours before she disappears?"

"Did it occur to you that maybe that's exactly what Liisa wanted? To make it look like I'm somehow involved."

"If so, she did a damn good job."

He looks up at her with pained eyes. "Why can't you just trust me?"

"I . . ." Holly spins away and hurries out of the restaurant. She doesn't stop until she reaches the traffic light on the corner. She glances over her shoulder, but Aaron is nowhere to be seen.

As she walks along the side street to her parking spot, she reviews their conversation in her head. She wants to believe Aaron, but she can't risk doing so blindly. Not with such a huge unexplained coincidence like Liisa's call to his office hanging over them.

As Holly reaches her car, she hears a noise and turns toward it. She can't see much in the weak glow of the streetlights, but she hears what sounds like the rapid patter of footfalls. She thrusts a hand in her bag and fumbles to find the small can of pepper spray that she always carries. But the footsteps fade away.

Holly hurls herself into her car and slams the door shut, locking it immediately. Her hands shake as she yanks the car in gear and jerks it away from the curb.

Am I being paranoid?

She realizes there could be multiple harmless explanations for what she just heard. But she can't help thinking of the glasses case she found lying outside her car door. And she remembers how Detective Rivers said that whoever broke into her car would have either used a sophisticated tracking device or one of Holly's own keys.

Her hands freeze on the wheel.

I left my backup key at Aaron's when I moved out.

CHAPTER 51

Friday, April 26

"Where's Salvador?" Baljit demands, as she strides past Simon and into his house, clasping an aluminum mug that wafts the scent of espresso behind it.

"Didn't you see the group text?" Reese asks from the chair where she has been sitting since she arrived five minutes earlier.

"Nope," Baljit says. "I decided not to read the obits today."

"Does everything have to be a cruel joke with you?" Reese snaps.

"Enough, you two!" Simon has to stop himself from adding a comment about catfights. Just the idea makes him imagine the two of them leashed and oiled up. But he forces the invasive fantasy out of mind. "Salvador said he had a work emergency."

Baljit plunks herself down on a chair across from Reese. "An emergency for a fashion designer? That's a thing?"

Reese shrugs. "Maybe he's just scared of being anywhere near the rest of us."

"Can you blame him?" Baljit asks.

It's hard to argue Baljit's point. Especially when Simon considers that, according to the Newport Beach Police Department's Twitter feed, Liisa is still missing.

Reese looks from Simon to Baljit and back. "Maybe we should go speak to that detective who came to see you, Simon?"

Baljit grimaces. "And tell him what?"

"What we know about Liisa," Reese says.

"Like what?"

"Among other things, like how she suggested that Dr. Danvers might have molested me, too, while I was under ketamine."

"Not you, too?" Baljit squints at her. "She pulled that same crap on me!"

"You serious?" Simon groans. "Liisa was deliberately spreading false rumors about Dr. D?"

"She must have tried to plant that seed with all the women in the group," Reese says. "Who knows if Elaine would've ever gone down that rabbit hole without Liisa's encouragement?"

"Why would Liisa be stirring all this shit up?" Simon asks, but he's really thinking of the two women who just extorted a king's ransom out of him.

"Jealousy?" Reese shrugs. "Two therapists. One's a Xanax addict, the other's famous for her successful treatment program. Maybe Liisa was envious?"

"Then why sign up for therapy with Dr. D in the first place?" Simon asks.

"To undermine it?" Reese suggests.

"That's your theory?" Baljit rolls her eyes. "First, Liisa talks Elaine into thinking she was molested. But then Elaine overdoses—or someone does it for her—before she can 'expose' Dr. Danvers. You can't pin that on Liisa. Why would she kill the one person who was going to take down her nemesis? Besides, how do you explain JJ?"

"Liisa's an experienced therapist," Reese argues. "She would know exactly what buttons to push. Maybe she got JJ drinking again. And then convinced her to jump."

Baljit scowls. "And then Liisa just what? Fakes her own death and disappears? That makes no sense, Counselor. God, I hope you don't practice criminal law."

Simon, sensing Armageddon, leans back and waits for Reese's response.

"Do you have a better theory?" Reese asks calmly.

"All I know is that Dr. Danvers assembled this group," Baljit says. "She heavily medicated us to the point where some of us don't even remember some of the sessions. And then the deaths and disappearances began."

Simon turns to Baljit. "You're saying that Dr. D has been manipulating us all?"

She holds up both palms. "Who knows? I was only trying to stop gambling. I never signed up for the rest of this snake pit."

"Why don't we at least talk to Dr. Danvers?" Reese suggests.

Baljit frowns. "Do you still trust her?"

"I do," Reese says without hesitation.

"Do you?" Baljit asks Simon.

Simon mulls the question over. Dr. Danvers has helped him. A lot. Maybe more than anyone else since Jeremy. But he also can't forget what she did to him at their previous session, adding that sedative on top of the ketamine. "Not sure I do anymore. Dr. D basically roofied me the last time I saw her. Why would she do that if she has nothing to hide?"

"Fine," Reese says. "I'll speak to her myself."

They lapse into morbid silence for a few moments. Simon considers again how effective that combination of medications had been in smudging his memory—and how useful it could be under different circumstances.

"I'm not sure I'll be able to do it without her," Baljit finally murmurs, her head hung, and her eyes glued to the floor.

"Do what?" Reese asks.

Baljit looks back up at them with uncharacteristic vulnerability. "Stay out of the casino."

Reese shows her a small smile. "Took all my willpower not to stop at the liquor store on my way home from work last night."

Simon nods. "Yeah, my . . . urges are coming back, too."

"What a sorry lot we are." Baljit chuckles grimly. "We can't live without her. But no guarantees we'll live at all if we stick with her."

CHAPTER 52

"Papa?" Holly calls out from his doorway but gets no answer.

She became concerned when he didn't answer her last two calls. Now her worry only grows as she moves from the kitchen to the office without spotting Walter. There's a bowl with remnants of granola on the counter.

Has he fallen somewhere?

She rushes out the back door and into the garden. It's not until she hurries past the flower beds and around the corner of the house that she spots Walter at the far edge of the hedge. Wearing a white undershirt and old jeans, he is stooped over, pruning the bushes with a pair of shears.

"Papa!" she calls. "What happened to your gardeners?"

"Hello, Koala." Walter struggles to cut another twig off one of the bushes before he turns to her. "This? This isn't gardening. It's therapy."

She chuckles with relief. "Sure looks like gardening from where I'm standing."

"The professionals are coming soon. I hope. They never tell me. But it's vital to prune back the junipers and the yews at this time of year. Helps with new growth."

Holly extends a hand to him. "How about you take a break and let me have a little therapy?"

"I'm never one to turn down free help," he says, as he hands her the shears and then carefully lowers himself onto the portable chair that he set up beside the shrub.

Holly opens the blades over a bushy branch and clips the twigs and leaves. She trims a little more before she says, "I'm not sure if I can trust Aaron."

Walter chuckles. "Why didn't we have this conversation ten years ago?"

"No, not as a husband," she says as she continues to prune while speaking over her shoulder. "I found out yesterday that Liisa called his office on the day she disappeared."

"The psychologist?"

"Yup. The one who was trying to sabotage my group from the inside, trying to convince the other women that I might have molested them under ketamine. And now Liisa is missing."

"This group of yours." He groans. "And why would Liisa call your husband?"

"No idea. When I confronted him, Aaron claimed he didn't speak to her. That he wasn't even aware she called."

"And what do you believe?"

Holly cuts aggressively at a thicker branch, satisfied by the crisp snap it makes before it topples to the ground beside her foot. "Aaron taught Liisa years ago. He thinks she might have deliberately reached out to him through his office number, knowing the call would be traced."

"That's not what I asked."

"Honestly, at this point, I don't trust my intuition. That's why I've come to you." She lowers the shears and turns to face him. "There's something else, too. Remember how someone broke into my car?"

"The wandering glasses case, right?"

She nods. "Whoever did it probably used a key. I had mine with me the whole time. But I remember now that I left my spare key at Aaron's when I moved out."

The wrinkles around Walter's eyes crease so deeply that his eyes turn to slits. "Why would Aaron break into your car?"

"Good question." She sighs. "Besides, he wasn't the only one with access. His son has free rein of the house, too."

"Oh. The problem child."

"I wouldn't put it past Graham at all. He's toxic. Always looking for an angle. Always looking for someone else to blame for his personal failings."

"Have you gone to the police?"

She nods. "Detective Rivers was the one who told me about Liisa's phone call to Aaron's office."

Walter's intense blue eyes fix on her for a long silent moment. "No," he finally says.

"No what?"

"I don't think you can trust Aaron."

She sighs. "Me, neither."

"Time for a tea break," Walter says as he pushes himself to his feet and turns toward the house.

"I could use a little more 'therapy,'" Holly says, focusing her attention back on the shrub. "But I'll join you soon."

Holly trims more leaves and branches, moving from bush to bush. She gets so lost in the chore that when she finally stops to consult her watch, she realizes that if she doesn't hurry, she will be late for her first appointment of the morning.

In the light traffic, she reaches her office in under fifteen minutes and enters through the main door. Her first client of the day—Howard, a meek, balding man with a debilitating obsessive-compulsive disorder—is already seated in the waiting room, crossing and uncrossing his legs. Holly is surprised to see Reese seated two chairs over from him, but the lawyer is so focused on the computer on her lap that she doesn't look up as Holly strides past.

Behind the reception desk, Tanya motions to a Post-it note on the desk that reads, "She just showed up."

"It's OK, Tanya." Holly taps her watch and then holds up three fingers.

Three minutes later, Reese is seated in the interview chair across from Holly. "What brings you in today?"

Reese interlocks her hands in her lap and offers a wisp of a smile. "I'm back to represent the tribe."

"Regarding?"

"We heard Liisa is missing."

"Apparently."

"Are you worried about her?"

"Very," Holly says, seeing no point in hiding it.

"It's strange, isn't it, Dr. Danvers? These happenings in our group."

"That might be the understatement of the century, Reese."

"Do you think it could all be connected?" she asks. "Elaine's and JJ's deaths? Liisa's disappearance?"

Holly feels as if she is being cross-examined. "Can you be more specific?"

"We heard the police are still looking into JJ's death," Reese says.

Holly only shrugs.

"A detective spoke to Simon. He was asking questions about JJ."

"That may be," Holly says. "But I don't disclose my clients' names to anyone. That detective tracked down Simon on his own. If that's what concerns you."

"Simon had to go tell the world about his therapy, didn't he?" Reese sighs. "No, it's not that. He made his own bed."

"What then?"

"Simon told us that during one of the sessions you were questioning him about the rest of the tribe. He can't remember the specifics because he was quite . . . sedated."

Holly's stomach flip-flops. "I can't discuss other group members with you." But even as she utters the sentence, she recognizes how convenient it must sound to Reese.

"Even though you were questioning Simon about Liisa and the rest of us?"

"I had my reasons." Holly feels too sheepish to meet Reese's gaze.

"All right," Reese says evenly. "Can you at least tell us whether you think Liisa was involved in Elaine's and/or JJ's death?"

"The detective is looking into the possibility. But as far as I know, he hasn't found any concrete connections. Besides, Liisa's well-being is the more immediate concern."

"No one's heard from her?"

"No." Holly hesitates but decides there's no harm in elaborating. "And I can't see Liisa abandoning her daughter like this. Not voluntarily, anyway."

Reese's shoulders straighten. "You think she was abducted?"

"I'm sorry, Reese. I can't be any more forthcoming with you and the group. I hope you understand."

"I get it. I do. I deal with very sensitive and private matters in my work, too." It's Reese's turn to look away. "Besides, there's something I haven't told you. Or anyone, for that matter."

"About Liisa?"

Reese shakes her head. "JJ."

Holly straightens. "What about her?"

"JJ and I, you know, we . . . bonded. We became friends. We even used to hang out outside of therapy."

Holly nods. "I'm sorry you lost a good friend, Reese."

"After Elaine overdosed, JJ took it so . . . personally," Reese continues. "She felt extremely guilty. The rest of us all knew there's no way you would have . . . could have molested Elaine. But somehow JJ felt it was her responsibility to disabuse Elaine of the notion that you might have hurt her. JJ thought that if she had put more time and effort into persuading Elaine, then maybe she wouldn't have OD'd that night . . ."

Holly feels almost relieved. "That's what you've been keeping to yourself, Reese?"

She hesitates. "There's more."

"What else?"

Reese finally says, "I have no idea if this is relevant or not . . ."

Holly forces a smile. "Tell me."

"The last time I spoke to JJ—the day she jumped—she told me she got an unexpected visitor. And it really spooked her."

Holly tilts her head. "Who visited her?"

Reese looks up at her. "Your husband."

Holly goes cold. "Why would Aaron go see JJ?" she mumbles, more to herself than Reese.

Reese shifts in her seat. "JJ told me about the vaping incident. How she walked in on you in your office."

Holly's cheeks burn. "She was my last appointment that day. The office door was already locked. I assumed everyone was gone. Besides, what does that have to do with Aaron?"

"JJ mentioned that the cleaner let her back in to get her jacket. Apparently, your husband thought JJ was planning to do something about what she had seen."

Holly's heart slams in her chest. "Like what?"

"Report it."

"What exactly did he say to her?" Holly asks in a voice barely above a whisper.

"I'm not sure of his exact words, but JJ thought he was trying to intimidate her."

Holly's head spins. *"Intimidate? How?"*

"It's all hearsay." Reese holds up a hand in disclaimer. "And JJ was definitely not herself when she told me. In retrospect, I wondered if she'd already been drinking at the time. But JJ said your husband warned her the group would collapse if she told anyone about you vaping DMT. And if that did happen, it would not be good for JJ. Not good at all."

CHAPTER 53

Holly's phone vibrates again, but recognizing the distinctive ringtone indicating Aaron's number, she lets the call go to voicemail. It's the third call from him this morning. She has ignored them all. Each one has made her angrier than the previous. She's tempted to pick up, if only to respond to his plaintive query at the restaurant and scream, "Now do you see why the fuck I couldn't *just* trust you?!"

It's barely eleven o'clock, but as she walks along Laguna's boardwalk the sun is beating down on her neck, promising a hot day. The coffee cup in her hand is only an accessory, a habit from previous beach strolls, and she hasn't drunk a sip. It was her idea to meet here. She needed to escape the suddenly claustrophobic confines of her office after Reese dropped her bombshell revelation.

Holly spots Detective Rivers striding toward her in another tailored suit, this one light blue. There's no swagger in his step, although she would understand if there were. They meet near the basketball courts where a loud two-on-two game is being played between four shirtless, sweaty guys.

His mouth curves into a welcoming smile. "G'morning, Dr. Danvers."

"Thanks for meeting me, Detective," Holly mutters, unable to match his friendliness.

"It sounded important."

"It is."

He waits for her to elaborate.

"My husband, Dr. Aaron Laing . . ." The detective must recognize the name from Liisa's earlier phone call to the office, but he doesn't show a response. "Actually, Aaron and I are separated."

"All right."

"But we're still in close touch. He's been very supportive throughout this whole ordeal . . . or so I thought."

Recognizing Holly's distress, Rivers motions to a nearby bench. "Why don't we sit?"

After they're both seated, he says, "Maybe it would be best if you just started at the beginning."

"Probably." Holly finally sips her coffee, primarily for something to do with her hands. "I've been confiding in Aaron from the outset. Ever since Elaine leveled her allegations."

"When you say confiding . . ."

"Sharing details about the group. The challenges." She lowers her voice. "The crises."

He leans closer. "Including their names?"

"Yes. First names, anyway. For the most part."

Rivers cocks his head.

"After all, Aaron's a psychiatrist, too," Holly says. "Bound by the same rules of confidentiality. And since most of the clients are recognizable, at least locally, they wouldn't be hard to identify by their first names alone."

"I see."

She hesitates. "There's something else I haven't shared with you yet."

"About your clients?"

"No. Me." She turns her free palm over on her lap. "I didn't think it was relevant to your, um, investigation."

He offers her an encouraging nod. "Go on."

"One evening—about a week before her death—JJ walked in on me while I was using psychedelics."

"Using how?"

"Smoking. Vaping, technically. DMT. The active ingredient in ayahuasca. But you have to understand, my office was already closed for the day. A cleaner let JJ in. At the time, I didn't even realize JJ had seen me."

He only nods.

"The last time I saw JJ, I was pressing her for details about Elaine's death," she says. "Too hard, in retrospect. And JJ freaked out. She became very agitated. And defensive. She went on about how inappropriate it was for me to be vaping in my office. Which, honestly, is impossible to argue with."

Rivers studies her for a daunting moment. "And how is all this related to your husband?"

"I told Aaron how troubled I was by what JJ had seen. And what she might do about it."

"Such as?"

She shrugs. "Tell the others in the group. Report me to the Medical Board."

"Did you ask Dr. Laing to intervene?"

"God no! I mean Aaron has always been super-protective of me . . . But I had no idea he might take matters into his own hands."

Rivers sits up straighter. "And how did he do that?"

"I only found out this morning. Aaron confronted JJ. He apparently warned her not to go public about me and the vaping."

"Dr. Laing told you this?"

"No. Someone else did. And please," she holds up a hand, "don't ask me who. I can't say."

"Another client, I presume," he says with a small sigh. "And when did this confrontation between Ms. Jang and your husband take place?"

Unable to meet his eyes, Holly's gaze falls to the bench. "The day JJ died."

CHAPTER 54

Aaron has been distracted all morning. At one point, he even wrote the wrong dose on a prescription refill and was mortified when the pharmacist called him to clarify that Aaron didn't actually intend to triple his patient's antidepressant dose.

Why did Holly bolt from the restaurant last night? And why has she avoided his calls since?

Holly and her goddamn psychedelics! They have been the source of so much grief. For both of them. All those bad decisions. Not to mention everything he has had to do to support her through the cascade of catastrophes they instigated.

Sitting at his desk, Aaron is about to pick up the phone and try Holly again when his assistant buzzes through. "There's a detective from Newport Beach here to see you," Amy tells him in her perpetually upbeat tone. "Can I send him in?"

"Please do," he says with an ease he doesn't feel.

Aaron greets the young detective at the door and leads him to the seat across from his desk. After introductions, Detective Rivers says, "Thanks for taking time to see me, Dr. Laing."

"Of course."

"I've been investigating the death of Justine Jang. I believe you're familiar with the circumstances?"

"Some of them, yes," Aaron says with a smile to hide the fact that his stomach has just leapt into his throat.

"You're also aware that Ms. Jang was a client of your wife's?"

Aaron leans back in his seat. "I am, yes."

"As I understand it, Dr. Laing, you were a bit of a . . . sounding board for your wife during the time of Ms. Jang's death."

Did Holly tell you? "Yes, despite our temporary separation, Holly and I are still close. And Holly has been distraught over recent . . . happenings with her clients."

Rivers nods. "The deaths of Ms. Golding and Ms. Jang?"

"And the disappearance of Liisa Koskinen," Aaron adds, realizing that the detective must know about that, too.

"My focus is Ms. Jang."

"All right."

"I understand that you spoke to her on the day she died."

How does he know?

Aaron takes a slow breath, warding off his sudden sense of claustrophobia. "I did, yes," he says, realizing it would only be worse to deny it.

"Were you acquainted with Ms. Jang?"

"No, I was not."

The detective's expression doesn't change. "Where did this conversation take place?"

"At the Laguna Art Museum. There was an event there that afternoon. The Jang family had donated two major works to the gallery."

"And you were a guest at the event?"

Aaron wavers. He had not even attended the event. Something that Rivers could easily verify. "No, I ran into JJ outside the museum."

Rivers raises an eyebrow. "Ran into her?"

"I . . ." He clears his throat. "I went to the museum to see her. I thought she might be in attendance."

"Why did you want to speak to her?"

Aaron studies the cop's inscrutable expression, searching in vain for nonverbal clues. "I have no problem telling you, Detective. But I'm not sure how much, ethically speaking, I can divulge. You see, Ms. Jang was a client of my wife's. And, as a colleague of Holly's, I was privy to certain confidential details about her."

"Like, for example, that she had discovered your wife vaping DMT inside her own office?"

Aaron is unable to mask his surprise. "You heard?"

Rivers nods. "How did Ms. Jang seem that afternoon? In your professional opinion."

Aaron considers his answer carefully. "Distracted. Flustered, maybe."

"Because of your interaction?"

"No, no. She was like that from the moment I approached her. Signs of anxiety and low mood. Poor eye contact. Tentative replies. Soft voice. Her overall body language gave me the impression of . . . angst."

"Did you think she might've been drinking, too?"

"That didn't occur to me, no."

"Thank you, that's helpful," Rivers says. "But what exactly did you hope to accomplish by confronting her, Dr. Laing?"

Aaron can feel his pulse pounding in his ears. "I didn't 'confront' her. We had a conversation."

"OK, then. What was the purpose of your conversation with her?"

Aaron does the calculation in his head. If Rivers is aware of the DMT, then he must already know why Aaron went to see JJ. "I wanted to convince her that it would not be advisable to disclose that she had seen my wife vaping."

"Because of the damage it would do to your wife's reputation?"

"Obviously, yes." Aaron clears his throat again. "But also, as I understood it, her group was in crisis after Elaine's overdose. I tried to make JJ see how counterproductive it would be to go public about my wife's DMT use in her office."

The detective's gaze locks onto his. "You went there to warn Ms. Jang? To intimidate her?"

"Not intimidate, persuade. To make her see the obvious."

Rivers frowns. "You didn't tell Ms. Jang that bad things would happen to her if she were to speak out?"

Aaron's chest is thudding now, but somehow he conjures a smile. "I'm not sure where you're getting your information from, Detective, but it's inaccurate. I told JJ that it would not be good for the group—and I suppose, by extension, her, too—if she did go public. Which was the truth. Nothing more."

"And you never saw Ms. Jang again?" Rivers asks pointedly. "After you left the museum?"

"No."

"You've never been to her home?"

"I only met her the once."

The detective eyes him steadily. "And where were you later that same evening?"

"At home."

"Alone?"

"Until Holly came over, yes," Aaron says, feeling his guts clench. "To wake me up and tell me about JJ."

"All right." Rivers stands up from his chair, and Aaron follows suit. "Oh, one last thing, Dr. Laing. You didn't happen to speak to either Elaine Golding or Dr. Liisa Koskinen, did you?"

"No." And then, remembering that the detective was the one who originally told Holly about Liisa's phone call, Aaron volunteers, "Apparently, Dr. Koskinen tried to call my office a few days ago. But I didn't even know that until Holly told me days later."

"Why do you think Dr. Koskinen was looking for you?"

Aaron remembers the hypothesis he shared with Holly: how Liisa might have been deliberately trying to create a traceable record back to him, to implicate him in some way. But to recount it now might sound like overcompensation. All he says is "I have no idea whatsoever, Detective. She never did reach me."

Rivers extends his hand. "Thank you for your time, Dr. Laing."

Aaron hopes his palm isn't sweating as he meets the other man's firm handshake. "Feel free to reach out anytime, if I can be of more help."

"I'll keep that in mind," Rivers says, turning for the door.

"Detective," Aaron calls out to his back.

"Yes?" he says without turning around.

"I never told my wife about my conversation with JJ. I thought it would . . . upset her too much."

"Hmmm."

"Does she happen to already know?"

"I'm not at liberty to share that. Ethically speaking, and all."

CHAPTER 55

Holly returns to the office just after lunch. She instructs Tanya that if Aaron shows up at the office she's not to let him in. "And if he insists, Tanya, please call 911."

Her assistant blanches with fear, practically vibrating in her seat.

But as the afternoon wears on, there is no sign of Aaron. He even stops phoning and texting. Holly suspects that Detective Rivers must have already spoken to him.

She manages to plod through her schedule, but Aaron is at the forefront of her thoughts and suspicions. The evidence against him is impossible to ignore or to explain away. He threatened JJ on the day she died. And Holly no longer buys his explanation that Liisa's phone call to his office, on the day of her disappearance, was a mere coincidence. If Aaron had been willing to confront JJ, why wouldn't he have done the same with Liisa or even Elaine? And just how far had he taken it?

Aaron must have intervened out of some twisted sense of protectiveness over her, but it doesn't make the act any less egregious. Whatever he did, he did for himself. To subjugate her to his wants and needs. He has always known how to capitalize on her vulnerability. And his plan has already begun to pay dividends. Holly thinks, shamefully, of how easily she ended up back in his bed, despite her determination to move on with her life after their latest separation.

Why does she keep doing that? Why is she so weak?

At five p.m., Tanya heads home, reluctant to leave Holly alone. Holly stays behind to finish charting. But she can't stop reflecting on her marriage.

What business do I have treating clients when I've been blind to the manipulation of my own husband? What else have I gotten wrong?

Another intrusive mental image of that stretch of highway where her father died pops into her mind. They've been recurring all afternoon. And again, she has to fight off the urge to go visit the crash site. *Why now of all times? Why is Aaron's duplicity—his unimaginable betrayal of our trust—triggering all these thoughts of my dad?*

Shortly after six, Holly gives up on trying to finish her paperwork and heads down to the garage. As usual, at this time of the evening, there are only a few cars still parked there since the doors to the building automatically lock at six p.m.

Aside from the hum of an overhead fan, the garage is otherwise quiet, but Holly feels oddly apprehensive, as if exposed. She reaches into her bag for her keys as she hurries toward her car, parked nose-out in her corner stall beside the pillar.

As she nears the driver's door, Holly catches movement out of the corner of her eye. She jerks her head up to see a tall figure slide out from behind the pillar on the passenger side of the car.

Her breath catches, and she involuntary backpedals a step or two.

Even before she makes out the interloper's face, Holly recognizes him by his slouched stance and the belly that presses against his black hoodie.

Graham steps out of the shadow, keeping his hands tucked in his pockets. "Evening, Holly." His oily voice oozes insincere friendliness.

Her whole body tenses. "What are you doing here, Graham?"

He shrugs. "I haven't seen you at Dad's lately."

Her breathing quickens, but she manages to keep her voice under control. "You think it's all right to ambush me in a dark garage?"

"Ambush?" He chuckles. "I just want to talk."

She eases her hand into her purse, until her fingers wrap around her canister of pepper spray. "You realize how inappropriate this is?"

"What is appropriate these days, Holly?" he asks. "It's kind of hard to judge."

Holly steps up to the driver's door. "I'm leaving."

"You might want to hear me out."

She grabs the handle. "Not here I don't."

"Two dead, and one 'missing.' But come on? We both know what *that* really means."

Holly's hand freezes on the handle.

"That's right. I know all about Elaine, JJ, and now Liisa. Wow. That's some track record for a therapist." He whistles. "I wonder what the media who gushed over your miraculous treatment of Simon Lowry would make of all this death and tragedy in your practice. Especially that one local reporter. Katy Armstrong, isn't it? I hear she's skeptical about your methods. Wonder why?"

"How did you . . . ?"

"Or what the cops would think of all those coincidental deaths."

"Did your dad—"

"Dad didn't tell me shit!" Graham yanks a hand from his pocket, and Holly instinctively recoils. But it's only a phone. "I've been listening."

"Listening?"

He nods toward the car. "Your calls."

"You bugged my phone?"

"It's a lot easier to bug a car."

The glasses case! "You broke into my car!"

He laughs again. "Is it a break-in if you already have the key?"

"You're deeply damaged, Graham."

"You want to talk damage?" He snorts. "Do you have any idea how much damage you've done to my life?"

Holly has no words.

"As a kid, I never bought the whole evil stepmom thing in fairy tales. But then I met you." Graham shakes his head. "All you ever cared about was being dad's protégée. The center of his universe. Of course, Nate put up with your selfish bullshit because he gets enough attention on his own. He loves everyone, and everyone loves him. But not me. I always saw right through you. You never had two seconds for me. Treated me like a failure and a disappointment from day one. Always wedging yourself between me and Dad. You're so fucking needy."

"I'm the issue?" Despite how unsafe and exposed she feels, Holly can't contain herself. "All the toxicity that swirls around you. Do you ever hold yourself accountable for any of it? Do you ever recognize yourself as the common denominator?"

"You poisoned Dad against me!"

"As if!" she snaps. "If you're having trouble with your dad, it's only because he finally woke up to the truth. I'm happy to hear it, actually. That Aaron is no longer deluding himself about what a disappointing, entitled brat you are. It's been staring him in the face for years. Don't you see it? You cause chaos and destruction wherever you go. And then you act like you're the victim. You're nothing more than an emotional arsonist."

His face reddens. "I'm not my dad. I don't fall for your manipulative bullshit. And talk about chaos. Will *any* of your clients survive your treatment?"

She yanks the door open. "I'm done with you. And your father."

"You better fucking well be!"

"Or what?"

"You're gonna get hurt," he growls. "Badly."

Still holding the pepper spray, Holly drops into her car seat and slams the door shut. Hands trembling, she jerks the car into gear and hits the accelerator, screeching the tires and forcing Graham to jump aside as the vehicle hurls forward.

CHAPTER 56

Saturday, April 27

Holly gives up on attempts at further sleep and crawls out of bed just after six a.m. She didn't think she'd slept a wink overnight, but when she consults the app connected to her watch, it tells her she managed to bank about two hours, though it rates both the quality of her slumber and her daytime readiness as "poor." Which sounds right to her.

Her altercation with Graham loops in her head. It gnaws at her. She's still incensed that he thought he could blackmail her. But ironically, she's more than willing to comply with his demand to cut ties with his father. She's only surprised that he didn't demand money to keep quiet about her clients' deaths. At least the nasty encounter clarified one thing: that it was Graham, not Aaron, who broke into her car. But that doesn't absolve her husband of anything else. Or make him any less guilty for trying to intimidate JJ or Liisa.

After Holly showers and dresses, she heads down to her car with the intention of driving to her office early to prepare for the videoconference her editor requested. She hasn't been able to focus on her manuscript in weeks. Besides, how can she write a book about the power of psychedelic therapy now? What a hypocrite and a fraud she would be. Holly would willingly return her six-figure advance to the publisher, but she knows that would devastate her sweet, sensitive editor, who has such high hopes for the book. Stalling is her only option.

As Holly drives, she thinks about all the ways Aaron has manipulated and betrayed her. Her outrage intensifies, and she can't stop herself from heading over to his house. She unlocks the front door with her old key, half-hoping Graham will be there. She's ready to blast him again, too.

Holly finds Aaron alone in the kitchen, sitting at the counter in his black robe with a coffee cup in front of him. His cheeks are unshaven, his hair is a bird's nest, and his eyes are sunken. The resignation in his face makes him look a decade older. But he doesn't appear the least surprised to see her.

"I'm sorry, Holly," he says with a weak smile.

Multiple possible retorts come to mind, but she opts to let him do the heavy lifting. "For what this time?"

"Where to start?" He sighs a laugh. "How about for not telling you about JJ?"

She shrugs. "Probably just slipped your mind that you threatened one of my clients."

He sighs. "I didn't threaten her."

She stands by the door, keys still in hand, unwilling to move an inch closer to him. "No? What did you do then, Aaron?"

"I reasoned with her. Or at least, I tried to."

Holly only glares at him, making no effort to hide her contempt.

He shrugs. "You have no reason to believe me, but it's true."

"Why? Why the fuck would you track JJ down like that?"

"You were so distraught, Holl," he mutters. "When you thought JJ was going to report you. After what happened with Elaine . . . I was worried. I thought . . ."

"What did you think, Aaron? I'm curious."

"That I might be able to help." He rubs his eyes. "I didn't even plan on speaking to her. But then I saw this post online announcing this Jang family event at the museum that same afternoon. I thought JJ might attend. So I went. And then, when I spotted her coming out of the museum, I couldn't resist."

"Resist ambushing her?" She scoffs. "I think that impulse might run in your DNA."

He grimaces. "What?"

"Never mind. Go on."

"We just talked, Holly. In broad daylight in front of the museum. I thought I'd even struck a chord with her. As JJ was leaving, she told me she'd consider what I'd said."

"Which was?"

"That it would only hurt the group and herself, if she spoke up about your DMT use."

Holly isn't willing to believe a word of it without proof. "And you never saw JJ again?"

"Never." He shakes his head. "She had to hurry off. Apparently, she was late to meet a friend."

"Which friend? Where?"

"I didn't think to ask. I actually went home feeling a bit better about your . . . predicament. I had no idea anything happened to JJ until later when you woke me up to tell me."

"And Elaine?"

He frowns. "What about her?"

"Did you try to make Elaine see the light, too?"

"Honestly?" He reaches for his coffee cup, but his hand stops short of it. "I might have tried if I had known how to find her." He pulls his hand away from the cup. "No. I never met Elaine."

"And Liisa? That call to your office?"

He holds out his palms. "I still can't explain that one. I haven't seen Liisa in fifteen years."

Some of her anger seeps away, seeing how small and pathetic her husband looks. "Even if what you say is true, Aaron, and I'm not convinced any of it is . . . why? Why hide it from me?"

His chin drops. "Because I realized I'd made a huge mistake. That, despite my best intentions, you'd never forgive me for that kind of professional and personal transgression. Not after what happened to JJ."

"And if JJ had lived another day, I would have found out from her what you'd done." She pauses. "And you just couldn't let that happen, could you?"

His expression is one of pure defeat. "Actually, her death only made it worse."

Holly looks at him sharply. "Why worse?"

"Because I didn't know—I still don't—if it was something I said that made her jump."

CHAPTER 57

Holly is so distracted during her videoconference with her editor that the young woman stops mid-sentence to ask if everything is all right. Holly resists the urge to tell her that nothing is. That two of her patients are dead, another is missing, and her own husband might be responsible. But Holly blames her preoccupation instead on a poor night's sleep. And she agrees to submit two new chapters by the end of the month.

After the call ends, Holly doesn't even check her appointment planner. She didn't think any of the remaining tribe members would want to continue seeing her, so she's surprised to see Tanya escorting Salvador in as her first client of the day.

Aside from his ubiquitous ball cap, Salvador looks different. Not right. Holly realizes that it's not because of his pallor or even the deep bags under his bloodshot eyes. It's his body language. Where normally he would bound into her office, today he trudges in with his neck stooped and his shoulders low.

"Hello, Salvador."

"Morning, Dr. Danvers." Even his voice is subdued.

"What's going on?" Holly asks gently.

"I fell off the wagon last night," he says, taking a seat.

She can't help it. Her face falls. "Adderall?"

"And blow." He sniffles a few times as if to emphasize the point. "The only reason I made it here this morning is 'cause I never went to bed."

"What happened, Salvador?"

"Where to begin?" He starts counting with his fingers. "Elaine, JJ, Liisa . . ."

"Of course," Holly says. "But did something specifically happen last night?"

"Who knows? Maybe the last of the ketamine wore off."

"It doesn't work like that, Salvador."

"Nothing works at all now, Dr. Danvers! We were a tribe bonded by our weaknesses, our temptations, our shame. And now . . ." He tosses up his hands.

"Relapses are to be expected, Salvador," she says. "It's never a smooth road with addiction. It's part of the healing process."

"What process?" he cries, bobbing in his chair. "When's the next ketamine session? The next group therapy?"

She shakes her head. "I'm happy to continue working with you one-on-one, but group therapy isn't possible now."

"Just as well." He giggles nervously. "We don't have much of a group left."

Holly can think of nothing positive to offer, so she only nods.

"Next week was supposed to be a celebration," Salvador says. "Two months of sobriety. That little milestone would've fallen on the very same day my new line premieres."

"I'm sorry, Salvador."

"The irony is JJ was supposed to help me with the after-party for my show. I texted her about it only hours before she jumped. I still can't wrap my head around that."

"What did she tell you?"

"Practically nothing. Like one- or two-word answers."

Holly thinks of the empty bottles the police found in JJ's condo that night. "Did you get the sense JJ had been drinking?"

"Nah. And trust me, I've seen enough drunk texts to spot them a mile away."

"JJ didn't mention anything about a run-in with someone earlier that day?"

"Run-in?"

"Nothing about a Dr. Laing?"

He grimaces. "Who?"

"It's OK. Never mind."

"It was only a few texts. She barely said anything." Salvador rubs his eyes. "It's too bad, though. JJ was supposed to have met up with Reese that night."

"Reese?"

"Yeah. Imagine how different it might have turned out if they had."

"Why didn't they?"

He shakes his head. "Reese had to cancel."

"Reese told you this?"

"She told all of us. A legal crisis or something. She feels horrible about it, too. Even shittier because she canceled by text." Salvador snorts. "As if a phone call would've made any difference."

Holly only nods, blank faced, despite the alarm bells going off inside her head.

"Let's face it," he says. "We'd all noticed how off JJ was after Elaine's OD. And none of us lifted a finger to help her."

"Easy to think that way in retrospect," Holly mutters, totally distracted.

Salvador taps his chest. "But I'm dying, here, myself! When can I get back on the ketamine, Dr. Danvers? It's the only thing that has worked so far!"

"Not yet, Salvador. Not until we know how the ketamine has affected events. Meantime you and I can focus on cognitive-behavioral techniques if you'd like."

He looks forlorn. "Sure, why not? Sobriety is overrated anyway."

As soon as Salvador is gone, Holly grabs her phone and texts Aaron: *Question for you.*

He replies immediately: *?*

What time was it when you spoke to JJ outside the museum?

A little before six. Why?

And JJ told you she was late to meet a friend, right?

He replies with a check emoji.

She doesn't ask him the one question that burns in her brain:

If Reese really did cancel on JJ via text, then how did she learn the details of the conversation Aaron had with JJ only hours before her death?

CHAPTER 58

It's eleven in the morning, and Simon is still in bed. Back in the day, he rarely saw the morning, at least not this side of it. He was a nocturnal creature back then, staying up most of the night and not rousing until midafternoon. But Simon went to bed last night before ten. And it's not just his aching hip that has kept him there. He hasn't felt this low or helpless in ages. The tribe is crumbling. He no longer trusts Dr. Danvers, the one person he viewed as his savior. And worst of all, the urges and fantasies are beginning to assert control over him again.

I'm the train wreck you always expected me to be, Mom.

When his phone dings with a group text, he almost ignores it. Nothing good ever comes from them lately. But after three more dings, curiosity gets the best of him, and he reaches for his phone.

Salvador: I fell off TWO wagons last night! Sizzling hot mess that I am!

Baljit: Two?

Salvador: THE DOUBLE PLUNGE! Coke and Adderall!!!

Baljit: It happens, Sal. Don't beat yourself up. Not that you're capable of beating up anyone or anything. 😜

Simon is oddly touched by Baljit's small show of compassion.

Simon: She's right. I've got a permanent dent in my skull from falling off so many wagons.

Salvador: 😗

Salvador: Dr. Danvers is adamant. No more group therapy. No more ketamine.

Baljit: Got any more earth-shattering news flashes?

Salvador: She'll keep seeing us individually.

Baljit: Without ketamine? Thanks, but no thanks.

Simon finds it hard to imagine what his life will be like without Dr. Danvers or the tribe in it, but he's too proud to share that with the others.

Salvador: Dr. Danvers is still fixated on the night JJ died.

Reese joins the chat.

Reese: Fixated how?

Salvador: After I told her JJ and I exchanged a couple texts that evening, Dr. Danvers wanted me to spill on everything and everyone.

Baljit: What's left to spill?

Salvador: She asked me about some kind of run-in JJ had with another doctor.

Simon: What doctor?

Salvador: Lang or something? 🙍

The text chain goes quiet for a moment. Then another message pops up.

Salvador: Reese, remember how you were supposed to meet JJ that night?

There are a few flashing dots on the screen as Reese types her response. Then a pause. Finally, her text appears.

Reese: Don't remind me.

Salvador: Dr. D seemed weirdly focused on that, too.

Reese: I wish I hadn't canceled on JJ. Everything might be so different now.

The conversation goes quiet again. Simon can think of nothing else to add. The whole thing has the death throes vibe of a text chat between people after a breakup.

Simon drags himself out of bed and heads to the kitchen to brew an espresso. The second shot has just dripped into his cup when his phone sounds again, indicating the video doorbell on the gate. Opening the app, he recognizes Detective Rivers at the gate. "Come in," Simon says, buzzing him in remotely.

The detective refuses Simon's offer of a coffee, and they sit down across from each other in the velvet chairs. Rivers crosses one leg over the other, and Simon can't help but admire the slim cut of his suit. He can barely remember the time when he was that lean, though he has the photos to prove he once was.

"Thanks for seeing me again, Mr. Lowry."

"It's Simon." But he doesn't add the well-worn line he has used for decades: "Mr. Lowry would've been my dad, if I'd had one." *Fuck, I'm old.*

"I need your help, Simon."

"My help? How?"

"I'm hoping you can clarify a couple things regarding Ms. Jang and Dr. Koskinen."

Simon immediately feels on edge, though he's not exactly sure why. "Clarify?"

The detective's grin is benign. "For starters, were both of them in your group therapy? With Dr. Danvers?"

Simon hesitates, still feeling protective of the tribe's privacy.

"Dr. Koskinen hasn't been seen in four days, Simon." Rivers uncrosses his legs. "The clock is ticking. I'm hoping you might help me find her."

"They were in my group, yes."

"When was the last time you saw Dr. Koskinen?"

His unease rises. "Last week. Liisa was over here with the rest of the group. Friday, I think."

Rivers pulls out a small leather-bound notebook and jots something down. "Have you spoken to her since?"

Simon considers lying, but he suspects the detective might already know. "I called Liisa a few days ago."

"Which day exactly?"

"Tuesday."

"The day she disappeared?" Rivers's eyes never leave his notebook.

"The afternoon!" Simon shoots up a palm. "But she texted us all later that evening via our group chat."

"Your therapy group? You had a chat group?"

"Yeah. We started it a month or two ago. Clients only."

Rivers nods. "Why did you call Dr. Koskinen?"

Simon thinks of his panic following the ketamine session where his memory had been wiped out with midazolam. But he doesn't want to have to explain his fears of what he might have divulged while medicated. "I just wanted to, um, debrief after our individual ketamine sessions. We weren't going to have another group session for a while. After all, Liisa is a therapist, herself."

"I see," Rivers says. "Did Dr. Koskinen sound different to you?"

"Different?"

"Dejected? Scared? Worried in some way?"

Simon considers the question. "Yes and no, I guess. She's hard to read, that one. Always so inhibited. Maybe she was a little more on edge than usual?" He shakes his head. "Nothing like her texts later that night, though."

Rivers scratches more notes. "What was different about those?"

"She was fired up!" Simon blows out his lips. "Like fit to be tied. Liisa called Dr. Danvers toxic. She went on about how Dr. D was sacrificing us all for the sake of her career."

"Dr. Koskinen used that word? Sacrifice?"

"I think so, yeah." Simon shifts in his seat, wondering if he's disclosing too much. "Anyway, Liisa told us she was quitting the group and said we'd be smart to do the same."

Rivers taps his notebook. "Did Dr. Koskinen explain why she was so agitated?"

"No. She just dropped off the group chat. Went totally dark. Last any of us heard from her."

"Can I see this chat?"

Simon runs a hand over the phone in his pocket. He is more concerned about what the detective might learn about him from the texts than protecting the identity of anyone else in the group. "I don't feel right betraying the confidentiality of the group."

Rivers views him for a long moment. "I respect your desire to protect their privacy. I really do. But when it comes to missing persons, every minute counts." He shows Simon a sympathetic grin. "I'm not interested in anything unrelated to Dr. Koskinen."

Simon breaks off eye contact. "It doesn't feel right to me."

"I can get a warrant for your phone, if you prefer."

Simon shrugs. "You could try."

"OK." The detective exhales. "Maybe you can help another way? Aside from Ms. Golding, Ms. Jang, and Dr. Koskinen, I still don't know the names of the other group members." Rivers flips back a few pages. "However, I did get a warrant to access Dr. Koskinen's phone records. She had some calls and texts with some private cell numbers. It will be easier to track her down if you help me identify these numbers I've written here."

"I don't know," Simon says warily.

"You won't be breaking any confidences. I'll definitely be able to track the names down through their mobile carriers. But that could take a day or two. Time Dr. Koskinen might not have."

Simon wavers. "All right. Show me."

Rivers turns the page out. There are six handwritten numbers listed in a column. The last one is underlined three times.

"That's mine," Simon points to the third number on the list. But he has to cross-reference with his phone to identify the other ones. Two of them he doesn't recognize at all. "The first one there is JJ's. The fourth one, that's Salvador Jimenez." And he runs a finger over the last number. "That's Reese. Reese Foster. The lawyer."

Rivers writes down the names, and Simon can't help notice how he circles only Reese's. "That's a big help, thank you, Simon."

After the detective leaves, Simon pulls out his phone, opens the tribe's group chat, and starts typing.

Simon: Just got grilled by that detective again. A lot of questions about JJ and Liisa. You might hear from him, too. He's got most of our numbers.

CHAPTER 59

Sitting at her desk, Holly waits for Detective Rivers to return her call. She has no qualms over sharing her deepening suspicions about Reese. After all, the bounds of client-therapist confidentiality don't apply to homicide.

Her phone lights up with a call, but it's not from Rivers. It's from Walter's landline. Holly answers on the second ring. "Hi, Papa."

He doesn't reply, but Holly hears what sounds like heavy breathing for a few seconds. Then the call abruptly ends.

She calls him right back, but it goes straight to voicemail. Five minutes later, she tries again. Still no answer. Holly grabs her keys and heads down to her car.

Holly drives aggressively, weaving through the moderate highway traffic and growing more worried by the minute. She reaches his house in under fifteen minutes. It's quiet on his street, but that doesn't bring her any reassurance.

She lets herself in through the front door. "Papa?" she calls out.

No answer.

Holly heads straight to his office but finds it empty. Heading out toward the back door, she hears a sound from nearby. A low-pitched moan. Then she's hit by the acrid stench of DMT.

Papa, you didn't!

Holly rushes for the solarium. At the entrance, she stops dead in her tracks. Her breath catches. Walter is sprawled out on the beanbag. His eyes are open, but he stares at the ceiling, oblivious to her presence. Reese sits beside him on the floor, one long leg tucked up against her chest. A gun rests on the floor by her right hand. An old-fashioned, carafe-shaped, steaming hookah pipe stands on the floor between Walter and her with yellow rubber tubing curled up beside it. Old towels and rags are scattered near the base of the hookah. The bitter odor of the burnt DMT is even more intense than in the vaped form.

"It wasn't supposed to be like this," Reese says.

Reese.

"Papa!" Holly cries, taking a step toward him.

Reese lifts the gun and lazily points it at her. "Let him be. He's just tripping."

Holly stops, but the panic in her chest keeps rising. "Please, Reese. He's very old. He's all I have left."

"He's fine." Reese turns to him. "Aren't you, Walter?"

Walter flashes a lopsided, goofy smile but says nothing.

"Exhibit A," Reese says simply.

"Why?" Holly demands.

Reese shrugs. "In two words? Alcohol cessation."

Holly is having trouble processing what she's saying. She can only focus on her grandfather's narrow chest, rising and falling, wondering what she'll do if it suddenly stops.

Glancing over her shoulder, Holly considers trying to flee to get help for him but realizes she probably wouldn't get far before Reese took a shot.

"Closer!" Reese waves her inside the room with the barrel of the gun, and Holly takes a few reluctant steps forward. "I meant it when I told you I didn't think I'd ever stop drinking. That I'd die an alcoholic. I haven't failed at anything I've set my mind to. *Except* sobriety. I couldn't stop failing at that. Until I found you and ketamine."

"What does this have to do with him?" Holly whispers.

"This?" Reese grunts a laugh. "This is the culmination of some horrible luck. For all of us."

Holly gapes at Reese, to show she's giving her full attention, but she's desperate to find a way to get to the pepper spray in her purse.

"I didn't want any of this," Reese says. "And I certainly had no idea it would spiral so wildly out of control. But when that helpless moron confused her childhood trauma with our group therapy . . ."

"Elaine?"

"And her bizarre fucking paranoia. How couldn't she realize that even an apex predator wouldn't molest someone in a room full of witnesses?" Reese scoffs. "But do you think she'd listen to reason? Even after the whole group confronted her. Selfish cow! Determined to take us all down with her. An attention-seeking activist like that! What a mess it would've been. And all our work . . . my one shot at sobriety . . . would've blown up with her."

"So you overdosed her?" Holly says, playing along while calculating when best to make her move. "To make it look self-induced?"

"We talked about it, JJ and I. How easy it would be to make it appear as if Elaine had relapsed. Which, let's face it, was a foregone conclusion with that hopeless mess." Reese exhales. "JJ and I went back to see Elaine after the group intervention. To take one more stab at making her see the light. And I thought . . ." Her voice trails off.

If only I can get a bit closer. "Thought what?"

"That JJ knew what I was prepared to do. I told her I'd brought fentanyl." Reese shakes her head. "Predictably, Elaine wouldn't listen to a word of reason . . . Actually, it was even worse than that. She accused us of complicity in her molestation. Ridiculous! Apart from screwing the whole group over, all Elaine was ever going to accomplish with her hysterical charges was to discredit real abuse victims."

"So you injected her with fentanyl?"

"What else was I supposed to do? To save six other lives, we had to take hers. It's utilitarian when you think about it. You know, greatest good for the greatest number. And I thought I'd convinced JJ . . . but then she lost it. Acting as if overdosing Elaine wasn't even an option, let alone the *only* one. I had to practically wrestle the phone out of her hand to stop her from dialing 911."

Holly's insides go cold hearing Reese explain the mechanics of Elaine's murder in such a detached tone. Suddenly, Holly remembers Reese's cool detachment when she talked about retaliating against the cousin who blabbed at school that Reese's dad had died of alcoholism. Reese, the smart, quiet girl who became the ambitious, successful lawyer. The first of the group to admit falling off the wagon. Wise indeed to mix truth with her lies.

Holly glances down at her purse. "And that's why you had to get rid of JJ, too?"

Reese's eyes are glassy. "JJ was my friend! My only ally in the tribe. Someone who understood the grip of alcohol. The others?" Reese rolls her eyes. "Salvador is a man-child. Baljit, a bully. Elaine was a 'woke' nutbar and Liisa an uptight know-it-all—both of them lost causes. And Simon? Just an abuser who views himself as some kind of victim. Not JJ, though. She and I found sobriety together. It was as if I'd stumbled across a long-lost sister. Do you know what it's like to be alone in the world? Really and truly alone? JJ and I did. Until we found each other, and your treatment. But she just couldn't stop panicking about Elaine. And then your fucking husband had to accost JJ outside the museum. It made her lose her mind."

"You didn't really have a choice, did you?" Holly says gently, stalling for time. She scans the room again, looking for any distraction as she surreptitiously slides her other hand closer to her purse.

"Not after your fucking husband got through with her. You know, I'd expect you to have better judgment than to be with someone like him. JJ came back from that museum fundraiser absolutely convinced you already knew about us and Elaine. She was sure she had blabbed it all under ketamine, but she couldn't remember thanks to that god-damn midazolam." Reese takes a long, slow breath. "I didn't go over to JJ's intending to kill her. Christ, she picked me up and drove me there herself."

Which explains why you weren't seen on the lobby's security cameras.

"We were supposed to talk things through. I tried to reassure JJ that, if necessary, we could leverage your DMT use against you. But she wouldn't listen to reason! Her conscience was killing her, and she thought her only hope was to come clean with you." Reese runs her free hand through her hair.

"I'm not a fool, though," Reese continues. "I did go there prepared for other contingencies. I brought a couple bottles with me. And once it became clear I couldn't talk her out of her plan to turn us both in . . . well . . . JJ was such a trembling, guilt-ridden, helpless mess . . . it was dead easy to convince her to have a drink with me. Of course, she didn't realize I was drinking alcohol-free wine to her twenty-six ounces of pure vodka." Her gaze falls to her lap. "JJ was so drunk that I had to prop her up just to lead her out to the balcony. It didn't take much of a push to get her over the railing . . . In a way, I think it might've been a relief for her. You know?"

Holly swallows the lump growing in her throat. As frantic as she is to get her hand on the pepper spray, she can't help picturing JJ's last moments, and it's undoing her. She doesn't want to think about JJ's shock or her confusion—the wind in her hair on the way down—or worse, the moment of impact.

"And Liisa?" Holly croaks.

"Liisa!" A burst of laughter. "Could that have been a bigger comedy of errors? How was I supposed to know JJ had already confided in Liisa? Behind my back, no less. JJ had turned to that sketchy psychologist to ease her own conscience. She told her about Elaine and the fentanyl. And then after, of course, Liisa suspected I had to be involved in JJ's 'jump,' too." Reese shakes her head. "But did that fucking know-it-all fraud turn me in? No. Instead, she decided to blackmail me."

Holly closes her eyes and thinks of Liisa's client who had accused her of extortion. *It fits.* As sympathetically as she can, Holly asks, "What did Liisa want from you?"

"Money. And lots of it. Oh, our Liisa liked money. Apparently, her legal fees were through the roof. And something about her daughter's expensive medication. She just assumed that a greedy lawyer like me would have millions of dollars in disposable income lying around. But *a*, I don't have those kinds of funds. And *b*, I'm not partial to blackmail.

But I didn't share any of that with her until she showed up to collect her blood money."

"Where is she, Reese?"

Reese shows a tight smile. "Liisa's in Big Sur now."

"Dead?"

"It's a fair assumption. Liisa wasn't exaggerating. She can swallow a ton of Xanax, that one. They'll probably find her car first. Not sure her body will ever surface."

"Koala!" Walter mumbles, and Reese glances over to him, unconcerned. His eyes drift back to the ceiling.

"Why, Reese?" Holly motions to Walter. "This isn't necessary."

"I wish," Reese says wistfully. "But you weren't ever going to let this go, were you? I thought maybe if you found out your husband had ambushed JJ on the night she died, that might divert you. I even called his office from Liisa's phone to muddy the waters." She sighs heavily. "But no. You kept pressing and pressing. And once Salvador let it slip to you that I had plans to meet JJ that night . . . well, if you hadn't already figured out my connection, you would've soon enough. I saw it in your eyes yesterday. Your single-mindedness. It's like mine. Unrelenting. And I couldn't take the chance. Not with that detective already poking his nose around."

Holly takes another step toward her grandfather. "I don't care about any of it. I just want to make sure he's OK."

"Get back," Reese growls.

Holly again notices the old towels and rags on the floor near the hookah. And then it hits her. *A fire!* From a hookah pipe. That's how Reese plans to cover up their deaths.

"Now that I've poured out my soul, I have a few questions of my own." Reese levels the gun again. "I'm going to borrow your technique for cutting through all the BS. Like how you did with JJ and Simon. Your little truth serum."

Reese opens a small container beside her hip, scoops up a spoonful of whitish powder, and feeds it into the hookah. As she's focusing on the task, Holly slips a hand into her bag until her fingers wrap around the pepper spray canister. She eases her fist out of the bag, praying Reese hasn't noticed.

As the stink intensifies and the smoke begins to rise from the top of the hookah, Reese gets to her feet and takes a few steps away from Walter. She motions with the gun. "Please, Dr. Danvers. Have a seat beside Grandpa."

Keeping her fist closed, Holly lowers herself down beside the beanbag. With her free hand, she rubs his shoulder. "It's OK, Papa."

"More than OK, Koala," he says, slurring his words, a thin line of drool running from the corner of his lip.

Reese tosses her something that Holly recognizes as a blindfold as soon as it lands by her leg. "Put it on, please. But don't cover your eyes yet."

Holly struggles to keep the canister tucked in her palm with her fourth and fifth finger, as she slips the blindfold over her forehead.

Reese motions to the tubing with her gun. "Grab ahold of it, please."

Reese is still too far away to be sprayed. Reluctantly, Holly lifts the tube and brings the tip to her lips.

"Blindfold down, please."

Holly reluctantly complies, plunging the room into darkness.

"Set and setting, Dr. Danvers. Isn't that what you always tell us? Go to your happy place now. Maybe best to pick a time before the tribe, huh?"

This used to be my happy place, Holly thinks with bitter irony.

"It's time to smoke," Reese instructs.

Holly hesitates.

"The gun is pointed at your head!" Reese barks. "Grandpa's next."

Holly inhales a tiny breath, pretending to take more.

"*Deeper!*" Reese cries.

Holly inhales again, this time feeling the burn travel all the way down her throat. She coughs, and the smoke seeps out of her mouth and nose.

"Another!"

Holly complies. And she chokes again. As the DMT kicks in, Holly sees flashing lights in her periphery.

"Who have you told about me?" Reese's voice sounds as if it's coming through a tunnel.

"No one."

"Have you mentioned me to that detective yet?"

The room is spinning faster now. "No. I haven't reached . . . him."

"Have another drag, please."

Holly feigns inhaling, but this time she keeps her lips open. "It's not working," she croaks.

"It's working fine."

"No. It's plugged."

Holly hears movement and, sensing Reese's approach, shoots out her hand and squirts the pepper spray while she swings her arm wildly.

Reese shrieks. "You bitch!"

Holly hears something clatter and fall. She pushes herself to stand up. But her legs won't cooperate.

And then colored lights explode across her visual field as her trip launches into orbit.

CHAPTER 60

The radiance is so brilliant that it hurts Holly's eyes, but she can't look away. Then the lights begin to bend, meld, and swirl into a whirlpool of color, its dark center steadily expanding. She's vaguely aware that she is hallucinating, but it all feels so real.

Hollycopter! She hears the familiar voice before her father's translucent form materializes out of the vortex.

Daddy! Her chest soars with relief.

I've come to take you with me.

Holly inhales a plume of smoke, and she coughs. *Where are we going?*

He motions beside him, and suddenly their old station wagon appears on a highway. The wheels are turning, but it doesn't move away from them. With a sweep of her dad's hand, it bursts into flames again.

No, Daddy. Holly feels the heat of the fire and leans away from it. *Stay here!*

He nods to the car. *It's where we belong.*

Holly focuses on the flaming car. Suddenly, she can see a teenaged version of herself in the passenger seat beside her dad. Tears pour down Young Holly's cheeks and evaporate into steam off her chin.

I'm sorry, Holly. He reaches over from the driver's seat to stroke Young Holly's cheek, but she recoils from his touch. *So, so, so sorry.*

The young Holly sobs. *Is it me?*

No, Hollycopter. Never. Sometimes, two people . . . they fall out of love. Your mother and me, for us it happened a while ago.

And Mrs. Blake?

Sometimes, without ever trying, you just fall in love with someone else.

She's Nina's mom! Holly hears her younger self cry. *My best friend!*

I'm so sorry, Holly.

Please, Daddy. Please! Don't go.

Your mother and I, we agree. It's for the best. We both love you. But I need time to sort things out.

The smoke around Holly thickens as she stands outside the car, observing her younger self plead with her father inside the vehicle. Her eyes sting, and her breathing is heavier. She can hear a distant wailing. A siren?

You're choosing her over us? Young Holly whimpers. *Over me?*

Only for a while, Holly. You'll have your mom. And your grandparents. He extends his hand to her again. *I'll be back as soon as I can. Once I've worked it out.*

Young Holly grabs on to his arm and wraps herself tightly around it.

Holly, please! Her dad tries to wriggle his arm free of Young Holly's, but she hangs on for dear life.

Holly watches in horror as, suddenly, almost simultaneously, both heads inside the vehicle swivel toward the windshield. She spots the hazy outline of a deer on the side of the road. It leaps out in front of the car.

Her father yanks the steering wheel, and the car veers violently to the right.

Holly feels herself cartwheeling, as if she's trapped inside a huge barrel rolling off a cliff.

The tumbling stops as suddenly as it started. A shower of glass explodes around her, the shards floating as if in slow motion.

Everything goes dark again. It's unbearably hot. Holly thinks she might gag on dense tendrils of smoke.

Then she feels hands on her, gripping her arms and then her legs. And she feels herself being lifted.

CHAPTER 61

"Dad!" is the first word out of her mouth when Holly comes to.

Disoriented, she sees police cruisers, fire trucks, and ambulances everywhere. People in uniform mill around her. Everything stinks of smoke.

How did I get here?

The last thing she remembers is the heat of the fire threatening the overturned car. Then it all comes back to her. She's lying on a stretcher on her grandfather's front lawn. She turns just in time to see a cop protecting the top of Reese's head with his hand, as he loads her into the back of a cruiser, her wrists cuffed behind her back.

Before the cop shuts the door, Reese locks eyes with Holly. There's no remorse in her swollen, red eyes. If anything, she looks betrayed. As if Holly should have known that Reese did it all to protect her own sobriety and to validate Holly's method.

What utter bullshit! Holly wants to scream.

Is Reese a sociopath? she wonders. And if so, why hadn't she picked up on it before? Holly probes Reese's face and posture for a hint of shame, but finding none, turns her head away in disgust.

A shadow crosses her face, and Holly sees Detective Rivers standing over her. He wears a suit, as usual, but it has dark patches and stains across it and on his shirt. His tie is crooked. And blood is crusted over his right eye.

Suddenly she remembers. "Papa?"

"He's going to be all right." He kneels down to her level. "They took him to the hospital for assessment."

"What happened?"

"A fire. In that sunroom. The firefighters say it was deliberately set. Reese was trying to burn down the house."

With me and Papa inside. "How did you know?"

"I traced Dr. Koskinen's phone records back to some unlisted cell phones, including Reese's. When we triangulated the cell signals from the night of the group chat—"

"What group chat?" Holly asks, her brain still foggy.

"Among the group members. You weren't included. Anyway, after Dr. Koskinen was already apparently 'on the run,' both phones dinged to the same cell towers. Meaning—"

"They were together! Reese was the one sending the texts under Liisa's name to her daughter, right? She must have been pretending to be Liisa on that group chat, too."

"Looks like."

Holly exhales. "Liisa is dead. Reese told me as much. I think she drugged her and dumped the body in the ocean."

Rivers doesn't appear surprised. "Dr. Koskinen's car was found this morning by the highway patrol. Off the trails near Big Sur."

Holly tries to sit up, but her head spins, and he helps her lie back down with a gentle hand on her shoulder. "I still don't follow. How did you know where to find me? And Reese?"

"I tracked her phone to this house. When I saw that the home was registered under the name of Danvers, I rushed over. I smelled the smoke as soon as I pulled up. Once I recognized it was coming from behind the house, I raced around the side and ran into Reese out back, trying to rinse the pepper spray out of her eyes and nose with a garden hose. I cuffed her to the gate and then kicked in the back door. She had tipped the hookah over, and the rags were burning, but the fire hadn't consumed the room yet."

Holly looks at him in awe. "And you carried me and my grandfather out?"

He shrugs it off. "Luckily, you're both on the lighter side."

She smiles. But then, unexpectedly, her eyes mist over, and her throat thickens. "Reese killed them all."

"Your instincts were right about foul play."

She wipes her eyes with a sleeve. "Thank you for following up on them, Detective Rivers."

"It's Cal."

"Cal?" She cocks her head. "As in Calvin? Or Caleb?"

He shakes his head.

"Callum?"

He chuckles. "Just Cal."

"I'm Holly, Just Cal."

He nods to the pair of paramedics standing off to her right. "I'll come check on you in the ER. OK, Holly? Meantime, I've got to go process Reese."

"Yeah, of course." She touches his arm. "Thank you, Cal."

Another smile, and he's gone.

A female paramedic appears at Holly's feet and says, "We're going to take you to the hospital now, Dr. Danvers." And her partner pushes the stretcher from behind.

They wheel her toward the open back door of an ambulance. The shape of the vehicle reminds Holly of her dad's old station wagon. Suddenly, the vision from her DMT trip rushes back to her. And with it, the actual memories of the accident flood back, too.

Holly can feel her heart breaking again in the moment when her dad told her the news about her parents' separation. Even as a teenager, she had recognized how strained and loveless their marriage was. She didn't care that he had found another woman. No. What devastated Holly was the thought of her father, the most important person in her world, choosing to live with someone else instead of her. She remembers grabbing his arm and begging him not to go. She also remembers her anger.

But the DMT-induced hallucination didn't fully align with the recollection of actual events. Holly hadn't wrapped her whole body around his arm. She had only tugged at his sleeve, pleading with him. True, she had distracted him at the worst moment. But the deer had darted out of nowhere. And she clearly remembers that her dad's eyes were on the road when he yanked on the steering wheel.

The accident wasn't my fault.

CHAPTER 62

Wednesday, May 8

Simon has long suspected that Salvador is Dr. Danvers's favorite, not that the competition is all that fierce. But now he knows for sure. The session was the tribe's idea. What was left of them, anyway. Dr. Danvers had been reluctant to go along with it, and she only acquiesced after Salvador convinced her.

They don't use the group therapy room today. Too many uncomfortable memories. Too many ghosts. Instead, there are two extra chairs in Dr. Danvers's office, and they sit in a circle. She allows the other three to do most of the talking as she sits back and observes, her fingers interlocked on her lap, her legs crossed.

"In the end, it had nothing to do with the ketamine," Salvador argues.

"Yeah, your only real mistake, Dr. Danvers, was in trusting a lawyer," Baljit grumbles, and the others chuckle grimly.

"Speaking of," Salvador says. "I heard Reese pled not guilty."

"As if it matters," Baljit grunts. "She's not going to weasel her way out of three murder charges."

Salvador glances over to Dr. Danvers. "Not to mention two attempted ones."

"I still can't believe it," Simon says. "One of our own tribe."

"Can we please get over this whole tribe bullshit?" Baljit moans.

"We're not family. We were a nightmare from the outset. Our only connection? A desperation to kick our individual habits."

Simon grunts. "Find me a stronger connection."

Baljit shrugs. "A mother's love?"

Not bloody likely.

Baljit continues. "Fuckups and liars stick together because they've screwed over everyone else."

"Baljit," Dr. Danvers views the other woman over the top of her glasses, "that's a bit harsh."

"If the shoe fits . . ."

Dr. Danvers holds up a hand. "We could argue this all day, but the truth is, no one would've died if I hadn't assembled this group."

"Might as well blame yourself for chartering a plane that later crashes," Simon says.

"Hundred percent!" Salvador cries. "And if it wasn't the ketamine's fault, why stop it?"

"I wish it were that simple." Dr. Danvers uncrosses her legs. "Sometimes, in medicine, it's hard to tease out cause from effect. There's already an ethics review of my practice underway. And I won't—legally, I can't—prescribe psychedelics until it's complete."

Baljit stares at her. "Then what now?"

Dr. Danvers makes eye contact with each of them. "You apply what you've already learned. Help each other. Tap into your inner strengths."

Salvador pouts. "What if we don't have any?"

"But you do!" Dr. Danvers cries. "Each one of you does. I've seen it. The ketamine was never meant to be indefinite. Even if nothing had gone wrong, we would've continued it for another four to eight more cycles at most. Psychedelics work by opening new pathways in your brain. Affecting your neuroplasticity. They reprogram your consciousness to not depend on your habit for numbing the pain of past traumas. But the effect lasts long after your final dose. Sometimes permanently."

"Then why do we begin to slip every time we stop it?" Baljit asks.

"Partly, it's psychosomatic. You believe you're more reliant on the ketamine than you actually are."

Simon notices that Dr. Danvers hasn't asked any of them whether they have relapsed since their last session.

"I will be here for you," she continues. "Either to meet as a group like this or in one-on-one sessions. Of course, I'm more than willing to refer you to another counselor, too. It's probably for the best. I can even connect you with another psychedelic clinic. But at this point, I believe you can manage without ketamine."

"Don't bet the farm on that," Baljit says. "Although, God knows, with my addiction I just might."

Dr. Danvers looks around the glum faces before offering them a supportive grin. "You might not believe in yourselves. Not yet anyway. But isn't it worth something to know that I do?"

Despite his enthusiastic nod, Simon shares Baljit's doubt. His urges have resurfaced with a vengeance. Even now, the sight of Baljit's fitted top and Dr. Danvers's toned legs is stoking new fantasies. And he can't stop thinking about last night. That young redhead chained to his bed and moaning noisily, trapped somewhere between pleasure and pain. And fear. The whole thing was delicious.

But he has also learned from his experiences in therapy. Before taking her to bed, he spiked the girl's drink with heavy doses of LSD and Ativan—the closest thing he could concoct to match what Dr. Danvers used to wipe out portions of his memory. After it was over, the girl was still stunned, and repeatedly asked what had happened and where the marks around her wrists and neck came from—even as he dropped her off in the lane where he'd found her, a thousand dollars richer and none the wiser.

Maybe Dr. Danvers hasn't cured him. But she has addressed his biggest challenge.

He doesn't have to worry anymore about ending up back in his lawyer's office at the mercy of women tangled up in his sexual cravings.

From now on, they won't remember a thing.

CHAPTER 63

Wednesday, June 12

The hospital sits in the hills above the town, and Walter's bright room faces west, with a view down to the beaches and the ocean. But Holly doubts his eyesight is good enough to appreciate much of it. Besides, he has only been back to himself for the past few days.

After the paramedics brought Walter to the ER, he was diagnosed with a broken hip from his fall in the smoke-filled solarium. The surgery to pin the hip went smoothly enough, but afterwards he suffered an acute post-operative delirium that left him confused for weeks. Most of the time, he was convinced he was still in his own home, and he frequently called out for his long-dead wife.

Holly now finds her grandfather sitting up in bed, his untouched lunch tray in front of him. She kisses his forehead. "It's good to have you back, Papa."

Walter chuckles. "Speak for yourself."

"What does that mean?"

"At my ancient age, carbon monoxide poisoning wouldn't have been such a bad way to have exited stage left."

"No one's exiting anywhere. Even if you're ready, I'm not."

He shrugs. "Now that my brain is functioning at a level slightly higher than an ostrich's, remind me again what happened."

Holly summarizes the events from the day of the fire for him and then says, "Reese figured I was another loose end she had to tie up. And she saw you as the means to do it."

"There's kind of a rich irony to that. Using DMT to get rid of us."

Technically, the hookah was her means, but Holly understands his point. "Reese found a way to weaponize psychedelics."

His shoulders dip. "They're not the panacea we both hoped, are they?"

"Don't be so sure. After all, a huge part of Reese's motivation was her desire—her need—to maintain ketamine therapy. In her mind, it was the only thing keeping her sober."

"Now she has prison for that."

Holly pulls up a chair beside his bed. "I refuse to give up on the promise of psychedelics in therapy, Papa. Of course, they're not foolproof. What is? Besides, not all traumas are surmountable."

Walter nods. "And not all damaged souls are repairable."

"Agreed. Ketamine didn't turn Reese into a killer. Her desperate desire for sobriety did." She swallows. "There's something else, too. About my last DMT trip . . ."

His eyelids crease. "What about it?"

"I saw Dad again."

Walter's chin drops. "Haven't we've been through enough?"

She lays a hand on his shoulder, which feels even bonier than before. "The details from the accident came back to me after the DMT. The *real* events. I remember everything now."

"Maybe so," he murmurs. "But do I have to know?"

Holly considers her words carefully. Her grandfather doesn't need to hear about her parents' separation or the other woman in her dad's life, though Holly suspects Walter has always known. She doesn't plan to tell him about the conversation where she begged her dad not to go. But only after the fire did Holly realize just how much she had idealized her father since his death. He had been willing to leave her, which Walter never would have done.

And it wasn't only memories of the crash that came back to her. She now also recalls how withdrawn and unavailable her father had become in the months leading up to that fateful car ride, when he must have already been planning to leave.

Initially, after regaining the memories, Holly felt only relief. Despite what she had feared, she hadn't been responsible for the accident. She assumed that awareness would finally free her of the guilt she had been carrying most of her adult life. But over the intervening weeks, another realization slowly took shape. She felt it like a heat in her belly. Underneath the guilt, she had buried something even deeper: a fury that bordered on hatred of her dad for having chosen someone else over her.

And because she never had the chance to process that anger, it had lived with her in other ways and affected her life choices. Would she have ended up with someone like Aaron if she hadn't been trying to fill that gaping emotional void her father had created in the moments before he died?

Still, Holly has finally found peace over the accident. And that's all her grandfather needs to hear. She gives Walter's shoulder a small squeeze. "It was a deer, Papa. It came out of nowhere. And Dad tried to swerve at the last second."

Walter doesn't comment, but his face relaxes. They sit in peaceful silence, Holly's hand still resting on his shoulder.

Finally, he turns to her and asks, "Will I be able to go home soon?"

"There's been a lot of structural damage." In fact, the destruction was limited to the solarium, and the house is otherwise livable. But the geriatrician told Holly that Walter shouldn't be living alone anymore. "You can't move back in yet."

He's crestfallen. "You're not going to put me in one of those awful homes, are you?"

"I've moved myself. As a matter of fact, to Dana Point. I've rented a house near the water. It's not as fancy as yours, but it has three bedrooms and a garden out back that could really use your help."

"My help?"

"I want you to move in with me, Papa. After all, as we learned, Dana Point isn't the safest neighborhood to be living in alone."

Walter grins again, his relief practically palpable. "But . . . what about Herr Professor?"

Holly pulls her hand from his arm and stands up. "That reminds me. I've got to go. I'm going to be late to meet Aaron."

As she drives over to Aaron's house, Holly reflects on how she and Walter aren't the only surviving victims of her father's crash. Her mother has suffered, too. Largely, in silence. The poor woman, who was never equipped to handle intense emotions, not only had to cope with the death of her spouse and her daughter's depression, but she also had to carry the secret that her husband was about to leave her right before he died.

As Holly pulls up to the curb, she makes a mental note to call her mom again soon. Maybe even book a trip to visit her?

Aaron welcomes her at the door and wraps her in a hug. Holly is wooden in his arms, but she can't help herself.

"I'm glad you reached out," he says with a sheepish smile after he releases her. "How's Walter doing?"

"He's OK. Thanks. Pretty much back to himself."

"Good. Please wish him my best."

"I will. Thanks."

"I read that article in the *Orange County Register* last week." Aaron whistles. "Amazing. It just never ends with that tribe of yours."

Holly still can't believe it herself.

After deciding she couldn't hide from Katy Armstrong any longer, Holly had agreed last week to sit down with her in person for an interview. She arrived at the café bracing for the worst but was surprised when the first question Katy asked was, "Is Simon Lowry still a client of yours?"

"You know I can't answer that."

"Even if he was the subject of a criminal investigation?"

"He is?"

"He will be."

"For what?"

"Sexual assault. Involving multiple victims."

Based on all she knew, it shouldn't have come as a surprise, yet Holly still felt shocked. Not only over the accusations, but also the fact that Katy had been hounding her all along to discuss Simon, not ketamine therapy or any of her clients' deaths.

"If Simon hasn't been charged, then how did you find out?" Holly asked.

"One of his victims reached out to me a few months back when he first went public. After speaking to her, I tracked down others. A few of them were willing to talk on the record. They all corroborate the same story. Lecherous old rock star coerced them into sex that soon progressed to nonconsensual violence and humiliation. Your typical predator shit." Katy snorted. "Two of them were teenagers at the time. They signed an NDA, so I'm keeping them as anonymous sources. I could do the same for you."

"Anonymous or not, I can't speak about clients, past or present."

Katy tried a few other angles but eventually gave up, accepting Holly's stance and even paying for the coffee. Two days later, the *Orange County Register* published her exposé on Simon. It sent immediate shock waves through the entertainment industry. And at least three separate law enforcement agencies had since opened criminal investigations into him.

While Holly felt a pang of sympathy for Simon—a man who despite all his fame and fortune was thoroughly broken—she was also relieved that he wouldn't be able to hurt any more women.

Shaking off the memory, Holly clears her throat. "Can we talk inside, Aaron?"

"Of course," he says and leads her into the kitchen, where they sit side by side at the counter.

Holly pulls out his house key, which she removed from her key chain earlier, and lays it down in front of him. "I thought you should have this back."

Aaron stares at the key as if it might be radioactive. "I told you how sorry I was, Holl. How badly I feel for going behind your back with JJ. It's just that you were in such distress. I wanted to do something—anything—to help."

"I get it, Aaron." Holly summons a smile. "This isn't about JJ."

"Is it Graham? Because things are different now. He's not allowed over here without clearing it with me first. He won't have a blank check anymore. And he knows to leave you alone. I've set those boundaries in stone."

"That's great, Aaron. Honestly, I think it's what he needs." She doubts Graham is capable of respecting boundaries, but she doesn't push. He is not the impetus for her decision. And she had already decided to spare Aaron from learning how his son broke into her car and attempted to blackmail her.

"What then?" Aaron asks.

He looks so defeated that Holly can feel her resolve weakening. She pats the back of his hand. "This is long overdue, Aaron. It's time we stop repeating history. We both need to move forward with our lives."

He pulls his hand away from hers. "You said the same when you moved out. But then, after the wheels came off, who did you turn to? Who do you *always* turn to?"

"You're right. I did. I do. And I'm sorry. It's not fair."

"Fair?" He huffs. "You need me when you're vulnerable. When you're in crisis. But then you don't want me anymore when you're back on track."

And you need me to need you. But Holly doesn't verbalize the thought. There's no point in hurting him more than she already has. Instead, she says, "I'll never be able to thank you for how much you supported me through this crisis. Without you, I would've gone out of my mind."

He only stares at the key on the countertop.

"I care about you, Aaron. And I always will. But this . . . this is something I have to do."

She stands to leave, but he doesn't so much as look at her.

"Goodbye, Aaron," she says, brushing her hand over his back before she walks out the front door.

As Holly crosses the street and gets into her car, she takes stock of her life. Her marriage is finished. Her book deal has been rescinded. Her career is seriously stalled, if not in shambles, while her practice is under ethical review. And she is about to move in with her convalescing ninety-year-old grandfather.

Still, Holly can only smile to herself. She feels freer and more hopeful now than she has in a very long time.

ACKNOWLEDGMENTS

As usual, I have too many people to thank for helping me shape this story. If I try to name them all, I will end up inadvertently omitting a few, which wouldn't be fair. I would rather extend a blanket thank-you to the friends and loved ones who soldiered through the pitches and early drafts, offering constructive criticisms along with generous encouragement.

However, there are a few people I need to single out for their exceptional contributions. At the forefront is my wildly talented and dedicated editor, Adrienne Kerr. Adrienne helped me plan and execute every aspect of this story, from the initial outline to the final draft. The end result is infinitely better for our close collaboration and her unflagging enthusiasm.

As with most of my previous novels, I relied heavily on the wisdom of my terrific freelance editor, Kit Schindell, and my friend Mariko Miller, both of whom provided invaluable feedback and suggested improvements, chapter by chapter. I would also like to thank Robyn Harding, a friend and distinguished fellow writer, for her helpful insights.

I'd like to thank my agents, Carolyn Forde and Samantha Haywood, and the reliable and skilled team at Simon & Schuster Canada, including Natasha Tsakaris, Rebecca Snoddon, Randall Perry, Felicia Quon, Tamanna Tamanna, Aditi Dwivedi, Hunter Sleeth, and, of course, Kevin Hanson, whose feedback inspired me to add the prologue.

While this is a work of fiction, scientific accuracy matters deeply to me. I would like to acknowledge the numerous insightful books, podcasts, and documentaries that I drew on to construct an authentic and informed backstory around psychedelics. I can't recall all the works I consumed in my research, but for those eager to learn more about the captivating history and realm of psychedelics, I highly recommend starting with *How to Change Your Mind* by Michael Pollan.

Lastly, a heartfelt appreciation to you—the readers—who continue to inspire me. Your feedback and reviews resonate deeply with me, and I genuinely hope the time you invest in this book proves to be worthwhile.

ABOUT THE AUTHOR

DANIEL KALLA is an internationally bestselling author of many novels, including *Fit to Die, The Darkness in the Light, Lost Immunity, The Last High,* and *We All Fall Down.* Kalla practices emergency medicine in Vancouver, British Columbia. Visit him at DanielKalla.com or follow him on X @DanielKalla.

> "A skilled, intelligent writer."
> *New York Times* bestselling author
> **Marissa Stapley**

Also by DANIEL KALLA

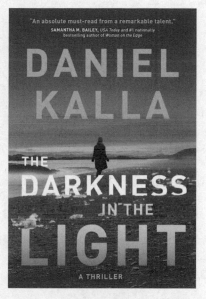

"The original and twisty plot helps this taut thriller stand apart."

Publishers Weekly

"One of [Kalla's] best."

The Globe and Mail

SIMON &
SCHUSTER